BROKEN MAN

MCCULLOUGH MOUNTAIN 5

LYDIA MICHAELS

BAILEY BROWN PUBLISHING

DEDICATION

To Gregory Payne.
May your dreams come true in every romance you write and
live.
~Lydia

*M**anhunt; Age 17*

TRISTAN'S back pressed into the tree. Pine needles prickled his front as the overgrown evergreen shrub swatted against his chest. It was dark and the scent of sap, sweat, and summer swirled around him like a swarm of gnats. His heart raced as he waited, crouching low in his hiding spot for the others to come.

Texas was dry, boring and hot in August, but manhunt was their favorite pastime. Other than sitting inside his family's dank ranch house, sweating his balls off playing video games, there wasn't much else to do.

The snap of a twig had his breath stilling in his chest. He crouched low, careful not to give away his location. A dry flake of dirt stuck to his lip and he quickly peeled it away.

Another step. His body became so quiet he could hear the on-comer's breathing. "Tristan?" a voice hissed.

He wasn't falling for it. Like a fox in a hole, he waited. Another crunch and then the shrub covering his location twitched. Like a soldier diving into a bunker, Jason shot behind the bush and chuckled. "Found you."

"You suck," Tristan said, unfolding his legs to stand.

Jason yanked on his shirt and Tristan dropped back down. "Wait. No one knows we're here."

Tristan frowned. There was a devious gleam in Jason's hazel eyes. Dirt and dust from a long sweaty day outside cluttered the sprinkling of boyish freckles on his cheeks. Jason was sort of the ringleader of their pack. He called the shots and the rest followed. Maybe the game had changed.

"You're still It, right?"

Jason nodded, but put his fingers to his lips warning Tristan to be silent.

"Who are we hiding from then?" he whispered.

Jason grinned. "Everyone."

His frown tightened, but he waited. "It's hot as hell. After this we should hit the quarry."

"Yeah," Jason whispered, but his eyes told Tristan he was thinking about something else. "Listen… I wanted to show you something."

Tristan's eyes skated over his friend's frayed cutoffs and settled on his hands. They were empty. The laces of his white Chucks, now faded and stained brown, were undone. "What?"

Jason shifted and their small hidey-hole seemed to shrink around them. "Why didn't you look when Timber showed her boobs?"

"I looked," Tristan lied, intuitively aware he had to do so. Boobs were weird. What was the point?

Jason's head shook meaningfully. "Nah. You didn't. I was watching you."

His gut tightened with the same anxious knot he always got when he thought his friends suspected something. "Yeah, I did. They were hot."

His friend's hazel gaze cut to his, challenging, knowing. Fuck. "No, you didn't, Tristan. You squirmed and sat there, lookin' anywhere else, 'til her shirt came down."

"I saw her tits, Jason. Jesus, why do you care so much?"

They were crouching so close their collective breath mingled. He could still smell cola on Jason's, sweet and syrupy. "I know."

Yeah, everyone knew Timber had the nicest rack in their grade. Tristan was the only guy who didn't—

All thoughts cut off as Jason placed his hand on his shoulder, a somehow gentle, caressing contact. Shit. What was going on? Guys didn't touch guys like that. They punched and shoved and sometimes horsed around wrestling, which was becoming more and more difficult to tolerate in Tristan's pubescent years, but the way his friend was touching him now... that shit didn't happen.

Brush it off. Get pissed.

"What are you—"

"Shh," Jason hissed. "I *know*. About you."

His breath quickened and his muscles tensed down to the soles of his feet, cramping painfully. Were they all out there, ready to kick his ass? Would this be the end of their crew? Who else knew? Maybe he was misunderstanding something?

Play dumb.

"Wha—" His words cut off as Jason's mouth pressed into his.

His heart beat so fast his ribs became a splintering vise on his lungs. Balance gone, he fell back into the tree, bark scraping his elbow, but none of that mattered. What was happening?

"I know," Jason whispered again, angling his mouth over Tristan's.

He'd never been kissed or kissed anyone else. Mostly because, since he was born, he'd liked boys. Never in a million years had he suspected Jason liked boys too. His instinct, growing up in a conservative, bible beating, redneck town, told him this was a trick and he should bale out right now and crucify his friend for being a homo. But something inside of him melted at the first touch of Jason's tongue.

He didn't know if this was a setup or a genuinely sincere moment. All he knew was that he didn't want to push Jason away. Something inside of him opened up. A weight that had been on his shoulders since the first hard on he got from watching a man on the beach, noticing every bulge and curve under his wet, clinging suit, suddenly slipped away.

This was right. *This* was him. This was everything he hoped to someday feel. Then his mind jolted as Jason's palm cupped him. His heart went ballistic. The dizzying effect of his friend's hand *there* nearly knocked him to his ass. This wasn't a prank.

I don't care.

Emboldened, he grabbed Jason by the back of the neck and deepened the kiss. He tasted of cola. His skin smelled like sweat and fresh air. His tongue was soft, but the kiss was hard. It was the most incredible moment of his life.

Then they heard the others coming and reality ripped them apart. Jason wiped his mouth over the back of his hand, lips parted, eyes wide. "Gotchya!" he yelled and stood.

Tristan barely had a chance to recover as Jason flung the branch out, exposing them to the others. Terror for what might happen next gripped Tristan, crippling his vocabulary in the face of fear.

"It's about fucking time," Tim shouted. "I was holed up in Old Man Hill's tree so long the dang branch started to give. You're It, Tristan."

He stood, still trying to comprehend what was happening. Glancing at Jason, ambling with the others, the picture of innocence, he caught the quick wink of his hazel eye.

Standing on shaky legs, he quickly turned and dropped to a knee, pretending to tie his shoe so he could buy some time and hide other unsightly situations going on below.

Mom. Grandma's underwear. Baseball. Barbara Bush naked. Jason's lips. Jason's touch. Jason's eyes. Fuck!

He stood and moseyed toward the woods, spit, and shouted. "Two minutes. Go!" The others took off running to their next hiding spot and Tristan caught his hand on the nearest solid object, hoping to find solid ground. Everything had just changed.

PART I
HIM

CHAPTER 1

*L*uke's thighs burned as fire pumped through his veins. He'd been at it so long it was a wonder he was still standing. His gaze shot to the clock then to the climbing numbers on the treadmill. He'd run just over twelve miles and his knee was killing him.

Don't be a pussy. Keep going.

Rage Against the Machine pounded into his eardrums as sweat burned his eyes. His arms pumped at his sides as he went at it like an animal.

Sixty thousand dollars a year and all you had to do was run hard and play harder and you fucking blew it, you useless pile of shit.

He'd been back in Center County for eleven months, surrounded by family and those who claimed to love him, but his childhood home had yet to calm his rage at losing the best opportunity of his life. Three years spent playing for one of the best colleges of the country and he'd lost it all. Everything. Lost the admiration he grew up seeing in peoples' eyes, lost the sense of potential he'd felt since childhood, lost his fucking grace and agility, all in the span of two seconds when he landed wrong and shattered his fucking future.

His life now sucked. He was working as a fucking logger like the rest of his family, which was fine for them, but he'd never seen that as his future. He'd been planning to play for the Steelers or the Eagles. Fuck, he'd even play for the damn Giants at this point, but they were all done with him. Every last one of them. He'd managed to go from one of the most sought-after recruits to being as useless as tits on a bull.

No one got it. His family sure as shit didn't. This town was like a coffin. Once people settled in they never left. He'd left and fate sent him back. Sometimes he wished they'd sent him home in a box, because that was how pointless his life had become.

Sharp pain shot up his heel and into his injured knee. *Son of a bitch!* His hand shot out and killed the machine, catching his weight in the last second. He panted, his chest heaving, leg throbbing, as his gone-to-shit body trembled.

Yes, he still trained. Yes, he was in better shape than most. To the naked eye he looked like a finely honed athlete, but those who knew him were aware those days were over. Never again would he run like he used to. Never again would he hear a stadium of fans chant his name as he scored the winning touchdown. Never again would he be the man he used to be.

Gripping his water bottle, he chugged the rest and

dragged his forearm over his drenched brow. His shirt was soaked through and he needed a shower before heading to his aunt's bar to welcome his cousin Ryan home from college.

As he made his way back to the locker room of the gym he grabbed his things and hit the shower. Did his family realize *his* graduation would have been this week too? He could have gone back, paid what the scholarship committee had revoked after his injury, but for what?

He wasn't smart like his brother Colin or his little sister Sheilagh. He was a football player. Everything else was second to the game and when a school like Notre Dame wanted you to play for them, you played with your heart. Everyone helped him manage the rest because they wanted to see their Fighting Irish win. Once he no longer played, all the other shit fell away.

Sure, his team came to check on him as he'd recovered, but as the news got out, those visits went to shit as well. His grades dropped when the responsibility fell solely on his shoulders and, like the pussy he was, he bailed.

Returning home was a metaphorical castration. He'd never felt like more of a failure or less of a man. The family was patient and supportive, but nothing hid the pity he saw in their eyes.

He'd hobbled around on his crutches for months and when his physical therapist finally gave him the go ahead to hit the gym, he hit it like a vengeful beast hoping to annihilate every obstacle that stood in his way. Problem was, the obstacle was himself. This was him now. This was his pathetic life.

No prosthetics or surgeons could repair what had been broken. So every God damn morning he woke up, strapped on his gear, and headed to the lumberyard like every other average Joe in Center County working to make an average fucking living.

Once he slid on his jeans he checked his phone. The party had already started. God, he hated family shit. It had been almost a year and everyone seemed to accept his lackluster return home, but he knew how they really saw him—a fucking failure. He'd go, make an appearance, congratulate Ryan, and say his goodbyes.

The barn across from his family home was almost finished. What had been his father's tool shed for the past twenty years was now in the process of becoming Luke's home. He didn't ask to make the conversion, just started cleaning it up and moving his shit out of the big house and into the barn. The plumbing was nearly done and this week he might actually be fully moved out of his parents' home and into his new place.

The big house was big, no doubt, but his family suffocated him. His youngest sister, Sheilagh, was seventeen. She was in that *the-world-revolves-around-me* stage. His other sister, Kate, was out of the house, making her own family. Colin, his oldest brother, was also out. Unlike Luke, Colin was fulfilling his dreams and on the last leg of his journey to becoming a priest. Kelly, his youngest brother, was now twenty-one and tending bar at O'Malley's, and Braydon, the next in line was in college on his way to becoming an architect.

Then there was Finn, Luke's twin. Finn was perfect.

He never wanted too much and seemed to get everything he asked for in life. He fell right into the logger role. Had himself a girlfriend named Erin who he'd likely marry and someday the business would be handed over to him. They were identical, but that's where their similarities ended. He loved Finn, didn't judge him for being content in their fishbowl town. It was Luke's envy of his twin's contentment that ate at him. He couldn't recall what it was to hold a sense of satisfaction in his life.

As he pulled up to O'Malley's his insides tightened. Instinctively, he wanted to blow off the night and bolt, but Ryan was his closest cousin growing up and it was only right to give him props after doing what Luke wasn't man enough to do.

He pulled the door open and a cacophony of voices greeted him. His family was good people, but they were loud as shit, didn't come with filters, and for the most part someone was usually drunk.

He went to the bar and nodded at Kelly. His brother poured him a draft and slid it over the counter. "Ryan here yet?"

"In the back. Mum was looking for you."

Luke rolled his eyes. "She can relax now. I'm here. Just like I said I'd be."

Kelly eyed him, but kept his mouth shut. Out of all his brothers, Kelly was the most easygoing. There wasn't much he took seriously, aside from getting laid. They all knew Luke had changed. He was glad they'd finally started to accept it. He wasn't putting on a show for anyone anymore and they could either deal with his surly disposition or keep walking.

He grabbed his beer and headed to the back of the bar. His aunts had put out a spread and he found Ryan sitting with his sister Sheilagh, and Patrick, Luke's other cousin. He clapped a hand on Ryan's shoulder. "Congrats, man. How's it feel to be holding that big fancy diploma?"

Ryan smiled. "Pretty damn good, Luke." They shook hands, gripping each other's fondly and pumping hard. "Luke, this is my buddy, Tristan. Tristan, this is my cousin, Luke."

Releasing Ryan's hand, Luke turned his gaze to his cousin's friend and stilled. A cool chill chased up his spine as the most startling set of eyes settled on him. "How ya doin'? You go to school with Ryan?"

"Yup. Good to meet you."

As they shook, Luke quickly removed his hand and stepped back, disliking the sensation shooting up his arm at the contact. Tristan spoke with a twang. His hair was longer and his face had its fair share of stubble. He wasn't as big as Luke, but he also wasn't small. His gaze caught on the large buckle of his belt. "Where you from?"

"Texas, but I'm gonna give Center County a try. Ryan's folks are putting me up for the summer and I'm gonna be logging while I look for a use for my degree."

"You just graduate too?" Luke asked, feeling slightly claustrophobic around so many success stories. He settled uneasily into a chair.

"Yup."

"Luke works at the lumberyard too," Sheilagh said.

He turned and frowned at his sister. "What's up with you?" She had some dumb ass look on her face and way too much gloss on her lips.

She scowled. "Nothing, asshole. I was just talking."

"Why you looking like that?" Seriously, he'd never seen her with that expression before. She looked like a cow-eyed idiot. His gaze narrowed as he saw her shirt. "You missed a button." Her boobs were out enough that he could see the lace of her bra.

Her face turned crimson and she mumbled, "You're a dick." She shoved away from the table and disappeared toward the bathrooms.

He glanced at his cousin, Pat. "What's up with her?"

Patrick shrugged and his little—drama queen—sister's presence was soon forgotten. Drinks were had and stories were told. Ryan was glad to be home, but much like the rest of the degree toting population of Center County he'd likely never do more with his diploma than cover up cracks in the drywall.

An hour later Luke was ready to go. He found his mother and said goodbye. She gave him the same disappointed sigh he'd been getting since returning home. Every time he made an excuse at a family function her mouth tightened with concern and the merriment that usually filled her green eyes faded a bit more. *Get used to it.*

As he left the bar he left behind a good deal of discomfort. There were just too many of them, all happy and content with their fucking success stories.

Plucking his keys from his pocket he turned toward

his truck and stilled. There was Ryan's friend, Tristan, smoking a cigarette in the shadows.

"Hey," Luke said, to be polite.

Tristan shifted and flicked away his butt, the red cherry smoldering on the ground, forming a coil of gray smoke. "Hey."

"You need a ride or something? I'm taking off." This had to be overwhelming for the guy. McCulloughs needed to be taken in small doses until one built up a tolerance. Being submerged into a bar full of them was probably like being pecked to death by a hoard of rabid chickens.

"Sure, if you don't mind. Ryan's my ride, but I don't think he's leavin' anytime soon."

Maybe it was because he smoked that Tristan had such a deep gravelly voice. Luke didn't stand around to think about it. He headed toward his truck and the other man followed.

As he pulled out of the parking lot, he noticed the deep woodsy scent coming off his passenger. It made no sense why he was cataloguing so many personal characteristics, but his mind couldn't seem to stop. For instance, Tristan wore a tethered leather bracelet around his left wrist. Guys in those parts didn't wear jewelry, but maybe it was a Texas thing.

His jeans were torn at the knee and his index finger had a silver ring. Luke couldn't make out the design on the band. His shirt was worn and tight around his toned biceps. And he whistled through his teeth.

"You like it here?" Luke asked, trying to break the silence and stave off the whistling.

"It's better than Texas."

"What's wrong with Texas?"

"Your cousin said you were gonna play for the NFL." *Nothing like avoiding the question.*

Luke's lips sealed tight. "*Was* being the key word."

"So how about I don't ask you about that and you don't ask about Texas?"

He liked this guy. "Sounds good to me."

He turned down his aunt's street and Tristan asked, "Am I gonna need anything for work on Monday? Ryan ain't starting for a few weeks, but I need the money. I don't much like being a free loader and I'd rather be workin' than sittin'."

"Good pair a boots, jeans that don't got holes, set of leather gloves, and a mindset to work your balls off will get you started on the right foot."

"Then all I need is some new jeans. Where can I grab a pair around here?"

"You got a car?"

"A truck, but it's busted. I'm working on it."

"Tell you what, I need some shit for some work I'm doing at my place. I'm headin' to Wells Borough tomorrow. They're some good places that sell good brands. If you want, you can go with me."

"All right."

"I'm leaving around seven, so be ready by seven fifteen."

"Sounds good." Tristan opened the door to his truck and hopped out. The ring—he saw once the interior light kicked on—had an upside down Y on it, sort of like a

Greek letter. Maybe it was from a college fraternity. "See you tomorrow, Luke."

His gaze ripped from Tristan's hands. They were strong hands and he'd be a good worker judging by the way they were calloused and slightly battered. When he met the other man's stare something tightened in his chest, sort of like the poignant and visceral adrenaline jolt one gets when they barely missed getting in a car accident. "See ya."

The door closed and he pulled away, unsure why he kept having anxious jolts in his chest. He hadn't felt anything like that since he'd last ran down the field at the snap of the ball.

TRISTAN SLIPPED out the front door and slid a smoke out of his crumpled pack, pissed he'd started up again. The house was still quiet, being everyone didn't get in until after two. He'd woken up to the sound of Ryan puking in the toilet and fumbling down the hall.

His lips closed over the end of his cigarette and he drew in a long pull of smoke as he waited for Luke's truck to show. Luke.

Fuck, the guy was a masterpiece. If he'd really blown out his leg like everyone said, there was no telling by looking at him. He was like a fine piece of chiseled flesh. Not gay though. Definitely not gay.

That was for the best.

College had bought him some time. He'd managed to

escape his past and be himself in an *ask don't tell* sort of sense for a few peaceful years. Tristan had known all along he couldn't go back home once he graduated.

Although his mother had sent him off with tears and hugs, his father banished him with a look of disdain, the same evil glare he'd given him that day in high school he'd caught Tristan with his hands in Jason's pants, right before...

His mind went back to that week and the weeks that followed, suffering the memory in order to remind himself this was a new beginning and he'd be wise to play it safe. Nothing had ever been more gut wrenching than those moments of his past, nothing more fundamental to his knowledge of human behavior.

HIS FATHER HAD BEATEN him so badly he'd lost consciousness. When he woke up Jason was gone and Tristan's body was black and blue, some parts of his skin split open from the latch of his dad's belt.

It took five days for him to leave the house and return to school. The most excruciating part of waiting for his body to heal was waiting for Jason to answer his calls.

The following week when he resumed school he was in no way prepared for the fall out of his father's rage. Sporting a shiner that wouldn't quit, he waited for Jason at his locker like he'd done every day in the months leading up to that moment. He still remembered the fear that his father might have hit Jason too.

His relief was a living thing as he caught sight of Jay

turning the corner with Tim and Kyle flanking him. All looked on the up and up from the outside. He'd caught the relief in Jay's eyes only a second before his expression shuttered and hardened with a scowl.

He waited for his lover to approach, hating that after the longest week of his life he couldn't take him into his arms then and there. Kyle whispered something as they neared and Tim snickered.

"What are you doing here, faggot?" Jason said and every pumping, functioning, twitching part of Tristan's body ceased moving.

"What?"

"You heard me," his lover said snidely. "We heard what you did and we don't want you hanging around no more."

"Checkin' us out and shit," Tim tacked on.

Tristan stepped back. "What the hell are you talking about?"

"Everyone knows it. Your dad caught you whacking off to guy-on-guy porn and beat your sorry faggot ass."

He blinked, because words weren't making sense. Not the ones meeting his ears or the ones ricocheting in his head. "Jason—"

"Dude, he looks ready to cry," Kyle said, making a sound of disgust. "Fucking pansy."

Tristan ignored him and drilled his gaze into Jason's. His mind pleading and his eyes begging him to stop. They could figure it out later, but stop this shit right now. It was only making it worse.

"If I didn't feel sorry for your pussy ass I'd kick it right now, but it looks like your dad did a fair job," Jason said and some-

thing inside of Tristan broke, snapping loudly and vibrating his soul. He couldn't breathe. "Now get out of here."

He was going to puke. Why was Jason doing this? They loved each other. They'd been through all the firsts together. They were best friends. Fuck. The pain only got worse with every breath.

He turned like a zombie and slowly took the first lurching step away.

"Cocksucker," Jason mumbled and something inside of him exploded.

Tristan twisted on his heel. His arm whipped out so fast there was no time to pull it back. Jason's sweet face connected with his fist and they were suddenly on the ground surrounded by a swarm of shouting students.

His ribs screamed as Jay's fist pounded into his side. He tasted blood and was pretty sure he'd be pissing it soon. A whistle blew and he was yanked off his back and tossed roughly to the lockers. Coach Brown scowled at the group of them.

"What the heck is going on? Tristan, get to Principal McLeay's office. Now! Jason, get to the nurse and then report to the office. Everyone else, get to class!"

THE RANCID TASTE of filter filled his mouth and Tristan tossed his butt in the street. Those days were long over. He'd heard Jason was married to a woman now and on his second kid. He wondered if his old lover was happy, being someone he wasn't. He wanted not to care, wanted to hate him for breaking his heart, but he did care and couldn't hate him no matter how he tried.

He never spoke to Jay after that and their year together was something his first lover would likely take to the grave. His father had been in too deep a rage to recall who the other kid was when he'd caught them. Tristan could have told, could have ruined Jason like Jason ruined him, but that was the thing with love. It made people incredibly selfless, most times when they shouldn't be, and Tristan protected Jason the way he believed one should always protect those they loved.

College had been amazing. He'd fucked around with other guys and gotten Jason out of his system. There had been a few encounters with the wrong friends, but on a campus the size of theirs, there were plenty of others.

He'd met Ryan sophomore year, but it wasn't until they roomed together that his friend asked if he was gay. Tristan's stomach had knotted like it always did when confronted with that question and clueless how the other person would react. He'd debated lying, but something in Ryan's eyes gave him the confidence to come clean.

"Yeah. That a problem?"

Ryan shrugged as though he expected as much. Was he that transparent? Most women thought he was hetero. "So long as you know I'm straight, we're good."

He gave him a smug grin. "Ry, even if you were gay, you ain't my type. No offense."

His roommate laughed. "None taken."

· · ·

AFTER THAT THINGS went on as they always had. Ryan was a good friend and an even better surrogate brother. He'd become the family Tristan never had.

His scalp prickled and he turned just as Luke's truck pulled up at the curb. Excitement tunneled through him. He didn't know why he was so anxious to go shopping with the other guy, but he was. His body seemed to have its own personal high-speed reaction to the guy's presence, gay or not.

Taking even, measured steps to the curb, he rounded the truck. Pulling open the door he hopped in. Luke's intoxicating scent he recalled from the night before hit him like a ton of bricks. The trace of soap complimented his natural musk like nectar compliments the anther of a flower.

"Hey," he greeted, sliding onto the leather seat.

Luke nodded. "Hey. I grabbed you a coffee. Didn't know how you took it, so all the shit's there."

Tristan glanced at the center console. Two cups and a bunch of condiments sat in one of those coffee caddy things. "Thanks. How much do I owe you?"

Luke's eyes focused on the windshield as he pulled away. "Don't worry about it. Next cup's on you."

When they reached the stores Luke disappeared toward the hardware shop and Tristan went for a stroll in the Working Gear. Shit was fucking expensive. He'd have to take a trip back after his first paycheck because at the moment he could only afford two pairs of jeans and the necessities. His boots were taped at the toe and they'd have to hold a while longer. He wondered how much he'd be making at the yard and was pissed he didn't have the sense to ask when Ryan's dad had offered him the job.

Didn't matter. A job was a job and this was the only one on the table at the moment.

He found Luke in the hardware store looking at samples of tile. Tristan knew a thing or two about putting down tile. He'd done a job in high school when he'd worked for Habitat. The program teacher was a jack of all trades and taught him quite a bit about construction.

"You tiling something'?"

Luke turned, the bulk of his body rippling under his shirt as he faced him. "Yeah. I'd like to. I'm trying to figure out how much of a pain in the ass it'll be and if I'd be better off with laminate."

"Nah, you don't want laminate. Tiling's not too hard. You got a cutter?"

"I can rent one here for fifty bucks a day, but I'm not sure if I'm ready for all that. Never used a wet saw before."

"It's cake. I can show you."

"Really? You know how?"

"Sure. Show me what grout you're thinking about."

Luke debated over two samples and ended up going with an earthy design and darker grout. They rented the cutter and were on their way back to his place an hour later.

"You hungry?" Luke asked as they drove through town.

"Sure."

They stopped at a diner and Tristan had another coffee and a plate of sausage and biscuits. Luke ordered eggs and a ton of fruit. "That shit'll kill you."

"I'm a southern boy, my friend. Biscuits and gravy are in my blood."

"It's gonna be in your arteries."

Tristan eyed his companion as they ate, scrutinizing everything from the size of his arms to the methodical way he chewed a bite then stopped to swallow a sip of water. "I guess you're one of those gym guys."

Luke shrugged. "I like a healthy body. The gym's therapeutic for me. Can't sit for too long or I get squirrelly. Gotta let off some steam once in a while, you know?"

Tristan was more of a lose yourself in the outdoors sort of guy. He enjoyed vigorous activities, but would never pay money to a building to run on a machine. He'd rather hike or swim, anything as long as he didn't feel contained.

They put away the meal in no time and split the bill. It didn't take long to realize Luke operated everything he did like he was on a mission. He seemed to have a set of rules for everything and a certain mindset that if something couldn't be done right it wasn't worth doing.

When they reached the McCullough property, Tristan whistled at the sight of the cabin. "That your place?"

"My parents. I'm in the barn. Been remodeling it for the better part of a year."

He turned and checked out the old barn in the distance. There was a discreet door at the side and without being told, no one would know it was a house. This should be interesting.

They unloaded the truck and stacked the materials out

front as Luke unlocked the door. Nothing could have prepared him for what was inside. It was beautiful.

High sandblasted beams crossed the cathedral ceilings. The walls were sheet rocked and painted a rustic shade of red. Old farm equipment decorated the rafters and the floor was a fresh bed of cement.

"You did this?"

Luke nodded, but didn't seem to show any signs of egotism at the admiration in Tristan's voice.

"This is incredible." He moseyed over to the open kitchen, dragging his palm over the granite countertop. Logging must pay pretty well. Either that or Luke was loaded.

"You want a beer?"

"Yeah."

Luke pulled open the stainless steel fridge and plucked out two bottles. He handed one to Tristan and they twisted off the caps, drinking in silence. Their gazes crossed and Tristan stilled. Luke's rough throat rippled as he took one last swallow. The mouth of the bottle pulled away from his full lips with a pop. "I still got a ton of shit to do, but I'm getting sick of cement floors."

"It's amazing what you've done so far."

"I'll give you a tour."

They left their bottles on the counter and he followed Luke through the spacious area. There was little furniture, but Luke mentioned he was still in the process of selecting what he liked. In what would be the den there was only a large television mounted on the wall and a beat up recliner.

"I want to do hardwood in here. I started it in the bedroom, but stopped. Hauling shit in and out puts a beating on the wood."

"Yeah. Best to wait and do the floors last. You'll be glad you got the dark grout too. Shows less wear and tear."

Luke opened a door to a small bathroom. "I'd like to tile in here eventually too. I like those subway tiles, the long white ones."

"They're nice."

As he pulled the door closed Luke's broad shoulders brushed his front. Tristan stepped back and gave him space, but his body tightened at the slight contact. It was impossible to ignore how incredibly toned the man was. He wondered if that was from logging or football. Probably a little of both.

He followed Luke down the hall. His hand, rough at the knuckles, nails clipped to the quick, dragged over the spackled wall. A trace of white dust caught at the corner of his thumb. "I put these walls in to make the bedrooms. I only have two, because I wanted a killer master bath. I'm gonna paint them that gray color," he said, toeing the can of paint on the floor. A swatch was taped to the wall.

"That's a good color."

"This is the spare bedroom. It's my workroom for the moment. Probably will be the last to get done."

The room was a good size. The walls were still exposed and front and center was a sheet of plywood housing a table saw, supported by two sawhorses. Tools were neatly placed in various bins along the perimeter.

He wasn't prepared for the next unveiling. Luke

opened the door to the master bedroom and Tristan had a moment of *what the fuck?*

Exposed brick walls were painted slate gray. The floor was dark wood, pristine and polished. The beams and one accent wall were painted a deep shade of sapphire blue. It was definitely masculine, but there was something not so subtly stunning about it.

From the high ceiling hung a wooden wheel, stained dark and lined with hurricane vases. The rustic chandelier was centered perfectly over the focal point of the room, which happened to be an enormous king size bed.

The covers were pulled tighter than a virgin's ass and sewn in the same dark sapphire as the accent wall. "Jesus," Tristan muttered, because words failed him.

"My younger brother, Bray, is going to school for architecture. He helped me design it."

"It's awesome." He couldn't ignore the sense of disappointment tunneling through him at the realization that Luke hadn't come up with this design himself. For the briefest second he'd thought he could have misread his new friend and mistaken him as straight. Only a gay man could manage such cohesive interior decorating—a gay man or a fucking architect. Shit.

"Wanna see the master bath? I just finished it."

He didn't know if he could stomach any more. It was all so perfect. Seeing the inside of this man's lair was doing things to him. The Richter scale was probably picking up tremors from how hard his attraction gauge was rocking. "Sure."

Luke led him behind the partitioning wall and Tristan

shut his eyes. Like everything else Luke, it was fucking stunning.

Dark slate tile covered the walls. The shower was an open cavern, lacking curtains or any feminine frills. The vessel sink was hammered copper and he'd even managed to find a matching antique tub. The toilet was housed behind a frosted glass wall. It should have been in a magazine it was so fucking breathtaking.

There were few accents. Twin towels hung from a copper bar, each creamy white. The floor showcased a shag carpet cut in a shape to look like animal fur. "Did your brother design this too?"

"Nah, this was all me. I hired a crew to do it, but I fucking love it. They argued with me about the shower being so large, but I work out a lot. Showering is part of my regimen. I spend a lot of time decompressing in there."

Fuck. Images of Luke all sweaty from working out filled his mind. He could picture his incredible body, all that tight muscle and sinew swollen from exertion as he pressed his palms into the tile and let the dual shower heads beat over his skin.

His mind battled with the question of whether or not a straight man could come up with this design.

He's not fucking gay!

Tristan backed out of the bathroom and returned to the kitchen where he proceeded to chug his beer. Luke appeared a moment later with a tool belt strung over his shoulder.

"You ready to do this?"

"Yup." He just hoped once they got to work the

fantasies rolling through his brain like an oversized loco-motive wouldn't derail and leave him in dangerous terri-tory, split open and spewing worrisome contents.

They set the cutter up out front because it was messy work. Tristan ran the water needed to get started and Luke began placing the tiles on the kitchen floor to get an idea of measurements.

Watching him crawl around on the concrete had Tristan reaching for another beer. Luke stood and brushed the dust off his pants. "I think we're gonna have to cut all along this wall if we do them diagonal like this. I'm wondering if I should keep it straight."

No, don't keep it straight. "I like the angled look better."

"Me too. All right. Let's play with tools," Luke said, grinning in his direction.

Holy shit. That dimple should be illegal. He bent and grabbed a set of tiles and headed out front.

Once they had all their materials in place, he stepped up to the cutter. Luke rubbed his palms together and grinned. "All right, show me how this mother works."

Tristan shut his eyes and took a breath. "So, basically, what you have is a diamond blade. The ceramic gets hot and the water cools the blade so it doesn't burn and break the tile. It's abrasive, but packs a lot of heat."

He lost his train of thought the moment Luke crowded around him. He could feel his body heat through the cotton of their shirts and swallowed hard. "What's this?" Luke's hand snaked around his hip and picked up the pump.

Fuck. His dick twitched at the sight of those big

fingers curling around the contraption. "That's the pump. The key is to keep it primed."

"That plugs in here?" he asked, reaching for the power source.

"Yeah, just fit it in there and make sure you got a good flow."

Luke fit the pump to the power source and water spewed out of the reservoir, arcing onto the ground. Tristan chuckled and repositioned the hose. "Yeah, you got a good flow there."

"Shit," Luke laughed. "Should I have waited to do that?"

"No, that's all right. Things tend to get messy with big tools. You want to fit the nub into that hole."

Luke's large hands closed over the filter as he maneuvered the tip in the hole of the hose leading to the blade. "It's tight."

Kill me now. "That's all right. You want a snug fit."

Once he had the filter hooked to the hose, water trickled through the mechanism and over the blade. Luke grunted at the slight accomplishment. "Now what?"

"You want to give it a few minutes. It's not a bad idea to let the water run for a second, really prime the blade, and get rid of any debris maybe left from previous use." Fuck, why the hell was his neck on fire? Was he fucking blushing? "That's good enough," he quickly said.

Unplugging the pump, he fit the saw's extension cord directly into the power source. "Now you're ready to cut," he announced, stepping back.

"And that'll keep the blade wet?"

He swallowed again. Where the hell did he put his

beer? "Well, yeah. But if you're going at it hard and the blade looks dry, you gotta stop and prime the pump some more."

Luke's mouth kicked up and the dimple was back. "Things always run a little smoother with a nicely primed pump."

Tristan gave a nervous laugh. "You know it."

Luke loaded up the first tile and secured it in place. "Maybe you should cut the first one."

Tristan stepped forward, but Luke remained close, hovering over his shoulder as he adjusted the blade.

"There's the mark," he said, sending a long tapered finger into his space.

"I see it. Watch your fingers unless you want nine."

Luke stepped back, but not enough. Frazzled, Tristan grabbed a pair of safety goggles from the table. The blade fired to life and even the grinding of the wet saw couldn't shut out the roar of his heart beating in his ears.

The spinning saw dwindled to a dull reverberation as he reached the end of the tile and the ceramic split in two. "Beautiful."

"Nice," Luke said admiringly. "My turn."

Tristan stepped aside and Luke took control. He was a natural. The next hour was spent watching Luke expertly handle the powerful machine and shifting uncomfortably as every gesticulation of his fine body added pressure to the bulge growing in Tristan's pants.

As they gathered the last of the tile needing to be cut, Luke annihilated the remainder of Tristan's control by peeling off his shirt. Motherfucker. The guy had the most beautiful body he'd ever seen.

Smooth pecs cut above his tapered ribcage. He counted eight—motherfucking eight—perfectly sculpted abs. On his side was an enormous crucifix tattoo with writing scrolled beneath it and disappearing beneath the sharp contour of his hip.

"You want another beer? It's hot as fuck today."

Tristan's gaze jerked to his face and he nodded. Maybe he should switch to bourbon or straight up moonshine. A moment later Luke returned and handed him a bottle, cap already removed. "Thanks."

As Tristan's lips closed over the mouth of his beer, Luke's head tipped back as he gulped his own, a tiny bead of sweat traveling slowly down his rippling throat, distracting his gaze. "I like this machine. Like most machines. Something good about handling so much power. Makes you feel like a man."

Tristan swallowed a groan. "Yeah."

"Luke?" Turning at the singsong, female voice, Tristan spotted a woman he didn't recognize approaching. Where the hell had she come from?

She wore unlaced boots, a loose bun, and some sort of dress hidden under an apron. Her hair was copper and her eyes were creased with laugh lines. Was this Luke's mom?

"I saw you had a friend over, so I thought I'd see if you boys were wantin' some supper. I made dumplings."

Tristan nodded in greeting and stepped back. Luke's expression was blank as he pulled the last drop of beer from his bottle. If this was his mother, he didn't acknowledge her presence with any sort of real courtesy. Luke's gaze met his. "You hungry?"

"I'm always grateful for a home cooked meal."

The woman smiled, her face round and pleasant. "Now, that I have plenty of. Come along. Wash yourselves up and get eatin' before the gettin's gone."

She turned and briskly walked toward the log cabin in the distance. "Is that your mom?"

"The one and only. Come on. Let's get cleaned up."

Tristan didn't ask about the obvious tension. Rather, he followed Luke into the house.

"I got the plumbing shut off at the kitchen sink since we're working in there. You can use the master bath. Powder room sink isn't hooked up yet."

Tristan nodded and headed in that direction. After using the toilet he turned to the sink and paused. Luke was in the bathroom stripping away his jeans, his boots tossed carelessly on the floor. His heart raced as his gaze followed the long line of his spine down to the fitted elastic of his briefs. Short briefs.

His vision focused on the contour of the thick muscles roping through his thighs, evident even under the tight cotton. Luke twisted and Tristan nearly choked as his gaze snagged on the enormous bulge packed in the front of those shorts.

Pivoting, Luke put his back toward Tristan. Down went the briefs and the sexiest ass ever to exist suddenly became the complete focus of Tristan's mind. Twin globes of perfection had his jaw unhinging and then the vision disappeared as he stepped into the shower alcove.

What. The. Fuck.

Maybe he's just cool with being naked.

"I'll be out in a sec. I just needed to rinse the sweat off."

Tristan cleared his throat. "'Kay."

He blinked, dumbfounded. The room filled with steam and the intoxicating scent of Luke's soap. When the water shut off, Tristan flinched. He'd been standing there the entire time. Fuck. It was too late to make it out the door unnoticed.

"Toss me a towel."

Towel, bitch. Move! Snapping into motion, he yanked one of the thick towels off the rod on the wall and stepped toward the shower. When he turned, Luke smiled and held out a hand. "Thanks."

He pressed the terrycloth to his face and Tristan's jaw nearly fell to the floor. The guy was fucking enormous. No wonder he'd been stretching the life out of those tiny briefs. The towel came down and Tristan's head jerked up. Panic cut through his system as he met Luke's gaze. Yes, he'd been staring and there was no denying it.

"It's bad, isn't it?"

Confused, Tristan asked, "What?"

"My scar."

Contemplating the body in front of him, his scrutiny dropping to the jagged white lines of Luke's knee, Tristan swallowed. That scar was like a spot of black oil on a perfect canvas, but he was still beautiful. No amount of scarring could detract from that. "Nah. It's not bad at all."

Luke tied the towel around his waist and exited the alcove. It had to be an athlete thing. Showering in so many locker rooms with so many other men probably made him indifferent to nudity.

As Luke passed him, he stopped, patted his shoulder, and chuckled. "Relax, man. It's just a dick." And with that, he left.

Again. What. The. Fuck?

"I'll wait for you outside." Tristan quickly exited the house and when Luke met him out front he hadn't calmed in the least. If he was going to be this guy's friend it was going to be torture. As soon as the floor was done, he was out.

CHAPTER 2

"So my sister tells me you and Ryan were roommates," Mrs. McCullough blurted, her litany of questions, curses and arbitrary statements now encroaching on a ten minute span of babble without a breath of pause.

"Yes, ma'am."

"That's a nice thing, the two of you keepin' up your friendship after graduation. And Rosemarie tells me you'll be workin' in the log yard now."

"Yes, ma'am."

"Did you hear that, Frank dear? Tristan's going to be workin' for ya."

"I heard."

She turned back to Tristan. "He heard. I'm, always the last to know. Wouldn't know my ass from a hole in the ground if I didn't find out for myself. No one tells me a damn thing in this house..." She went on and he wondered if no one told her anything because once she started talking no one else could slip a word in edgewise.

He didn't know what was more awkward, the way Luke's mom wouldn't stop talking about every thought that flitted across her mind or the way his little sister wouldn't stop gawking at him. What was she, fifteen?

"Could you pass the salt?" Then there was this guy, Kelly. He was cool, sort of laid back. Tristan slid him the salt. Luke remained quiet and meticulously cleaned his plate. The girl kept staring. His new boss grunted and nodded on cue whenever Mrs. McCullough threw his name into whatever she was saying and so the meal went on.

After dinner, Mr. McCullough disappeared and the girl helped Mrs. McCullough with the dishes. Luke seemed anxious to get back to work on the floor. When he stood, so did Tristan.

"Thank you for the meal, ma'am."

Luke's mom turned and gifted him with a wide smile. "Of course, love. Livin' with my sister and all, you're like family now." She slapped his cheek. It didn't hurt. It was sort of an affectionate tap. "You come by any time and I'll feed you, dearie."

He smiled. It had been a long time since he'd felt as welcome, if overwhelmed, as the McCulloughs made him feel. "Thank you."

He followed Luke back to the barn and the moment they left the house he muttered, "Sorry about that. My family's—"

"Really hospitable?"

"I was gonna say crazy, but yeah, we can call it that."

"Luke, wait!" They both turned as his little sister came tearing out of the house. She skidded to a stop beside them and batted her eyes at Tristan. "What are you guys doing?"

"Working. So unless you wanna help, go away."

"Oh, Luke," she said, swatting his arm. "I'll help."

Luke frowned. "You'll be in the way, Shei-Devil. Go play."

"I'm not a kid, you dick."

Whoa. Tristan did a double take. This one had a mouth on her.

Luke continued walking. "Go home, fart licker."

She scampered after him. "Please let me help. I promise to behave and actually work."

"No, Sheilagh."

She stomped her foot. Tristan followed several feet behind, not wanting to get involved.

"Damn it, Luke. Why not?"

"I told you why. Now take off, kid."

She didn't seem to flinch at the way her brother talked to her, but Tristan was a little taken aback. Here was this great family and Luke didn't seem to want any part of it. Why?

As Luke disappeared in the barn he turned and Sheilagh's smile widened as her gaze connected with his. She skipped back a few paces and took up walking by his side. "He's always like that. I'm Sheilagh."

"I'm Tristan."

"I know. We met last night. So you're a college gradu-ate? That's pretty cool. By the way, I'm seventeen, not twelve like my dickbag brother treats me."

Oh boy, a whole seventeen.

"How old are you?" she asked.

"Twenty-five."

"So we're only, like, seven years apart."

"Eight."

"Not really. I'll be an adult in ten months. I'm almost seventeen and a half."

Jesus. Where the fuck was Luke?

"Since you're new around here, if you ever want to do something, I could do it with you—I mean—I'd be happy to show you around. Town." She frowned and he did the same. Only adding to the awkwardness, she announced, "I'm allowed out 'til eleven."

Luke returned and Tristan had never been more relieved to see someone before in his life.

"You still here, kid? I told you to go home."

"We're talking, scrotum breath!" she snapped then turned and sweetly batted her eyes at Tristan. "So, like I was saying, if you ever wanted to catch a movie or something…"

Aw, Christ. Glancing back at Luke, Tristan saw that he was preoccupied taking measurements. Hiding a grimace he pasted on a smile and said, "That's real sweet, baby girl. I'm gonna be busy gettin' settled and working, but if one of those times ever come up where I need a nice girl to show me around, I'll be sure to come find you."

Her lips parted and she blinked up at him in what

seemed like astonishment. "Uh…yeah…okay…great." She shook her red head and her smile was back in place. She was a very pretty girl, just not at all what he was looking to get into. Their contrasting ages being second in the reasons not to go there.

She bounced and said, "Perfect. I'll talk to you soon. Bye, Tristan."

Whatever he'd just started was a mistake. "Bye?"

After she pranced off he turned, confusion likely apparent on his face. Luke jotted a line on a tile and mumbled, "There's more of that *hospitality* you mentioned."

Hospitality being code for crazy. He laughed and Luke treated him to a spectacular grin.

He followed him inside and they dove into a night of newfound friendship and laying tile.

Several hours later Luke stood back to admire their handiwork. He tipped back his beer. They'd killed a case, but also knocked the shit out of his to-do list so it was worth it.

"I gotta say, that floor looks bad ass."

Tristan nodded, a satisfied smile on his face. For some reason Luke's attention kept snagging on the torn piece of denim he'd used to tie back his hair when he was grouting. "Sure as hell does. Cheers. Your first lay was a success."

Luke tapped his bottle to his and finished it off. Dropping his empty in the can he went to the fridge, which was now parked in the den, and retrieved two freshies. He passed one to Tristan and they settled in at the table shoved next to the fridge.

"You got yourself a nice place here, Luke."

"Thanks. It feels good to see it all coming to fruition."

They couldn't help admiring their work.

After a long bit of comfortable silence, he asked, "You planning on sticking around long, I mean in Center County?"

Tristan shrugged. "Got nowhere else to be."

"What about home, family and shit?"

"A little too much hospitality back in Texas."

"Gotchya. You gonna stay with Ryan's family?"

"For now. Eventually I'd like to get my own little slice of earth to call home."

"Nothin' better than having something to call your own."

Tristan nodded. "Or someone."

"You got a girl?" Luke asked.

"No. Been single for a long time."

"Me too. When I played ball, girls used to bang down my door. After I blew out my knee that shit all fell away like everything else in my life."

"You seriously can't ever play again? You're in impeccable shape."

Luke shook his head. "Nope. I push myself hard at the gym, but I still can't do more than fifteen miles without feeling like my legs gonna snap in two."

"Did you just say fifteen miles?"

He nodded. "Not much I enjoy anymore. Running's something I can't give up. Drove me nuts, the months I was healing, not being able to hit the track. I get cranky as shit, need that outlet, you know?"

"Sort of like sex."

Yeah, sort of like sex, Luke supposed, but not really. Even after sex he felt the need to run, the urge to escape. There had been one girl since he returned home and afterwards he wanted nothing more than to get the fuck away from everyone and everything close to him. Even fucking was different since he blew out his knee. Not that it was ever as spectacular as most made it sound.

Sex was a release. Maybe it was because he was such a big guy that he never felt like he let off enough steam. He was always afraid he'd hurt someone or maybe still not be able to feel what the rest of the world felt.

He reached for his beer and accidentally tipped it over. "Shit."

Tristan caught the bottle before it rolled to the floor and they both stood, searching for some paper towels. The flow of liquid curled over the edge of the table and just as it was about to hit the tile they'd just finished, Tristan grabbed the edge of his shirt and caught the spill.

Luke blinked as he wiped up the mess. "Thanks."

"No problem."

Once under control, Tristan stood and batted at the large wet mark staining his shirt.

"You're gonna stink like beer," Luke said. "I'll get you a

fresh shirt for the drive home, just in case you get pulled over." He disappeared into his room and returned a second later. "Here."

Tristan crossed his arm at his waist and peeled off the wet shirt. Luke stilled. He wasn't built like an athlete, but he wasn't built like a waif either. His abs were cut and shadowed with dark hair. His arms were toned and showed soft tufts of hair underneath. He wore a thick leather belt and there was something intriguing about the fit of his tattered jeans.

"Like what you see?"

What the fuck? Luke's gaze jerked to his, but his scowl was short lived. Tristan's chest lifted with each slow breath. A leather necklace tied to some sort of arrowhead pendant rested between his dark nipples.

Luke frowned. "What?"

"You're looking at me."

"No, I wasn't." Luke's brow tightened.

He stepped closer. Too close. Luke should take a step back, but for some reason he didn't. His breath came in short, clipped puffs as Tristan crowded him.

"Yes," he whispered. "You were."

Luke met his stare and frowned. He couldn't move, couldn't tell him to back it up. He just stood there, staring into his gunmetal eyes, mesmerized. Part of his dark hair had fallen from the tie. It dusted his shoulder just above a curled scar. Luke wanted nothing more than to trace his finger over that mark and ask what had happened—which made no sense.

His gaze shot to his chest. Another scar. This one a

divot. By his sternum there was another, exactly the same. A tiny little star of white. Once he noticed one, he noticed all of them.

Without thinking, his hand reached out. His thumb coasted over the white scar on his ribs, his fingers curling around Tristan's side. The other man's skin burned the inside of his palm. Tristan drew in a sharp breath and Luke asked, "What happened to you?"

"My dad wasn't a nice man and he liked to wear big belts."

His head jerked up and he checked Tristan's eyes for sincerity. "He hit you with a belt? That's what all these marks are?"

The stubble along his rugged throat shifted as he swallowed. "He wasn't happy when he caught me doin' something I shouldn't have been doin'—to his way of thinking."

"What were you doing?"

"This." He stepped close and his palm curled around the back of Luke's neck. A split second later—too quick to pull back—Tristan's lips met his.

Luke grunted and jerked away at the first stroke of the other guy's tongue. "What the hell are you doing?"

"I…I thought you wanted me to. You touched me."

He frowned. No he didn't. *Yes. You fucking did. You're still touching him.* He jerked his hand away. It was the beer! Shit, he needed to lay off the drinking.

"Luke, look, it's okay. I just thought with everything today—the shower—clearly I misread—"

"Are you dating my cousin?" he suddenly blurted.

"What? No. Ryan's straight." Tristan's answer shouldn't have relieved him, but it did.

"You're *gay?*"

Luke was distracted as Tristan took a deep breath. Tanned skin shadowed with hair drew his gaze to the cut of his chest glistening with a hint of sweat or maybe spilt beer. "Yeah, but it doesn't have to be an issue. If you aren't interested, we can act like nothing happened here and just go back to five minutes ago."

"Does Ryan know you're gay?"

"Yeah. He's fine with it. Most people are. It's not like I openly maul anything with a dick. I have a specific taste."

"Me?"

"Well…" He turned and forked a hand through his hair. "You're very handsome. Christ, I already saw you naked."

And for some reason Luke had purposely made sure he'd seen him. He wanted him to look, like it was some pissing match or something. Thinking back, it was stupid and nothing like he'd ever done before.

"I'll go," Tristan said, grabbing his soiled shirt.

Luke caught his arm. "Wait."

"For what, Luke? I clearly misread the situation."

"Did you think I was gay?"

"No, but then…I don't know. I thought maybe you were bi. You hear things about football players playing grab ass in the locker rooms and shit. I don't know what the fuck I thought. Then you touched me and I just… stopped thinking."

"You like being with men?" Well, no shit. That's pretty much what it was to be gay. He couldn't fathom it. Did

Tristan take the top or bottom? He didn't look gay, whatever that looked like.

"Well…yeah."

"What do you do with them?"

"Jesus, Luke, everything. What do you want to know?"

"Does it hurt?"

"Fuck no. It feels fantastic."

He stepped back, needing to do something, but not the type to fidget. "Have you ever been with a woman?"

Tristan's expression became serious. "No. It's always been guys."

"This is crazy. I need a beer." He turned and pulled out a new bottle. *He's fucking gay.*

Luke never met a gay person that he knew of. He lived in Center County, not the most liberal place. "Man, you picked the wrong town to move to."

"Tell me where the right town is." Tristan stepped into the den. "I'm just another guy, Luke. I just wanna work and live and have the right to the same happiness everyone else is looking for in this fucked up world."

Luke's gaze moved over his chest. There were over a dozen scars. "That's why your dad beat you, for being gay?"

"Yeah." There was so much gravity in that one little word something in Luke broke.

"I'm sorry."

"I'm not. Taught me a lesson I'll never forget. No matter how hard someone hits me, or shuns me, or calls me ugly names, I'm still me. They don't have to like it.

They don't have to live with it, but I do. And I refuse to be something I'm not."

Luke dropped into the chair. "How old were you?"

"When I realized I was gay? Probably four."

"No, when your dad did that to you."

"Eighteen. Five days later my lover tried to kick the shit out of me in front of the whole school and called me everything he was afraid to call himself. Three months later I left for college and never looked back."

Holy shit. "Did you ever think it would be easier to be straight?"

"I've thought lots of things. Sometimes I think it would be fun to fly, but that doesn't make it possible."

"No women?"

"No. Only men."

"I'm not gay." Luke stated, needing to hear the affirmation.

Tristan nodded. "And that's cool. I didn't mean to…"

"Right."

The silence stretched between them. Finally, Tristan said, "I'm gonna take off."

"Okay." He was in a daze. This was some heavy shit.

"Thanks for…"

"Thanks for your help."

They nodded at one another and Tristan slipped on his wet shirt. A moment later the door closed.

Luke sat there for probably five minutes just digesting everything. He liked Tristan. A lot. Just not in any sort of romantic way. He didn't swing that way. He liked pussy.

He was a boob man or maybe a leg man. Definitely wasn't a gay man.

He stood and went to hit the lights. He was way past the legal limit and needed to sleep. Maybe things would be clearer in the morning.

He dropped the empties in the bin and went to lock up. As he approached the door it suddenly opened. He stilled and Tristan stepped back in. Why was he back? His return sent a rush of blood pumping through Luke's veins and his breathing picked up.

"I don't have a car here."

Right. He'd picked him up. "I've been drinking."

"I could call a cab."

"Or you could crash here." He hadn't thought about his offer, it just slipped out.

"Or I could crash here."

Luke stared at him and waited. Sure, Tristan could crash. He could sleep on the recliner. Luke swallowed. He felt like he was doing something very wrong. Part of him was glad he couldn't drive. So glad, that when the thought of calling Sheilagh and asking her to take Tristan back to his Aunt Rosemarie's popped in his head, he immediately shoved it away.

"I was about to hit the sack anyway," he said.

Tristan nodded. "You got an extra blanket?"

"Yeah. I'll grab it. Make yourself comfortable."

He went to the closet in the hall and pulled out a spare blanket. When he turned, Tristan was in the den, kicking off his boots. "Here you go."

"Thanks, Luke. Listen, I'm sorry about all this. I hope—"

Luke slammed his lips to Tristan's mouth. He didn't know who was more shocked, him or Tristan. All he knew was the thought of Tristan, who'd taken his fair share of beatings for only being who he was, apologizing to him, cut him apart. He silenced him the only way he knew how.

Strong hands cupped the back of his head and he was walked backward through his house. His back slammed into the wall as Tristan's mouth slanted over his. His heart was going to beat out of his chest.

Sturdy hips pressed into his and his ass clenched. His cock filled his jeans in seconds flat. He didn't lift his hands or touch the other man, only let him do his worst.

Tristan's tongue stole into his mouth, hard yet soft. Their teeth gnashed and there was an unfamiliar nudge at his hip he didn't want to think about for too long. It was hard to think about anything. All he could do was feel. Feel how incredible Tristan's mouth was on his, the strength behind his hold, the forceful way he pinned him to the wall. Every part of his body was suddenly alive, pumping with the adrenaline of a million victories.

His shirt was stripped away and Tristan's mouth sealed over the pulse point at his throat. "Your heart's beating so fast. I can feel it."

He shivered as Tristan's gravelly voice whispered over the shell of his ear. So many foreign things were affecting him he couldn't keep up. There was the scrape of the other man's stubble along his shoulder, the scent of his cologne, the trace of a cigarette he'd likely smoked when he realized he didn't have a way home, his cock digging into his hip. Luke had never been more turned on in his life—or terrified.

Jolted into action by the pure eroticism of the moment, Luke grabbed the other man's shoulders and gave him a power drive into the adjoining wall. Things hanging from the sheetrock rattled and Tristan grunted.

"Sorry," Luke mumbled as he gripped Tristan's shirt and sealed his mouth over his.

Tristan moaned and bit his lip. "Don't be." His tongue thrust into his mouth. The kiss broke only for a second as Luke ripped off Tristan's shirt and tossed it aside. Skin to skin, chest to chest, his body caught fire. Their lips rejoined in a fury as his hands roamed over the other man's body. So hard. So strong. Nothing like a woman's.

He heard the clink of metal followed by the tug at his fly. Tristan's hands worked fast at getting him out of his pants. Before Luke could object, Tristan dropped to his knees and took his cock into his mouth, swallowing him back to the root.

Luke's knees trembled and he caught his weight against the wall and cursed.

"God damn, you have a beautiful cock." Tristan's breath cooled his wet flesh which was then engulfed once more in the heat of his mouth. He didn't suck him off like a woman. There was no toying around. Tristan swallowed him back and pumped his mouth over his length like there was nothing in the world he'd rather be doing than sucking his dick.

Finally, Luke grabbed hold of the hair that had been driving him crazy all night. He fisted the long, soft strands in his fingers and pumped Tristan's head over him. "Yeah, you suck my cock. Take all of it."

Slurping sounds echoed off the walls and high ceilings. His jeans were yanked down to his boots and warm fingers fondled his balls. He groaned as Tristan tugged at his sack. When his spine tingled and he knew he was gonna come, his fist tightened in Tristan's hair. Tristan sucked faster, harder, and Luke's toes curled almost painfully as he blew the most violent load of his life.

Tristan never stopped. He swallowed every last drop and Luke was shaking by the time he pulled away, licking the last bit off his shaft. Fuck.

Luke's fingers relaxed their grip in Tristan's hair and his hand fell away as he panted. Tristan stared up at him, lips swollen and parted. Luke stumbled back and the gravity of what they'd just done settled in.

Tristan seemed to register the change in his demeanor. Slowly, he stood. Luke wanted to bolt, but his pants were still twisted at his boots and his body was so strung out he couldn't move if he tried.

"Don't panic," Tristan whispered. "Everything's cool. Just give it a second."

He needed more than a second. He'd just let another man blow him. And he liked it. He couldn't breathe.

Tristan stepped closer and placed his palm over his heart. "Relax. Breathe. Everything's cool."

Astonishingly, his touch helped. Luke drew in one shaky breath after another as Tristan stepped even closer.

Lips brushed his and Tristan slowly pulled him into a hug.

Walls came tumbling down and something cracked inside of him. He let out a harsh breath and yanked Tristan close.

"It's okay," he whispered and Luke wrapped his arms around him tight. "You're still Luke. You're still you. Just let me hold you for a minute."

He broke. A sob he seemed to be holding in for a year tore from his chest. He gripped Tristan's head, hard, and buried his face in his shoulder. He couldn't let the other man see him break.

Tristan's voice continued to promise everything was fine and Luke cried for the first time in what felt like an eternity. He cried for the future he'd lost, for disappointing his fans. He cried for the pain that had been swallowing him whole since he'd come home and for the loneliness he couldn't escape nor wanted to leave. He cried, because, for the first time in his entire life, he'd understood what sex was supposed to feel like. He finally got it, but he got it from a man.

He wasn't sure how long they stood there in the hall, in each other's arms. He only knew he needed Tristan's strength in those moments and didn't want him to let go. Once he'd finally pulled himself together, Tristan ducked and removed Luke's boots and jeans. It was such a practical gesture, yet stunningly kind and touching.

They found their way to his bed and Luke shyly drew back the covers, instinct he didn't know he possessed taking over. Tristan kept his eyes on him as he stripped away his pants and, together, they climbed under the covers. Nothing else happened, but those hours that followed changed everything.

Tristan was able to hold Luke in a way no one else ever had. Their bodies curled into each other and something about his presence made everything—for the first time in a long time—seem okay.

CHAPTER 3

Tristan knew the moment Luke awakened, because his body immediately stiffened. Those strong arms and broad shoulders he'd been holding all night tensed and Tristan wasn't sure how to prepare for whatever came next.

It was obvious Luke had never been with a guy before. Tristan had been born gay, a belief he shared with most homosexuals, but Luke had obviously lived his life as a heterosexual man. Bi?

Bisexuality confused him. Tristan liked men. Women were of course beautiful, but in the way a sunset was beautiful or a flower. There was never any sexual chemistry between him and someone of the opposite sex. But maybe Luke was bi.

As the man in question grunted, Tristan slid his arm over that tapered hip that fascinated the hell out of him and teased the soft divot just before his fingers met the curve of the most impeccable abs he'd ever set eyes on. "Good morning."

Luke's shoulders shifted with each inward breath. Tristan didn't want him to freak out. Pressing his lips to the strong muscle of his back, he caressed his hip and snuggled closer. Sensing Luke's arousal, he nestled his bare hips into the flawless ass pressed to his groin. "Don't be scared."

"Uh…"

Shutting his eyes, he slid his hand lower and captured Luke's dick in his fingers. Yup. He was rock hard.

Luke hissed in a breath and tensed, but Tristan wasn't deterred. The other man was obviously bigger and stronger. He could throw him off at any minute. Tristan kept his touch light and slow.

Stroking his flesh, he pressed kisses at the back of Luke's neck and nestled closer. It only took a moment for Luke to roll to his back and face him. There was that beautiful face and those piercing blue eyes. His irises were dark like wet denim. His stare was filled with pain and confusion. Tristan rolled over his strong body and continued to touch him.

They were so close he could count each little lash. "You okay?"

Luke's gaze darted away, but he stretched and shut his eyes, signaling Tristan to go on. He shifted and scooted lower, kissing every decadent dip and bulge along Luke's chest and abdomen. Cool air teased his backside as the covers fell away and he came face to face with Luke's cock.

It was thick and long. A dark vein traveled up the length. Tristan breathed in his intoxicating musk, sending his eyes rolling back on a wave of ecstasy. He kissed the tip, dragged his tongue slowly up the side and explored the soft rim at the top. The sense of urgency that had driven them together last night was gone and Tristan took his time exploring and learning Luke.

Luke didn't touch him nor did he pose his body in a way that looked relaxed. Luke's hands remained fisted by his side as Tristan slowly took him into his mouth.

The other man's hips twitched and lifted as he worked his mouth down that column of flesh, stretching his lips wide. His fingers held and pumped with each languid stroke of his tongue. The sound of Luke's heavy breathing filled the quiet room. Tristan cupped his balls and massaged gently, pulling, tugging, rubbing until Luke's legs began to scissor slowly at Tristan's sides.

Tristan's body was so attuned to his. Every little breath, moan, and sigh sent a thrill up his spine, over his shoulders, and straight to his cock.

A moan slipped past Luke's lips as Tristan took him deeper. Luke's knees drew up and, emboldened, Tristan slid his finger past Luke's taint and smoothed a calloused fingertip over the taut flesh there.

Deep breaths echoed through the room, interrupted by the occasional curse. Tristan's finger traveled back between the cheeks of Luke's ass and found that tight little virgin knot.

"No."

He stilled and withdrew Luke's cock from his mouth.

Pulling back his hand, he returned his ministrations to the other man's balls. He wondered if—in the mind of Luke—anal play crossed a line he wasn't yet prepared to face. Luke was obviously having some issues with the fact that a man was currently sucking him off, but maybe he thought if he kept his eyes closed and didn't experience anything he couldn't experience with a woman, he was still safely hetero.

It pissed Tristan off. He was no one's vessel and no one's toy. If Luke wanted him, he'd have to own up to it and Tristan was determined to make it perfectly clear that it was him Luke was fucking around with.

Keeping his hand curled around his cock, he slid up Luke's hard body and pressed his lips to his. Those dark blue eyes flashed open. Tristan traced his tongue over his full lower lip and slid his own dick along Luke's.

Luke's breath quickened and his shoulders tensed. Sliding his legs along Luke's, Tristan dragged his mouth over the stubble covering Luke's throat. He kissed the curve of his shoulder and trailed his tongue up his neck.

Heat from their bodies turned to condensation below. Tristan's thumb rubbed over a pearl of precum as he slipped his hand between their bodies and massaged it into Luke's shaft. The slide of their cocks together was devastatingly erotic, but nothing felt better than when Luke's hands finally grabbed hold of his hips and held him close.

Their bodies dragged together in a slow, sultry rocking motion. When he caught Luke's half-lidded stare he paused. Luke met his gaze challengingly, seemingly waging some internal battle. Then, ever so slightly, he lifted his head from the pillows and pressed his lips to Tristan's.

Victory.

Tristan sealed his mouth to Luke's and explored with his tongue in fast, thrusting flicks. Luke's fingers tightened on his hips, slid down to his ass and soon they were kissing passionately with no thought aside from feeling each other's body.

Cocks ground over each other. Fluid seeped from his tip. His hand, still snaked between them, gripped both their dicks and he thrust his hips, jerking them both off as one.

Luke grunted and a look of euphoric pleasure took over his face. His mouth opened. Kiss-swollen lips parted, as his head tipped back in a silent cry and his release covered Tristan's fingers.

His body quivered and tightened as Luke rode out his climax. Warm, pulsing jets of come shot from Tristan's dick, mixing with Luke's. Fuck. It was incredible.

Their bodies continued to rock in a slick slide as he flattened his palm over Luke's hard stomach. His mouth brushed over that strong jaw, all sharp edges and stubble. He nipped his chin with his teeth and dragged his tongue to the cleft beneath that perfectly plump lower lip.

"Like I said. Good morning."

Luke's mouth quirked in the slightest smile and his lashes lowered bashfully. *That's right, mister. There will be no hiding from me or denying anything we share. Get used to it.*

He rolled to his side and rested his head in the crook

of Luke's arm. With halting movements, Luke slowly curled his arm around Tristan's shoulder, as though deliberating each tiny encroachment. When a hand closed over his shoulder, holding him to Luke's side, Tristan shut his eyes and sighed. He'd be patient, because this man was definitely worth it.

HE WAS SOBER. The easiest excuse slid off the table and Luke frantically searched his brain for another.

His body and mind were still reeling from the incredible orgasm he'd just had. Come, his and Tristan's, still remained in a sticky smear at his hips. These were new sheets and that should have bothered him, but there was something erotic about Tristan's scent clinging to his bed, that his mark was all over his skin.

Fuck!

He should say something. Pull away. Punch him in the face. Anything. What the fuck was happening to him?

Luke's mind continuously reassured him that his front door was locked and no one knew Tristan was there since Luke had driven them. But his cousins would know Tristan didn't come home. *Shit.*

He needed to get him out of there. "People are probably wondering where you are."

"I texted Ryan late last night and told him I spent the night with a friend. He knows what to do with that."

"What do you mean?"

"If anyone asks, he'll say I met a girl."

"Do you lie a lot?"

"I only lie about that. Mostly because it's easier for me to lie than for outsiders to hear the truth. I don't like it, but it's what's easiest for everyone."

Luke understood privacy. He coveted it and respected it, but continuously lying wasn't something he was into. He was raised to believe if something had to be kept a secret it wasn't something he should have. This was new territory and he didn't know how their relationship applied to that rule.

Didn't matter anyway. After today it was over. Whatever had just happened couldn't happen again. They'd experimented. He'd heard something once that one out of four men had gay experiences. This was obviously his. But he wasn't gay. He'd merely let Tristan kiss him and blow him. That's all it was, just another blow job.

Like a Filofax, his mind shuffled through women he knew. He should go find one and fuck her brains out. That's what he'd do. After Tristan left, he'd shower, put his kitchen back to rights, and later he'd go out trolling.

He realized it was Sunday and lamented not many people would be hanging out at O'Malley's. That was all right. He'd call someone. As a matter of fact, he'd call Tiffany. She'd come over. He'd fuck her on every hard and soft surface he could find, and then he'd parade her in front of his family so everyone was clear.

Tristan's soft lips pressed into his chest and Luke's dick twitched. "You want to go to breakfast?"

"I have stuff to do. There's food in the fridge if you want to grab something on your way out."

His head lifted and steely eyes bore into his. "Are you kicking me out?"

Luke shrugged and slid out of bed. "Like I said, I got shit to do."

He sat up and Luke struggled not to fidget under his scrutiny. "At least let me help you get the kitchen back in order. There's no way you're moving that fridge on your own. I don't care how ripped you are."

"That's fine, but then I have errands to run. I gotta jump in the shower."

Tristan's gaze darted to the sticky smear at Luke's stomach and the side of his mouth kicked up. "Need any help?"

"No, I'm set." He turned before he could see the dejection in Tristan's eyes. It was good that he realized now that this was a mistake. Luke wasn't gay.

An hour later the kitchen was back in order and Luke was anxious for Tristan to go. It was only nine in the morning, but soon others would be getting up and he didn't need anyone to see them emerging from the barn together or him dropping Tristan off at his aunt's.

He grabbed his keys from the bowl on the counter. "You ready?"

The other man's expression was unreadable. "Yeah."

Luke felt like he was forgetting something, but couldn't figure out what. They headed down the hall and when he opened the door Tristan's large palm slammed it shut.

Luke turned and found Tristan's hard gaze drilling into him. "Are you at least going to kiss me goodbye?"

Yes. No. Fuck. He didn't want to reopen that can of worms. He wanted to seal it shut, wrap it in duct tape, encase it in a box of unbreakable cement, and throw it away in the deepest crevice of the ocean. "Tristan—"

"Is that it then, Luke? I suck you off, we spend the night in each other's arms, and you toss me out like yesterday's garbage and forget how much you enjoyed it? Out of sight, out of mind?"

"I'm not fucking gay!"

"My memory calls you a liar."

His eyes narrowed, his gaze sharpening. "You don't know me."

"I know enough. I know you've never been with a man before and it terrifies you because you liked being with me. I know you aren't such a hard ass underneath all that bulk. Don't forget it was my shoulder you cried on last night."

Luke's arm shot out and he shoved him. Unprepared for the blow, Tristan stumbled back a few steps and caught his hand on the table. His eyes narrowed and his lips tightened.

"You gonna hit me now too?"

Fuck. He hadn't meant to lash out. His heart beat erratically. He bit back his apology. He felt like the horrid character in some animal movie throwing stones at the poor family dog so it ran away and returned to where it was meant to be.

Tristan rose to his full height. "You aren't going to push me around, Luke. You throw a punch and I'll swing back. I may not have as much mass as you, but I ain't no slouch."

"I'm not gonna hit you."

"You sure about that?"

He shut his eyes, wishing he could hit himself. "Look, last night…I've never done anything like that before and I don't plan on doing it again. I'd appreciate it if you kept it to yourself."

Tristan's nostrils flared. "Are you suggesting I'd otherwise inform the town—who by the way is all strangers to me—that I was used and tossed out on my ass the next morning when my lover's shame set in?" He laughed dryly, harshly, and without humor. "Yeah, I'm good with keeping that little tidbit to myself."

They weren't lovers and it pissed him off that Tristan had used that term. Before Luke could reply, Tristan snapped, "Just take me home."

They rode in utter silence. Tristan didn't even whistle like he often did when the quiet stretched on. Each time Luke glanced his way he noticed the hard set of his jaw and the tightness around his eyes.

When he pulled up at his aunt's he turned to make some excuse, but Tristan was out of the truck before he had the chance, slamming the door in his face. Great.

"Luke, take Tristan over to the shed and get him suited up. Why don't you work with him today and show him the ropes of climbing. He's gotta ring the bell a dozen times before we can give him a chainsaw."

Luke sighed and headed to the shed. He wasn't going to argue with his dad. That would stir up questions. As he passed Tristan, he snapped, "Come on."

In the shed he dug through the equipment racks searching for lanyards, proper sized cleats, and a decent harness. "What size are your shoes?"

"Thirteen."

His brow lifted as he kept sorting. Thirteen was a big foot. He found a set of cleats in the back that would work, but they needed to be sharpened. "How much do you weigh?"

"Around two hundred. Maybe two ten."

That surprised him as well. Tristan wasn't bulky. He was lean. He was obviously hiding some muscle mass under all that firm flesh. "How tall are you?"

"Six-three."

They were the same height. He grabbed the right strength J hooks and the right weight harness. "Get your-self some glasses and a hard hat from the pile."

They left the shed and went to the hanger where all the lockers were. Luke grabbed his spikes and handed Tristan the wide stirrups to support his size thirteens. Settling onto a bench, careful not to make eye contact, he with-drew two gaff gages and tossed one at Tristan. He caught it without flinching.

"All right, this is your standard spike. You got the shaft, that's this long part that runs along the inner calf, the cup, that's the soft part that supports the climber under the knee, and the stirrup, that's the part that fits under the boot. Most climbers get their own spikes once they learn their preference of support."

He held up his gage. "This is your gage. It keeps you alive and you use it every day, no matter what, before you leave the ground. Once a gaff blade is replaced it's garbage. Do *not* toss it back with the others."

He knew he was going fast, but he wanted this done with. He pointed to the blade at the bottom of the stirrup. "This is the gaff. You want to check its radius, width, length, and sharpness. A chiseled point gives you easy penetration." He swallowed.

Keep it about trees.

"Yours probably needs to be sharpened. I'll show you how to use the vise."

Tristan silently followed him to the sharpener in the back of the shop. He instructed him on how to effectively clamp the spike in place between two blocks of wood and unrolled his sharpening tools.

"You got your smooth cut file, honing stone, and gage." He ignored the sensation thrumming through his body as Tristan crowded behind him. He reached for the file. "Take your file in both hands and draw from heel to tip in a smooth, over and down motion along the underside."

Was it his imagination, or did Tristan just step closer? Sweat beaded at his temples as he gripped the file and indicated the proper procedure.

Clearing his throat he said, "You don't need to exert too much pressure." His voice sounded constricted as the words rasped out. "Next slip it in the hole of the gage and check the fit. You wanna also check the thickness and width to make sure there's no difficulty penetrating." *And there was that word again...*

Luke quickly finished checking his spike and removed it from the vise. Grabbing the plank of soft pine on the table, he lined up the shaft. "To test the tip, you want to line up the wood. You shouldn't need to use too much pressure. A good point will penetrate easily, sliding through the wood."

Fuck. Is it a thousand degrees in here?

Once he was finished, he stepped aside and nodded in Tristan's general direction for him to try. Tristan fit the climber into the vise, tightened, measured, filed, and sharpened with little issue. He quickly completed the process with the other climber and removed the equipment. "Done."

His voice was clipped and indifferent as though they were merely strangers, one orienting the other with job and safety procedures. Good. That was likely the best way to go about business, regardless of how much his gut seemed to squeeze in protest.

They left the hanger and Luke led him through the forest to the practice tree. He sat on a nearby stump and latched up his straps, rings, and fasteners, monitoring Tristan's actions to see that he was keeping up. When he glanced at his profile it was set with focus and there were no signs of anything other than determination.

Luke secured his harness and approached the tree. "Bell's at the top. You got to ring it a dozen times before we let you play with the big tools. I'll show you how it's done."

He flicked his lanyard around the trunk and planted his spikes in place. Taking quick steps, he shimmied up the hundred-foot tree in a matter of minutes. Fisting the rope of the bell, he gave it a hard ring and shimmied back down.

Landing on the ground with a crunch that jolted his bad knee, he smothered the urge to wince. "You ready?"

It would likely take Tristan a day or two to build up the technique and stamina to reach the bell. Most guys weren't given saws until their second or third week of training.

Tristan stepped in front of the tree and checked all his gear. Without comment, he mimicked Luke's example and swung the lanyard around the trunk, locking it into place. His first step was smooth and he wasted no time leaving the ground.

Luke frowned as he crossed the halfway mark without pausing for breath. He was speechless when he heard the echo of the bell. His lips twitched, wanting to praise Tristan, but he bit back any compliments.

Tristan shimmied back down in no time. His spikes cut into the soil as he reconnected with solid ground. He nodded in Luke's direction, not boastfully, just assertively. "Eleven to go."

It took only a few hours for Tristan to ring that bell twelve times. Luke knew his body had to be feeling it. Even though he'd met his quota, he wouldn't be playing with tools today. His limbs needed to be rested and sure.

There could be no room for slip-ups fifty feet in the air while operating a power tool capable of killing a man.

When he was making the final trek down, Luke's father approached. "Been hearing a lot of ringing. What number's he on?"

Eyes focused on Tristan's body smoothly descending, he said, "This is twelve."

His dad let out a slow whistle. "That's a first. Think he's trying to prove something?"

Maybe. But it wasn't about proving what his dad might think. He lied anyway. "I think he's trying to prove he's capable and prepared to work."

Frank nodded. "Good. We need more guys of that mindset. Don't let him get near the tools today. Tell him to organize the equipment room until it's time to clock out." With that he returned to his truck and drove away.

Tristan turned and faced Luke when he made it to the ground. A hard glint resonated in his eyes. His hair was tied back and sweat left his throat damp. He guzzled water from the bottle that had been holstered to his utility belt and said, "That's twelve."

"Come with me." Luke led him back to the equipment room. "You can hold onto those spikes if you're comfortable with them. Get yourself a lock for your locker. The rest of this stuff needs to be organized and the floor needs to be swept out when you're done. That should take you until five."

"What do I look like, the janitor? Give me a real job."

Luke bristled. "This is a real job. You don't like it, door's that way."

"You're sticking me in here on purpose. What the fuck?"

Luke took a quick step forward and pointed in his face. "I'm sticking you in here because after exerting yourself all morning it isn't safe to send you up again with a saw. This is a family-run business and as such, we all pull our weight. Broom's in the corner. Get to work."

He turned and grabbed his hard hat on the way out and nearly crashed into his brother, Finn. "Yo, bro, where you rushing off to?"

"Sorry. I've been training all morning. You know I hate that shit."

Finn eyed him curiously. "Ryan's friend, right? I heard he got his twelve in record time. Pretty impressive."

Luke shrugged as if it made no difference to him. "Where's everyone working?"

"Just got back from the 246th Acre. I need to switch out my gaffs then we're heading over to 247 to clear out those oaks. Got room in my truck if you want to wait."

"Nah, I'll meet you there."

"All right."

He pressed past his brother and didn't raise his head until he got to his truck. Jamming his key in the ignition, the engine rolled over, and gravel spewed from his tires as he backed out of the lot. After making it to a rarely used road, he jerked the wheel and threw the truck in park.

His palm stung as it slammed down on the steering wheel. "Fuck!" He hit it several more times and was panting by the time he calmed himself.

He should not be having these thoughts. He liked

women. Tiffany sang his praises all night after he'd blown off Tristan. He wasn't fucking gay!

Scraping his hands over his face he fisted his hair and growled long and hard. *"God damn it!"*

Gripping the back of his neck, he stared blankly at his lap. Visions of Tristan's hands, eyes, lips, arms, and hair bombarded him. He could still conjure the incredible scent of his skin, recall the unmatchable feel of his mouth. Yet he had no recollection of Tiffany's body from the night before.

Probably because every time you fucked her you had your eyes screwed shut and were imagining someone else.

No. That wasn't true. But it was.

He hit the wheel again and cursed. He just needed to get over this. He'd fuck everything with tits until the sheep were scared, if that's what it took. He was Luke fucking McCullough for fuck sake. McCullough men were virile, potent, and strong, not fucking pansies.

CHAPTER 4

The following six weeks followed the same format. Tristan had mastered everything at the yard, including organizing the tool room better than anyone else ever had. Meanwhile, Luke was losing himself in a revolving door of pussy and on the brink of having a major meltdown.

His eyes stared out the windshield as the female head adorned with blond curls bobbed over his cock. He focused on the security lights at the back of O'Malley's as his own head rested on the back of the seat and his beer dangled from his fingers hanging out the window.

Slurping sounds and soft keening noises rose up to his ears every few minutes, but other than that he could have been at the dentist for all the pleasure he was feeling. Tanya or Tina or whatever was doing a fine job. She got an A for effort, but Luke really didn't give a shit if she finished or left him like that.

The back door of the bar opened and Kelly stepped out hauling a bag of trash to the dumpster. He paused when he saw Luke's truck and shook his head. His brother hurled the bag into the bin and slowly approached.

Kelly's palm banged twice on the hood. "Wrap it up. This ain't no disco. This ain't no country club either. And this sure as fuck ain't L.A. so either get a room or say goodnight."

That blond head popped up, eyes wide and lips glossy. She dragged her hand over her mouth and cursed. Kelly raised a brow, but kept his distance.

"You better pack it up, sweetheart," Luke suggested without emotion.

"Isn't that your brother?" she asked.

"Yeah, but he makes the rules here. How about I call you tomorrow?"

"You don't have my number."

Because he didn't want it. He slid her his phone. "Plug it in."

Dainty little fingers moved over his phone. "There. Now you have it." Smiling, she pressed a kiss to his cheek. "Sorry we couldn't finish. Tomorrow you can come to my place."

Not likely. "Sounds like a plan."

As she slid out the passenger door, Luke stuffed himself back in his pants, lifting his hips to right his zipper. He wasn't even fully hard. Once Curls made it back to her Ford Focus, Kelly approached his window and tapped his beer.

"You can't have beer outside the bar. You know that,

Luke." Ignoring his brother, he took another swig. "What's going on, Luke? You were bad before, but now you're worse. It's a different girl every week."

He scoffed. "Like you can talk. I have yet to meet someone who hasn't made your acquaintance."

"That's different. They know what they're getting with me. I make sure they enjoy themselves."

"I haven't gotten any complaints."

"That's because you're gone the second you finish. I hear them talkin'. Even saw a few of them cry."

Luke should feel bad, but he didn't. "I ain't forcing nobody. I can't help it if they're easy."

"That's fucked up and you know it. When are you gonna stop acting like a prick and go back to the old Luke?"

The old Luke was gone and never coming back. "Do yourself a favor, Kelly, and stop waiting for me to be something I'm not. The sooner all of you accept this is who I am, the sooner we can all get on with this shitty thing called life."

"I'm cutting you off."

His eyes cut to his brother's and saw steely determination he wasn't used to finding there. What did he know? He was still a kid.

Finishing his beer he shoved it in Kelly's direction. His brother caught the bottle and Luke started the truck, pulling away before Kelly could give him shit for drinking and driving. He didn't need to listen to that crap. He backed out of the lot and drove until the sun came up the following morning.

Sunday morning he went with his family to church. Luke wasn't a bad guy. And once his sodden brain dried out, he didn't like the cloudy memories he'd created over the last few weeks.

Sheilagh sat beside him in the pew as Father Mark carried on with his homily. She looked different, refined or something. Her makeup wasn't as all over the place as it usually was and she didn't seem to radiate awkwardness. This summer had definitely changed her. She was growing up.

His mom and dad sat side by side before them and Luke knew without looking that they were holding hands. That was right. That was what love looked like. Kelly, as usual, wasn't there, but Finn was.

He and Erin sat motionless across the aisle. He wondered how long until his twin married his high school sweetheart. She was cute, but not much of a prize. She sort of bossed Finnegan around and undervalued him. Luke didn't know why his brother didn't tell her to knock it off.

His gaze moved to the back of the church. There was his Aunt Rosemarie, Ryan, and Pat. No Tristan. He saw Tristan from time to time at O'Malley's and avoided him whenever at work. Twice, his presence at the bar had spurred Luke to openly proposition whatever female was next to him and twice the repercussions had left him with an acidic sensation in his gut.

Tristan wasn't shy about watching him. His mouth

never quirked in a smile when he was around. His eyes were always focused, seeing, and scrutinizing. Luke knew he was a prick to flaunt other hookups in his presence, but it had to happen. Tristan had to understand Luke was straight and whatever they shared meant nothing but too many beers.

That was bullshit. He fucking dreamt about the guy. Not just in a sexual sense either. He dreamt of them hanging out, driving in his truck, and lying close in the warmth of his bed.

When Tristan was around, Luke couldn't help but stand to attention. His neck prickled with awareness and his pulse quickened and then there was the way his body hardened every time he sensed his presence. It was fucking killing him.

Dear God, make it end. Either make the feelings go away or let me end this miserable existence.

Things were getting so bad he didn't even want to go to work. Ryan had started, and he and Tristan had a great friendship that grated on Luke's last nerve. His cousin didn't seem to give a shit if Tristan fucked women, men, or goats for that matter. To Ryan, he was just Tristan and that was enough.

None of the other guys at the yard appeared to know about Tristan's orientation. Whenever the topic of sex came up, he seemed to roll with the punches like any straight man would. He didn't have to like tits in order to comment that they were big. He tossed out a comment here and there and that alleviated any possible questioning glances, which never came.

When mass ended he went to his truck. "Luke, can I get a ride back with you?"

He turned and found Sheilagh at his heels. "Yeah. Where's your car?"

"The belt broke again."

They climbed into his truck and he backed out. Once the parade of church traffic dissipated, he took the back road home.

"Can I ask you something?" Sheilagh said in a small voice that sounded nothing like her usual one.

"Sure."

"Do you think I'm pretty?"

"I think you're beautiful, Sheilagh. Why? Do I need to kick someone's ass?"

"No. It's just… I like this guy and whenever I see him around he doesn't seem to notice me."

"Then he's an idiot."

"I think it's because I'm immature."

He glanced at her then returned his eyes to the road. "You're going through a tough stage. You're almost an adult, but still very much a child. Don't get pissed. It's true and we've all been there. Before you know it, you'll get a handle on all these new feelings. You'll understand your body is its own work of art. And that guy will eventually see he's either got a shot at the best girl in Center County or he missed his chance, because she's found someone better. Just don't go giving it away for free. You make them work for it, you hear? And if any guy gets a little too fresh, you tell me. You got five older brothers. A guy would have to be a complete sadist to treat you wrong."

He paused and frowned. "Scratch that. Maybe you should just hold off for a while on the boy stuff."

She snorted. "Like the rest of you held off on the girl stuff? I'm not deaf, Luke. I hear about you and Kelly."

He inwardly flinched at being placed in the same category as his reprobate brother, Kelly. With three other brothers to emulate, Kelly's behavior toward women was probably the least flattering. "Just...just keep your legs shut."

"Ew! Please stop talking now."

They were silent for a moment. God, was Sheilagh having sex already? "Do you know what an STD looks like? You should look it up on the internet."

"*What?*"

He couldn't stop thinking about his little sister having sex and he needed to make sure she didn't. Ever. "Then there's pregnancy. After that your life and dreams come second and your body's never the same."

She scoffed. "And you know this because you've carried how many babies to term? Jesus, Luke, I thought we could talk about this seriously. I should have gone to Kelly."

"Do *not* get dating advice from Kelly." That would be a huge mistake. Kelly slept with anything female. *Yeah, sort of like you've been doing.* Damn it! He gritted his teeth. "Fine. We can talk about this. What do you want to know?"

"Really?"

"Yes, but keep it PG."

"What do guys find attractive in women?"

"Brains."

"Luke!"

"I'm serious. Intelligence is the greatest turn on. Nothing's sexier than a smart girl. A smart *virgin* girl."

"I'll ignore that last comment. What *physical* traits do guys find sexy?"

He let out a slow rumbling breath. "A smile is usually the first thing I notice. If a girl's frowning I tend to think she's a bitch."

"Maybe she's just sad."

"Maybe."

"What else?" she asked.

He thought for a minute. What did he find sexy? Broad shoulders, toned arms, capable calloused hands. Fuck. "Boobs."

Sheilagh frowned, her chin dipped as she peeked down her blouse. "Do you think a certain color hair is pretty?"

Yes. Brown hair with sun bleached highlights, long, down to the shoulders, and tied back so he could see the hard line of Tristan's jaw and every flex of his throat. "Hair's hair."

"Do you think red hair is ugly?"

He scowled and faced his sister then turned his focus back to the road. "No, I don't think red hair is ugly. What the fuck, Shei? Every woman in my family is practically a red head and I think they're all beautiful. Who's putting this shit in your head?"

"No one. I'm trying to figure out why no one sees me."

"Maybe they see too much of you. Try reeling it in a bit."

"I have been. I hate that I'm always the loud one. I've been trying to act a little more…classy."

"Well, classy might be pushing it. You are, after all, a McCullough. Just be yourself and when the right guy notices you, it'll be because who you're naturally attractive to him. No one wants to be in a relationship with someone fake."

"Do you think age matters?"

He was grateful they were almost home, but he slowed down, because that was a question that needed his full attention. "How old?"

She shrugged. "It's just a question." She was lying. She had her eye on someone older.

"You aren't an adult yet. It's statutory rape for a man to be with you."

She rolled her eyes. "It was just a question, Luke."

"Bullshit. How old?"

"Just a few years. It doesn't matter anyway. At the pace he's moving, it'll take him eight months to get there. By then I'll be an adult."

"No one's moving anywhere. Especially not some old clown after your V card."

"How do you know that card's not punched?"

He growled. "Not funny, Sheilagh."

She snickered. "It's a little funny."

"Jesus. Just…don't rush into anything."

He pulled up in front of his parents' house and she hopped out. "I won't. Thanks for talking to me, Luke."

He hesitated. He didn't want to suffocate her or himself, but this was his baby sister. "Sheilagh, if you ever need anything, even if it'll make me mad to hear about it, you know you can count on me."

She smiled and he felt like the biggest prick in the world. Whatever he'd just said, he meant, but it seemed like his little sister had been waiting a lifetime for that reassurance. "I love you, Luke."

"I love you too, Shei-Devil. Now go say the rosary or something."

She laughed and shut the door. He drove to the barn and sighed. There. That wasn't too difficult. He actually felt a little proud of himself. He'd done something good for a member of his family and it had nothing to do with stats or touchdowns or colleges. It only had to do with him.

TRISTAN SLIPPED UP the stairs and into the bedroom that had become his over the past few months. His head was spinning from the overflow of relatives there for Rosemarie's birthday. It was only polite that he help out and share the meal, but after that part was over he wanted to flee. It wasn't his family anyway.

Once in his room, he sifted through his drawers and pulled out a thick sweater. In his closet he found his sleeping bag. As autumn was closing in, he felt a pull to be outdoors before the snow came and made that impossible.

He had everything together and was lacing his boots when there was a knock at the door. "Come in."

Sheilagh, Luke's little sister, slipped inside and shut the door. "Hi, Tristan."

"Hey, baby girl. What's happening?"

She looked at his bed and saw the rolled sleeping bag. "You going somewhere?"

"Just taking a little overnight trip."

Her smile faltered. "Oh. With a girl?"

He laughed. "Nah. I don't got a girl."

Her grin returned. "Oh, well, in that case… Where're you going?"

"Wherever I land."

"Can I come?"

Fuck. "Uh…" He stuffed his keys in his pocket and pulled her to the bed, wedging the pile of his things between them. "Look, Sheilagh, I think you're real sweet, but you're not my type."

"Why?"

"Well, for one, you're still young. I don't think your family would appreciate that."

"I won't be a kid forever."

"I know. And I bet, when you're older, you'll be fightin' off more guys than you can handle. But do me a favor and just be a kid for now, okay? All the other stuff can wait. Have fun and be young. You only get one shot at it."

She nodded quietly and he noticed how different she looked from the first time he'd met her. She had the perfect complexion of lily-white skin. Her lips seemed permanently stained with berries and her hair was the most radiant shade of copper. He had no doubt she'd be fighting them off.

He squeezed her hand. "We're friends, right, baby girl?"

She gifted him with a brilliant smile. "Of course."

"Well, as your friend, I wanna tell you that if you ever need anything, I'll be there. One of those boys your age comes knocking and you want them to leave you be, you tell me and I'll handle it."

"Okay," she said almost breathlessly.

He stood. "Now I gotta get going, but you come talk to me whenever you need a good ear."

"What if I can't find you and something's wrong?"

He went to his nightstand and jotted down his number. "There. Now you'll always be able to find a friend when you need one."

After she left, he sighed. He knew the girl had feelings for him, but she was too young. It didn't matter what type he liked, she was far too young to even think about, so there was no point in telling her he liked men. She'd eventually get over her little crush and find a nice boy her own age.

Grabbing the last of his things, he slipped out the back of the house and found his old bomber truck parked in the midst of the rest of the cars. He managed to back out without doing too much damage to the lawn, and as he took to the road he sighed at the sense of freedom approaching.

He didn't know where he was heading, but once he found it, he'd recognize it. There was plenty of open state land in Center County and he was bound to find a small place to hunker down for the night.

As he waited at the light at the edge of town, he

spotted Luke's truck and his gut clenched. Moisture beaded his brow as every emotion elicited by this man's presence took over his body and his conscience battled to logically outsmart chemical attraction. Luke equaled rejection and pain. Self-preservation had him gritting his teeth and refusing the temptation of vulnerability.

Even from across the intersection, heading in the opposite direction, that man triggered something inside of him. But that was just it. They were headed in the opposite directions.

He was done playing games. Luke clearly regretted their encounter and Tristan had no desire to see him take off with yet another willing female. It hurt, but the pain was slowly subsiding. Or so he told himself.

Luke's truck idled on the other side of the traffic light, likely heading to his Aunt Rosemarie's for the party. As they waited for the light to turn green their eyes met. He kept his expression blank and prayed the light would change soon.

When it did, he let out a breath he didn't know he was holding and proceeded on his way. The sound of tires squealing pulled his gaze to the rear view. Luke's truck fishtailed and was suddenly barreling after him. "What the fuck?"

Tristan tried to ignore the truck trailing him. *He probably just forgot something and was heading back to the barn.*

When he pulled onto the jug handle leaving town, he was surprised to see Luke speed up. The road opened up and Tristan increased his speed. Luke trailed him for a quarter mile then moved to the passing lane. Tristan's truck couldn't go past sixty-five and Luke probably had places to be.

When Luke cut in front of him in the pokey lane he frowned. "Come on, man, don't be a dick."

His taillights kicked on and Tristan pressed his foot into the brake. Their speed dropped down to forty. When the blinker went on, Tristan slowed some more. Luke's truck pulled onto the shoulder several yards ahead. Was he having car trouble? Should he keep going?

He didn't know what to do and really didn't feel like fighting. It would be dark soon and he wanted to find a place to settle in. With a tightness in his chest he didn't like, he hit his turn signal and pulled up behind Luke's truck.

He waited and the knot in his chest constricted. When Luke's door finally opened he stopped breathing. Their eyes met and Tristan couldn't make sense of the blank expression on his face.

Nerves knotted his stomach at the thought of a possible oncoming argument. He got that the guy wasn't gay. It wasn't like Tristan needed the message drilled into his head.

He rolled down his window as Luke approached. "Party's that way," Luke said.

He kept his tone light and non-confrontational. "I have somewhere to be. They're all still there."

"Where?" Luke asked, his jaw tightening.

Tristan frowned. "At the party. It's still going on."

"No. Where do you have to be?"

"It's personal."

His eyes narrowed. "Meetin' someone?"

Seriously? "What if I was?"

"Who?"

"Jesus, Luke, why do you care?"

"Just curious?"

He shut his eyes and counted to ten. If he wanted to count higher he could just count all the woman Luke had fooled around with in the past month. "What do you want?"

Luke didn't answer.

"Look, if you don't need help and you just pulled over to interrogate me, I gotta go."

"You."

Tristan turned at the whispered word. "What?"

"You. I want…you."

His stomach dropped out. He couldn't go through this again. "I'm not some thing you get to play with and toss away when you're bored, Luke. Go find someone else to occupy your time."

He shook his head and worked his jaw. "It doesn't work. I know I've been a complete asshole these past few weeks and I'm sorry. This isn't me. None of it is."

"Do *you* even know who you are?"

"No!" he said, staring back with such desperation his fear was obviously genuine. "I don't fucking know. I thought I did, but then everything changed. Then you came along and I don't understand any of this. I don't look at men. I don't notice them. It's always been women, but you…you I see. I see you in my dreams and I see you when I'm lying in bed at night wishing you were there. It doesn't matter who I'm with. I shut my eyes and I know it's not you and I hate myself that much more in the morning."

Sometimes emotions in a relationship took time to develop, but sometimes they didn't. In cases like Luke McCullough, the chemical reaction was impossible to ignore. However, Tristan spent weeks convincing himself those feelings were one sided. What if they weren't? It was a risk linking his happiness to someone as confused as Luke. The man changed his mind as often as most people changed their socks.

"And what if I believe you? You gonna run the next time things get a little hard?"

"No."

"I don't know if I can trust that, Luke. You fucking hurt me."

His sad gaze settled on Tristan. "I'm sorry."

Tristan sighed, his head falling back. Shit. "Luke...I know this is all new to you. I know you aren't *gay*, all right? But I need to know you at least have an open mind. There are gray spots. No one ever said sexuality was black or white. Maybe you're bi."

"Maybe I am."

That surprised him. He hadn't expected his agreement. Pressing his luck, Tristan went all or nothing. "I don't do casual."

Luke's jaw twitched and his nostrils flared. "Good, because the thought of you runnin' off to meet someone else puts me in a rage, Tristan. I don't play well with others and I've never been much for sharing."

Something fluttered in the pit of his stomach and his cock twitched. "Women either, Luke. I won't be filler."

"Just you."

Could this really be happening? He warned himself not to put too much trust in it. Luke was confused and having somewhat of an identity crisis since being injured. This could all be part of it and Tristan could wind up trampled once he got back on his feet. "Now what?"

"Where're you going?"

"I just wanted to take off for a while. Someplace quiet, to think, where the world doesn't know I exist."

"Where?" Luke's blue eyes lit with intrigue and Tristan smiled, liking that Luke valued seclusion as much as he did.

"Haven't found it yet."

"I know the perfect place."

He lifted a brow. "Yeah?"

"Yeah. Do we need anything before we go? It's about fifteen miles from here."

We. God, he wanted to be a complete fruitcake and throw out something like, *All I need is you, baby.* But they definitely weren't there. They might never be. "I'm good."

Luke grinned and slapped his hand on the base of the window, "Then follow me, cowboy."

His mind jolted as his heart did a little flip. Cowboy. He'd never ridden a horse in his life. Those big bitches scared the shit out of him with their wild eyes and skittish legs, but if that's what Luke wanted to call him, he definitely wasn't going to object. *Maybe I'll take you for a ride...*

He followed Luke back toward town. When it

appeared they were heading to his place, Luke suddenly turned down a beaten path that was hardly a road. His truck slowly barreled over the pocked thoroughfare and even if they'd only traveled a few miles it took the better part of a half an hour.

That was good. It gave him time to think and pull himself together. He didn't want to get too far ahead of himself. Just because they said they were going to do this didn't mean they had to do everything in one night.

When the road became more obscure Tristan started to hear dueling banjoes in his head. Where the fuck was Luke taking him? Finally, the truck in front of him stopped and Tristan had no fucking clue where they were.

When Luke climbed out of his vehicle, Tristan followed. "I'm having memories of *Deliverance*."

Luke laughed. "Not quite." He pointed to a small cabin in the distance. "That's our hunting spot. This is our property. No one comes up this way unless it's open season. It's private."

Okay. Private was good. He reached for his bag and when he turned Luke was right behind him. Tristan drew in a breath, his heart picking up pace.

Luke's feet shifted and he stepped closer. Tristan saw the vulnerability in his eyes, the fear, the courage. He didn't move, wanting to see what he'd do.

When they were standing close enough that their breath mingled, he thought his heart would explode if Luke didn't kiss him soon. He didn't disappoint.

Soft lips brushed his and Luke whispered, "I missed you."

Tristan's eyes fell closed as his head tilted and Luke's mouth sealed over his. His hands slid over the collar of Tristan's shirt until his fingers tightened in his hair. He pulled him close and their bodies pressed tight, thigh to thigh, shoulder to shoulder.

A thousand jolts of energy elated inside of him and his blood pumped hard, arousing him instantly. Tristan's arms wound around the other man's back and massaged all the tight muscles there. Luke was an incredible kisser. His lips were full and soft and his tongue knew exactly what to do. Within minutes they were both breathing hard and he could feel Luke's arousal pressing against the bulge in his own jeans.

Luke slowly pulled away and licked his lips. His hooded eyes were sapphire blue and watched Tristan under thick lashes. He was beautiful. "You gonna show me inside?"

His mouth quirked—and there was the dimple. Luke surprised him by sliding his hand over his and relieving him of his bag. Unprepared for such a caring gesture, Tristan turned and grabbed his sleeping bag. He needed a second to compose himself.

Luke frowned. "What's that for?"

"It's my sleeping bag."

"Uh-uh. You're in my bed tonight."

Okay then. He smiled and tossed the bag back in the truck.

Following Luke into the cabin, he was greeted first by the musty sent of unused space. There was an old wood-stove in the center of the room and a dated kitchenette along the wall. Across from that was a futon. The floor was wood and aged. It wasn't much, but Tristan immediately liked it.

A small table with only three chairs was pressed against the wall by the door. The cabinets didn't have doors and were filled with enamel-ware and metal dishes. One shelf was stocked with canned goods.

Luke dropped the bag on the futon. "There's a bedroom back here. It's not much."

He followed him into the back room and stopped abruptly. There wasn't much room to walk. Two twin beds formed an L and a large trunk swallowed the rest of the floor.

"It'll be dark soon. We should carry in some wood so we can have a fire. Temperature drops to the forties this time of year once the sun sets."

"I'll keep you warm." He winced. Maybe he shouldn't say stuff like that just yet.

Luke stilled and turned. His lips seemed set in an almost smile. "Will you?"

Afraid the littlest show of emotional affection could scare him off, he swallowed. "I want to," he rasped.

And there came the full blown smile he'd been hoping for. Christ, he'd never survive this guy.

Luke pivoted and slowly stepped in front of him. His eyes searched over Tristan's face. What he was looking for? Trust? His hand lifted and cupped the side of Tristan's jaw. "I'm glad you're here."

He had no idea. "I'm glad too."

His lips brushed slowly over Luke's in a chaste kiss and

he growled. "Mmm, let's go get the wood so it's done. Then you can show me how you intend on keeping me warm."

"Okay." He couldn't breathe at that one, succinct word.

They carried in the wood in record time. Once Luke stocked the woodstove and stuffed it with paper, the nerves really began to rattle. For some reason this was different from every other encounter Tristan had ever had. It meant something. He didn't know why he was putting so much significance in one moment, but everything seemed important. He felt like a kid again going through his first time. Maybe because this might be Luke's actual first time and that put a lot of pressure on him. He wanted to do everything right.

"You hungry? I ate at the party, but I could eat again." Was he buying them both some time?

"Sure. You wanna put something on? The front burner's busted so use one of the back ones."

Tristan sorted through the selection. Beans, beans, and more beans. No, no, and no. In the back he found some canned chicken soup. That would work. He pulled down the—

His motions stilled as Luke's body pressed into his from behind. Strong arms wrapped around his front and squeezed gently. "Do you mind?"

Tristan swallowed. "Not at all."

Luke's face pressed into his shoulder. "I like being able to touch you without worrying...sorry. Forget I said that."

Unfortunately, he knew exactly what he meant. "It's okay. I know what you mean. I like when you touch me."

"You do?"

Was he insane? "Uh, yeah. A lot."

Luke's hand flattened over his stomach and dragged up his chest. Tristan's body hardened. The hand moved over his shirt, bunching the fabric into little ripples and sending chills up his spine.

"What about when I touch you here?" The hand slid over the bulge at his crotch.

Oh, God, yes, please. "That's good," he croaked.

"I'm not that hungry anymore."

Tristan's hands dropped from the cabinet onto the counter, bracing his weight as he lowered his head. "Okay."

Luke stepped closer and the ridge of his cock pressed through his jeans. "Turn around, Tristan."

Slowly, he pivoted. The hunger in Luke's eyes nearly knocked him to his knees. "God damn." Tristan breathed as he slammed his mouth over his.

Luke's hands forked through his hair, pulling the tie away. His kiss was hungry, beyond hungry, starved, and Tristan met his tongue thrust for thrust.

His hands were everywhere, on his shoulders, under his shirt, at his belt. Tristan backed him against the wall and their bodies crashed together in a collision of need. Luke shoved him toward the futon. "On your back, cowboy."

He shivered and dropped to the old sofa. Luke stood, peeled off his shirt, and kicked something on the side of the frame that had the futon sliding into a double bed.

Luke's eyes drilled into his as he toed off his boots and

undid the top snap of his jeans. Tristan wanted to be naked too. He stripped off his shirt and the minute he tossed it aside, Luke's body blanketed him, hot skin to hot skin.

Their mouths reconnected in a fury of passion. Nipping and licking, their tongues dueled as they groped every bit of exposed flesh they could get their hands on. Without releasing Luke's mouth, he kicked off his boots and twisted until his socks disappeared somewhere.

Dropping back to the cushions, Luke's mouth worked over his chest. His tongue swirled at his nipple and Tristan arched into him. His eagerness stunned him. Strong fingers tugged at his belt and once the buckle was undone, the leather slid through the loops in a fast slither. Rising to his knees, Luke tugged at Tristan's jeans.

When they bunched at his thighs, boxers tangled in the mix, everything stopped. He watched as Luke looked at him for the first time—*Please don't stop*—and waited.

The silent, still, moment carried on too long and fear reared its ugly head. He closed his eyes, not wanting to see the moment old Luke returned and looked away. Then the heat of Luke's hand traced, feather light, over his shaft and his eyes shot open.

Luke wasn't looking into his eyes, but rather, at him. He didn't fist him or even try to cup him. He simply dragged the pads of his fingers slowly over Tristan's rigid flesh as if he'd never seen a cock before.

"You're big," he whispered.

"I've seen bigger," he joked and Luke seemed to get he was referring to him.

His cheeks flushed and he returned to his slow perusal. "I've never touched someone else's."

"I know. We don't need to rush."

Blue eyes locked with his. "I want to. You have no idea how much. So much it scares the fucking hell out of me. I'm just not sure I know how."

"Just…do what you're comfortable with. Do what you like."

"I like your mouth on me."

Tristan smiled and chuckled. "I like that too."

"I can't believe this is happening."

"Why? It happens all the time, Luke."

"Not with me. Not like this."

That hurt. "If you want to stop, we can stop. But this time, when you walk away, do me a favor and don't trample me in the process."

Luke's hard scowl cut into him and he snapped, "What the fuck are you talking about? I meant I never feel this sort of connection with someone."

Relief and regret tunneled through him so fast he wasn't sure which emotion was responsible for the tight pinching in his chest. "I'm sorry. I thought—"

"I wouldn't have brought you here if I wasn't sure this was what I wanted."

"How am I supposed to know that? You're asking me to go by the last hour and forget everything you showed me in the last two months."

Luke licked his lips as if considering that. "Trust. I trust you, Tristan. No one else gets this side of me, but you do. I'm trusting you not to…"

Tell.

"Okay. But you have to give me a chance to catch up. You hurt me, Luke. Bad. I'll give it a second chance, because I feel it too. All these emotions are intimidating and coming at me faster than I can process. You're different. I like you way more than I probably should."

"You do?"

"Fuck yeah. It killed me, these past two months."

"I promise, I'll never do anything like that again. Hurting you…it didn't feel good. It hurt me just as much."

"You're gonna have other moments that freak you out. I can't help you through them if you shut me out, Luke. You have to give me your word, that if something comes up and you get spooked, you'll talk to me."

"I promise."

Tristan wasn't sure there was a way to express how much his promise meant. "Kiss me."

Luke grinned and lowered his body to his, his mouth making slow, sweet work of unraveling Tristan's senses. They kissed, simply kissed, for a long time. Luke's body curved and arched over his, his nipples dragging teasingly over Tristan's skin.

Fingers wrapped around his wrists, pinning them into the space above his head and Tristan arched as he ground his cock into Luke. No one had ever treated him with such sensual tenderness. Every look, every caress, and every kiss, was a prelude to something incredible. Something neither of them was prepared for. Luke's seemingly innate touches left him in awe.

Luke's body slid lower. Soft kisses pressed into Tristan's stomach. The drag of Luke's wet tongue was perhaps the most incredible sensation he'd ever felt. Then his strong fingers wrapped around his cock. They tightened and slowly tugged at his flesh. And when Luke's mouth closed over the tip, Tristan nearly came.

"Jesus."

Luke smiled. Tristan felt the curve of his lips as he licked over his flesh and experimented with taking him into his mouth. It wasn't fast and it didn't have to be. It was amazing. Luke's innocence and inexperience showed, but only in the most charming sense.

"This is different," he said, licking up Tristan's shaft. "There's so many things I want to try, I'm just not sure where to start."

He was starting off just fine.

Sliding lower, Luke stroked him. He'd yet to take Tristan fully in his mouth, but that was fine. It felt incredible. His balls lifted and Luke pressed an open mouth kiss to the crease of his thigh. Tristan's knees drew up, opening himself to that exploring mouth.

"I love your scent here. It's you, but a thousand times stronger."

"Keep talking like that and you're gonna make me come."

Luke's hand tightened on the base of his cock. "Not yet."

His body shivered at the commanding tone. That amazing mouth traveled up his shaft, over his balls, and across his hips. It was the longest foreplay he'd ever tolerated. He wanted it to end and wanted it to last forever. His body was so turned on, his mind beyond seduced, he'd never felt such pleasure and they hadn't even done anything yet.

"What about here?" Luke asked quietly, his finger grazing the throbbing knot of Tristan's ass.

"There's good too…" he could barely talk.

Luke's body slid off the futon and onto the floor. Tristan spread his legs as they were given a little nudge. His balls lifted and cool hair teased his thighs as Luke's head lowered.

The press of his finger was subtle, hesitant. Tristan patiently waited for him to go on.

"Roll to your stomach."

Easing up, Tristan turned, positioning himself on his stomach at the edge of the mattress. Luke gripped his hips and slowly pulled him back until his knees were also on the hard floor. His palm flattened on his back and rode up his spine until his chest was pressed into the mattress.

Large hands smoothed over his ass. Two thumbs parted his cheeks and then that wicked tongue traced from the back of his balls all the way to his hole. Tristan grunted and moaned.

"This okay?"

Jesus. There had never been anything better. How was this man so gifted when he'd never had a gay experience before meeting Tristan? He wondered if it was an innate part of Luke, something that had been repressed for far too long. "Everything you're doing feels incredible."

Sharp teeth nipped his cheek as strong hands spread them, pulling his skin tight, opening him more. Tristan rocked his hips into the low frame of the bed as Luke slowly kissed those tender muscles.

He heard the slurp and pop of Luke's mouth and then there was a wet finger pressing into him. "Is this okay?"

"That's fine," he rasped, breathless.

Luke pressed deeper. It was slow and euphoric. Monumental. He didn't stop until his knuckle budded up against his rectum. Tristan's eyes closed. He could feel them rolling back in his head.

"You like that?"

"I love it."

"What does it feel like?" Luke slowly withdrew and pushed back in.

"Good. Deep. Full. Fucking amazing."

"When you…have sex, are you usually on the top or bottom?"

"Top."

His motions stilled, as he seemed to process this. "All the time?"

"I've bottomed, but I usually like to feel in control."

"I want control," Luke whispered and pressed his finger deep.

He couldn't fucking concentrate with his finger up his ass. He was about to blow all over the fucking mattress. "We'll figure it out later." His voice sounded guttural to his own ears.

Luke grunted. "Yeah we will. I plan on having you begging for my dick inside that sweet ass."

Holy fucking shit. Tristan's brain short-circuited. He

cursed, reached under his body and squeezed his cock hard so he didn't come. Luke noticed and chuckled.

"That turn you on? Thinking about my cock drilling into your tight ass?"

"Fuck, Luke, you're killing me."

"The first time I make you come, you're gonna blow so hard you'll never forget it."

His finger yanked out of his ass and his tongue was suddenly there, impaling his soft flesh. Tristan's hand was jerked away and replaced with Luke's. Strong fingers tightened on his cock and tugged hard. Three strokes and he was shooting like a fucking teenager, all over the bed.

His body twitched and shivered as Luke bit his ass and kissed up his spine. This was not the man he'd been with six weeks ago. This was not the unsure, diffident, scared guy who'd blown him off. This was a new Luke. A Luke that knew exactly what he wanted and was determined to get it.

As Tristan caught his breath, his mind spun. He wanted *him.* His desire was almost painful to process. The intensity of his yearning was terrifying, because in that moment he wanted him *forever.*

CHAPTER 5

"This soup is terrible," Luke said, shoveling in another bite of the watered down noodles.

Tristan smirked, a soft crease around his eyes, and a devastatingly handsome quirk to his lips. How had he resisted him for so long? Luke's mind was still reeling from watching him come apart beneath him, feeling him lose himself under his touch. It was the most sensual moment of his life.

"What's your favorite food?" Tristan asked.

Luke tipped his head in contemplation. "I love my mum's chicken casserole."

"How does she make it?"

"I have no idea, but it's like biting into heaven. You'll have to try it."

Tristan's expression suddenly shifted from easy going to burdened. Quietly, he asked, "Will you tell them? Your family?"

Luke stilled. Absolutely not. He wasn't ready to tell anyone. His decision was pure instinct, but there was more to it. He wasn't ready to share this part of himself with anyone aside from Tristan. He wasn't ready to share Tristan. "Maybe in time."

Tristan's eyes moved over him as if contemplating his answer. "Your family's pretty liberal."

"Yeah. But they're also Catholic."

"Do they see homosexuality as a sin?"

Homosexuality. For some reason that label didn't encompass what he felt about Tristan. It was still sinking in and Luke wasn't sure if he'd ever come to terms with that classification. "I don't know. It isn't something that comes up often."

Tristan pushed his soup away. "When I was younger I always had this fantasy in my head that I'd bring home a lover, maybe when I was older, perhaps coming home for Thanksgiving or some shit. He'd stay at my house and together we'd tell my parents we were in love. They'd be shocked, my dad more than my mom, but then they'd come around and we'd hug it out and eventually all be sitting around watching reruns on late night television like the perfect modern family. I never got that. I under-stand why certain things are private."

"Do you ever talk to them?"

"No. I send my mom a card every Christmas. It's generic and only has my name. But it tells her where I'm living and that I'm alive. That seems to be enough for her. She never writes back."

"What did she do when your dad caught you?"

"Cried. I wasn't hospitalized, but I was in bad shape. After that day, nothing was ever the same. If I walked into a room, he walked out. I'd catch her wiping her eyes and sometimes I told myself it was because she hated her husband, but I was never sure if it was because she hated him for what he'd done or me for what I was. I don't know if I'm strong enough to ever ask the truth."

"There was a gay guy in our high school," Luke said quietly, remembering what his team had done to him and how he laughed with the rest of them. It wasn't funny now. It stopped being funny the day they read the kid's obituary—at least for most of them.

"I'm not going to ask you about that, because by the look in your eyes it isn't a memory you want to remember. People change, Luke. No one has the right to throw the first stone because no one's perfect and none of us even know what perfect is. Society is the last measuring stick we should use. Just take a look at the horrid beliefs we've applied over history."

He lost his appetite. "Is this…are we a couple now?"

Tristan's brow shot up. "Uh, yeah."

He nodded. Good. He was hoping that was the case, but this was so different from any other relationship he'd ever had. He wasn't remotely close to understanding the dynamic and who fulfilled which role.

He'd always imagined settling down with a wife. She was stacked, could bake, and knew how to decorate the shit out of a Christmas tree. Never in a million years had he contemplated any future remotely close to this. Although, this was far from the outcome. This was the very beginning, but he wanted it to last—for at least a while.

"What are you thinking about?"

"How life is surprising."

"I think it's all planned," Tristan said. "I think the bad things that happen are actually good things disguised as challenges to make us stronger and carve us into who we're meant to be. Destiny."

"Do you like sports?" Luke asked, preferring to leave Tristan's deep insight for another time.

He chuckled. "Did you think I pranced around in high heels and painted my nails in private? Yes, I like sports. But be fair warned, I'm a Dallas fan."

He groaned. "That's gonna be an issue."

Tristan laughed.

After they cleaned up from dinner, Luke took a shower in the tiny bathroom that barely fit his body. His heart started racing as he was drying off. Outside the door was Tristan. Tall, handsome, southern twang talking, all kissable lips, Tristan.

He gripped the lip of the tiny wall mounted sink and breathed. He couldn't seem to catch his breath. His eyes shut and he experienced the same rush he got running through the tunnel onto the field. Anxiety, adrenaline, and anticipation churned inside of him making him dizzy with a rush unlike anything he'd ever known.

He swallowed and glanced at his reflection. His jaw was shaved, hair trimmed. Unsure what would come next, he hesitated leaving the small room.

The scent of burning wood greeted him as he quietly

cracked the door. Easing into the tight hallway, he caught sight of Tristan's bare back leaning over, his jeans slung low at his tapered waist, as he twisted paper and fed it into the woodstove. He'd gone outside for more wood. He'd also found the linens in the chest and made up the futon bed.

Luke's stomach flipped as he took in the scene of shadows playing over his lover's tanned skin as flames flickered through the opening of the stove. Tristan shut the grate and stood. When he turned, he stilled, realizing he had an audience. "Hey."

Luke's throat dried like the Sahara. "Hey," he rasped.

"I made the bed."

"I saw." He also noticed his bag was tossed conveniently close. Did they need anything? Fuck, condoms would've been smart. His insides seemed to take a dip at that thought.

"I think I'll grab a quick shower too, if you don't mind."

That was good. Give him some time to process. "Okay."

Tristan passed him and Luke sucked in a deep breath as he dragged the tips of his fingers over the lower part of his sternum. His cock came to attention and he caught Tristan's wrist, pulling him close for a brief kiss.

Tristan smiled against his lips and nibbled, then stepped back. "Five minutes."

The door to the bathroom closed and Luke debated staying in his towel, losing it, or slipping back into his jeans. He dropped to the low bed and eyed Tristan's bag. Listening for the running water, he tipped his finger in the open zipper compartment and peeked in without disturbing much.

Looking back at the hall to make sure he was alone, he leaned over to scope things out. There was a sweater, a book and a small black toiletry case. He slowly undid the toiletry zipper. Travel toothpaste, a toothbrush in one of those plastic caddies, three condoms, deodorant, and—oil. Thank fuck.

Quickly zipping up the bag, he scooted over on the bed. He looked around the room and waited, tapping his fingers on his thigh anxiously. They were gonna do this. There'd be no going back, no erasing it. Shit. Part of him wanted to bitch out and part of him just wanted to get it over with.

He was suddenly very aware of his body. His cock was hardening and he thought about every part of him, parts of Tristan, and how this whole thing would work.

The water shut off and Luke's breathing sped up. The door to the bathroom opened and Tristan came out wearing a towel. Luke watched as he came closer, taking note of his rigid abs, strong chest, cut arms. He'd bulked up a bit since working in the lumberyard. Then there were all those little white scars, each one a badge of the condemnation he'd lived through. Tristan was a lot stronger emotionally than he came off. He was stoic.

"You okay?" Tristan asked, coming to stand by the bed.

"Yeah. Little nervous," he admitted.

Tristan stepped in front of where he sat. His hand cupped his jaw and his thumb rubbed gently over his cheek. "Your eyes are incredible. You probably hear that all the time."

He didn't and hearing it from Tristan did things to him. He lifted his hands and gently rested them over the towel at Tristan's hips. His thumbs massaged lightly. His skin was smooth, different than a woman's though.

Fingers sifted through his hair and he shut his eyes for a brief moment, luxuriating in the feel of those hands on him. Luke pulled away the towel and there he was. It was still disorienting having all that manliness in his face.

His thumbs ran over the dark hair at the root of Tristan's shaft. It was trimmed short. Tristan's cock lifted and twitched as Luke placed a kiss on the tip. The sound of Tristan sucking in a deep breath had his own body tightening.

Luke's palms glided to his thighs and he opened his mouth, catching the broad end on his tongue. Fingers tightened in his hair. The head was smooth against his lips, odd, but pleasant.

Mouth closing over Tristan's girth, he slid his lips lower. Tristan's hips flexed and pressed deeper, causing Luke to jerk back. His throat constricted, the sudden stab cutting off his air supply making his eyes water.

"Sorry."

"It's okay."

He took him in his mouth again and Tristan's hold on his hair gentled. His palm traced down to the back of Luke's neck and guided him closer. Luke pressed forward, taking him deeper, and adjusted to the feel of him in his mouth. Each time the head bumped the back of his throat he retreated, but tried again.

Saliva built and the friction eased. His lips stretched and tightened as he adjusted his hold on Tristan's thighs.

It was a foreign act, but familiar in that Luke had been on the receiving line and knew how good a blowjob could feel. The idea of giving Tristan such pleasure motivated him to do his best.

"Your mouth feels incredible," Tristan forced out through gritted teeth, as though pleasure made it difficult to form words.

The praise knifed through him like a warm blade into butter, sinking right into his needy, vulnerability. His grip tightened and he increased his rhythm, really getting into it.

Tristan's fingers curled around the back of his neck, pressing him faster, up and down. He sucked harder. Fuck, he loved sucking his cock.

Grunts filled the air and he moaned over the stalk of flesh, knowing exactly how good that slight tingle of vibration could feel.

"Touch my balls, baby," Tristan whispered and Luke nearly preened at the endearment. It didn't feel girly. It felt affectionate. Right.

His hand lowered and cupped the supple sack. Tristan had a good set on him. The soft, warm flesh filled his hand and he slowly stroked the sensitive weight with gentle tugs. Tristan's hips began to rock faster. With each second Luke grew more aroused.

He swallowed back and took him as deep as he could

manage, sending Tristan up on his toes as he held him there, his lips pressed to the firm base, the hair at his pelvic bone tickling his lip.

Tristan let out a guttural moan and Luke drew in a breath through his nose, running his tongue back and forth over the underside as he slowly pulled back. He became drunk on his lover's heady scent.

"Do you want me to come?"

Mouth stretched and full, he glanced up at Tristan as his head fell back with a moan. When he set his eyes on Luke again, he said, "Baby, you keep lookin' up at me with those sweet blue eyes and I won't have a choice in the matter. If you don't want me to explode we should slow down."

He pulled back and released his cock with a slow kiss. "I want you to come. On me."

Tristan's lips parted and his chest rose as he breathed deeply. Catching the back of Luke's head, he pulled him back on his cock. "Open your mouth."

Luke obediently parted his lips and Tristan shoved his cock deep. His scalp tingled as his fingers tightened. Tristan was in complete control and, surprisingly, Luke liked it. He released Tristan's sac and gripped his hips. Both of Tristan's hands held his head, dragging him forward again and again as he fucked his mouth.

Tristan lurched away, startling Luke and rapidly began jerking his cock. "Lay back."

Luke eased backward and caught his weight on the mattress as the first rope of hot come shot across his belly. Fuck. It was the sexiest thing he'd ever seen, Tristan's mouth opened in a silent cry of ecstasy, his eyes closed in pleasure, his throat and chest working as he breathed hard.

When he finished, they both remained silent. There were no words, at least not for him. It was incredible. All Luke could think about was how bad he wanted to fuck him.

Glancing up at Tristan who was still breathing hard, Luke grinned. "I want to be inside of you."

Tristan panted and blinked then slowly nodded. "I have what you need."

Licking his lips, Luke twisted and pulled the towel off his hips. He blotted up the mess on his abs and said, "Get it."

Tristan slowly bent and sifted through his bag. When he stood he held a condom and a small bottle of oil. Luke relieved him of the things they'd need and tossed them on the mattress. He kicked the pillows onto the floor and held out a hand. "Come here, cowboy."

Tristan kneeled on the bed and Luke rose to eye level. Cupping his face, he kissed him deeply. His cock was rock hard and pressed into Tristan's hip. His hands roamed across his lover's body, coasted over his smooth shoulders, traveled down his spine, to grab a delicious fist full of ass.

Tristan moaned. "I need you."

Luke turned him and he settled on his forearms. Reaching for the lube, he snapped open the cap and drizzled a small amount at the base of Tristan's spine. He had an incredible ass. Smooth, round. He wanted to smack it and bite it. But mostly he wanted to bury his cock in it.

He'd done everything on the menu with women, but this was much different. It felt different, somehow more satisfying. He shoved the thought away for another time, returning his focus to Tristan's pleasure.

Dragging his finger through the puddle of oil, he found the tight little knot of muscle nestled between those perfect cheeks. He added more oil to his fingers and rubbed it around until his fingers held a glossy sheen. Wasting no time, he lined his fingertip up with his hole and sank it in to the knuckle.

Tristan's initial grunt turned into a deep baritone moan. "Fuck. Yes."

He withdrew and pumped the digit back inside. His path was slick and smooth, allowing Luke easy penetration. He bent and placed an open mouthed kiss on Tristan's left cheek, sucking his flesh and leaving a slight hickey. *That's my ass.*

He spread Tristan's cheeks and added a second finger, which seemed to really please Tristan. His hips rocked as he backed into each forward thrust of Luke's wrist. He knew there was some trick with the prostate, but he didn't know the details yet, so for right now, he simply fingered him hard and stretched that tight little hole.

Reaching for the oil he used his teeth to flip open the top. He was afraid to hurt Tristan so he added a bit more before tearing open a condom and sliding it on with one lubricated hand.

Adrenaline pumped through him the closer the moment came. Such delicious anxiousness, nothing like he expected. There was no fear, only absolute desire.

Withdrawing his fingers, he lined up his cock. There was a moment, only a second long at best, but he saw everything in that split glimpse of reality. The first time he shook Tristan's hand and the thrill he felt, but didn't yet understand. The first time he saw him smile. The moment he admitted he was his friend. The way he showed him how to use a water saw and how he laughed when Luke accidently sprayed the water all over. The shock that rushed through him when Tristan first kissed him. The moment he knew he wanted to kiss him back. The way he held him when he fell apart and how it felt so terrifyingly right waking up in his arms.

It occurred to him then, in that split second, that he was in love with his friend.

His hand coasted over that long length of back, slowly, affectionately, and he pressed his cock inside by slow increments. His eyes rolled shut at the splendid ecstasy of such heat and compression. His body closed around him like a tight glove and they both sighed.

"Oh, fuck."

His hands rode over Tristan's hips and he squeezed. It was better than anything he'd ever felt in his entire life. "Tristan." His breath escaped in a plea as though saying grace for the incredible feelings bombarding his mind and body.

His hips pulled back and slowly drove forward. The tight friction was almost intolerable. It felt so incredible. He took it slow, savoring the snug grip of Tristan's ass over every smooth ridge of his cock.

Mesmerized, he watched his flesh withdraw and sink

back inside, deep, smooth, right. His hands gripped and curled over his lover's back, petting admiringly over his strong form. Pacing each stroke, embracing each thrust, he made love to this man like he'd never made love to anyone else.

Sweat trickled down his brow and glistened on Tristan's back. His body was like a large cat, angled and graceful. Snapping his hips forward in a hard, measured thrust, Tristan cried out against the tender assault. Luke's balls tapped against his taint as he thrust again. Each penetrating stab of his cock was a reverent show of power, steeped in emotion, drenched in sexual promise. He never wanted to give him up.

The slapping sound of their flesh filled the room. Tristan's voice grew hoarse and Luke's name was the only mantra it sang. He watched as Tristan's fingers tightened over the blankets, pulling them between his knuckles and he drove in hard, swirling his hips as he buried himself as deep as he could go.

His spine tingled and his nuts drew up tight. He was going to come. Withdrawing to the tip, he thrust hard again and again, now drilling his cock into him. "You're mine, Tristan," he hissed as he plowed into him. "*Mine.* You got that? I'm never letting you go."

"I won't let you get away. Fuck. I don't think I'll ever survive losing you again."

Luke's eyes shut and he roared, body twitching as his hips jerked, cum rushing out of his dick. Every nerve fell into a spasm and jangled like he'd been electrocuted with pleasure. Tristan groaned long and hard. His shoulders heaved and tensed as an evident chill took hold of him.

Luke collapsed over him and kissed those broad shoulders reverently. His arms pulled Tristan close, sealing his chest to his strong back. His eyes and mouth screwed shut so he didn't start spewing off things better left unsaid.

With a reluctant sigh, he slowly extricated himself from Tristan's body. He made the sweetest little keening sound, as Luke pulled out then rolled to his back. Tristan wore a soft smile on those incredible lips. "You're amazing."

Luke grinned. He had no idea. Touching his jaw lightly, he said, "Let me clean up and I'll be right back. Do you need anything?"

"Only you."

His words did inconceivable things to him. He nodded and quickly went to the bathroom. Wasting no time, he returned to the bed in less than a few seconds. Tristan hadn't moved. He stared at the ceiling, an expression of pure, satiated bliss on his face.

Luke climbed in beside him and drew up the covers. Tristan adjusted his arms and pulled him to his side. It was amazing how perfectly Luke fit in the crook of his arm.

He thought they'd talk about it, but they didn't. They merely laid in silence and enjoyed the moment. Tristan's finger's traced over his bicep, a seemingly unconscious caress, and Luke shut his eyes, resting his face on his chest. *This* was what he'd always been missing.

CHAPTER 6

Tristan awoke in the dark, taking only a second to recall where he was. The side of his body Luke was curled around was burning up. The rest of his body was freezing. The fire had gone out and Luke slept peacefully beside him. Of course he did. He had all the covers.

Trying not to disturb him, he found a corner of blanket and tugged. Luke grumbled in his sleep and Tristan stilled. He was a fucking ox and the blankets weren't budging.

"Luke," he whispered, but the man didn't move. "Luke."

"Hmm."

He smiled. "You're hogging the covers. It's fucking freezing."

Luke's chest rose as he drew in a deep breath. Without a word, he shifted. Lifting the covers, wrapping a big arm around Tristan's chest, he drew him into the heat of his body. Stubble dragged over his shoulder and warm lips pressed into his skin. "I'll keep you warm."

Tristan blinked, fighting the strange sensation of tears prickling his eyes. How had he gotten here? Never in his life did he imagine this was where last night would lead.

The emotional realization was cut short as Luke made an indignant grunt and flexed his hips, almost playfully. His cock nudged his backside. "You woke me up," he mumbled against Tristan's shoulder. "I'm horny. Wanna fuck?"

Tristan's breath caught at the basic statement, said with a level of ease he never expected from Luke. "Sure."

The bed squeaked as Luke turned. The sound of a zipper buzzed through the quiet cabin followed by the shred of foil tearing. A soft click rent the air and then Luke's body was crowding his back again.

Strong hands dragged over his thigh and caught him below the knee, lifting his legs as Luke pressed close. The heat of Luke's cock fit in the crack of his ass as his hand reached around and cupped his dick. Tristan pressed into his palm and sighed as Luke's fingers curled around him and stroked slowly.

His hips ground into him and after a few minutes Luke rose to his knees. Tristan squinted through the darkness. Blue shadows from the moon pooled through the curtain casting dappled silver highlights on his skin.

Eyes never leaving him, Luke's fingers found his ass and teased. Firm hands gripped his calf and lifted it to his shoulder while Tristan's other leg rested on the mattress just outside of Luke's knees. He licked two of his fingers then wedged them into his ass. Tristan arched as he fucked them into his tight hole.

"You like that?"

"God, yeah." That might be an understatement.

"You want my cock."

His skin pricked with excitement. "Yes."

"Beg me for it."

Lifting a brow, he grinned at the ballsy bastard, but appeased him anyway. "Please put that big cock in me, Luke. I need it, need to feel your hard body pounding into mine."

His teeth flashed white in the darkness and Tristan's leg stretched as Luke bent forward. The blunt end of his dick nudged his opening and he sucked in a fast breath. Luke was enormous in every sense of the word.

His body relaxed and he pushed back into him, and their bodies united as one. Such fullness. He sighed and Luke's labored breath panted out of him, fingers flexing on his calf.

"Can I be rough?"

"Be you. I can take it."

His hips drew back in a slow glide and snapped forward, filling him to the hilt. Flesh smacked against flesh and Tristan grabbed his own cock. His hand jerked hard over his own length as Luke slammed into him again. This time was fast and furious and he loved seeing Luke on the brink of savage.

His name whispered over his lips. "Luke."

"That's it. Say my name."

Rapid thrusts pumped into him and he was out of his

head with lust. Again and again he called Luke's name, the word torn between a curse and a prayer. His hand moved faster as his body tightened.

Luke lifted Tristan's other leg bringing them both to his sides. His strength was impressive. He held him wide and the first jets of hot come tunneled out of Tristan's cock and over his stomach. Luke growled and pounded into him. He was an untamed animal and Tristan couldn't get enough.

His head kicked back and he shouted. "I fucking love being inside of you."

Tristan's insides flew apart as Luke's body locked over his in the rawest display of masculine beauty he'd ever seen. His cock pulsed deep inside of him and he collapsed, catching his weight at the last moment on those strong arms. He breathed hard.

"Look at me," Luke demanded and Tristan focused through the darkness, finding those sharp blue eyes, intense with something unnamable. "I'm in love with you."

Holy shit. His body went cold with a rush of fear, affection, and emotions he'd never experienced before and had no name for. All he could manage to do was breathe.

"You don't have to say it back," Luke quickly said. "But you have to know it. I won't let you go."

His brain was absolute mush. It was too soon. This was all new to Luke. It wasn't safe to trust his confession right after such mind blowing sex. But he wanted to.

He wanted to believe that this incredible man could love him, would take care of him and be humble enough to let Tristan take care of him too. It was a lot. Too much for this heady moment to handle. He gave the only reply he could manage honestly. "I'm not going anywhere."

LUKE WAS A UNIQUE GUY. He liked manly things, shooting guns, the NFL, horsepower, and red meat. But he also had softer sides Tristan suspected most of the world missed when they saw him.

They'd stayed up the rest of the night talking. Holding each other close and whispering about life. They talked about Luke's family and the way he felt he'd let them all down after his injury. He was supposed to be the McCullough's shining star in his mind and he'd burned out before age twenty-five.

They talked about his decision to move out and his need for isolation. Tristan was surprised to learn he was the first person to actually break through the cage Luke locked himself in.

There were parts of Luke that were inherently sad, doubting, in a way Tristan knew only Luke could figure out how to come to reconcile. Then there were funny parts too.

Luke teased him about his southern drawl and Tristan admitted to never having ridden a horse in his life and finding the nickname cowboy, quite amusing. Luke's only reply was to mimic his accent and say, "Well, I'm gonna ride your ass like Sea Biscuit 'til the cows come home."

They laughed and in the morning, as the sun pressed

its pink fingers through the veil of night, they made love. Luke again took him, but this time gently, slowly, tenderly. Tristan never wanted to leave that little cabin in the woods. He was afraid of how Luke would be once the outside world crept back in.

Yes, he was falling in love with him. There wasn't much not to love. He was rough and had a cynical outlook on the world, but Tristan saw the scared boy inside. All he could do was hope that one day Luke would love *himself* enough to let go of the anger and forgive himself for the things beyond his control.

When they had the cabin cleaned and all traces of their visit removed, Luke carried his bag to his truck. "Will I see you tonight?" Luke asked, placing the bag on Tristan's passenger seat.

"That's up to you."

Luke stepped close and pressed his nose to his throat, breathing deep. "I want to," he whispered.

"Maybe we could grab dinner."

Luke's blue eyes moved as he considered the suggestion. "A date?"

"Yeah. Sort of. Nothing wrong with two friends grabbing some food and beer."

"All right. How about I meet you at O'Malley's at six?"

"Sounds like a plan." He turned and caught Luke's mouth in a kiss, not knowing the next time he'd have the opportunity.

Luke cupped his face and pressed his lips hard to his. His hands held him by the jaw as they shut their eyes and breathed each other in. "Thank you," Luke whispered and Tristan felt his gratitude down to his soul.

Yeah. He loved him. Someone had to. He was too much man wrapped up in too many knots to handle it on his own.

He kissed the corner of Luke's mouth. "Thank *you.*" Stepping back, he said, "I'll see you at six."

On the way home his phone buzzed. He frowned when he didn't recognize the number. "Hello?"

"Tristan?"

"Speaking."

"It's Sheilagh…McCullough."

"Hey, baby girl. What's up?"

"How was your trip?"

"Great. How you doin'?"

"I'm good. Bored."

"Not gettin' into trouble, I hope."

She laughed. Now that he was dating Luke, he thought it was sort of sweet the way his little sister looked up to him. Sort of like he had a little sister of his own.

"No. Not getting into trouble. I…um…wanted to know if you knew anything about cars."

"What do you need?"

"The cooling belt broke on my truck. I can take it to the mechanics, but he'll charge me—"

"Nah, don't go to a mechanic for something as simple as that. What kind of car you got? I'll swing into town and pick up a belt. I could probably have you up and running sometime today."

"Really? That'd be great."

"Hey, what are friends for?"

He loved the idea of having a reason to pop over to Luke's neck of the woods. He was doing Sheilagh a favor so there was no guilt about using her as an excuse. This way, he got to see Luke and everybody won.

He found the belt Sheilagh needed at the auto parts store. Thirteen dollars later and he was on his way up McCullough Mountain. As he pulled onto the long driveway leading up to the big house, his eyes spotted Luke's truck parked by the barn.

He parked on the side where there was no mistaking his vehicle and wished he could somehow let Luke know he was there. The front door of the big house sprung open and Sheilagh came prancing out, a great big smile spread on her face.

He grabbed the bag with the belt and climbed out. "What are you all dressed up for?" She wore a pale lemon colored dress with a sweet little white cardigan to match the ribbon tied in her hair.

"Nothin'. Just felt like lookin' pretty."

He grinned. "Well, you sure managed to accomplish that."

Her face flushed and she blinked at him, lips still parted in the same smile that hadn't left her face. "Did you get the belt?"

"Yup." He held up the bag.

"How much do I owe you? My purse is inside."

He shook his head. "Not a thing."

"Tristan, I'll give you the money. You're probably saving me, like, fifty bucks anyway."

"Nope. Your family's been good to me. It's my pleasure to give somethin' back. Now, where's this car?"

She led him over to a dated Blazer. "That's a lot of truck for a small thing like yourself."

"I don't mind big."

He glanced over his shoulder and shot her a sidelong glance. She grinned wickedly. "No wonder they call you Shei-Devil."

He lifted the hood and went to work. Sheilagh stuck by his side except for the times she went in to get him a glass of lemonade and make him a sandwich. A white Taurus pulled up while he was eating the turkey and mustard on rye and Sheilagh, who was eating beside him on the front porch, groaned.

"Who's that?" he asked, unable to make out the driver.

"That's Erin. Finn's girlfriend. She's a bitch."

He raised a brow and bit his sandwich. The girl climbed out of the car and marched toward the house.

"Hi, Erin," Sheilagh greeted, none too friendly.

The girl stopped as though just noticing them. She didn't return the greeting, but smiled as she took a long, perusing gander at Tristan. "Who's your friend, Shei?"

Sheilagh's eyes narrowed. "Erin, Tristan. Tristan, Erin," she snapped out. Then with more emphasis, she said, "Finn's inside. You know…your *boyfriend.*"

The girl scowled at Sheilagh and Tristan thought she might be right. This girl looked like a bitch.

"Of course he is," Erin huffed, rolling her eyes. "Where else would he be?"

"He's probably hiding from you," Sheilagh grumbled

under her breath, shoving the last bite of bread in her mouth.

Tristan's lip twitched. She was a fiery little thing and he liked it.

When Erin stomped in to the house, he turned to Sheilagh and jokingly said, "You're mean."

She lifted her chin, long locks of copper hair shaking out over her shoulder, and smiled sweetly. "I happen to be very nice, actually, but Erin doesn't respond to nice. She's a bitch to my brother, so I'm a bitch to her. Besides, I've actually gotten a lot nicer to her."

He arched a brow.

Sheilagh's lips pressed in a tight smirk. "I used to kick her under the table and stick things in her hair at church."

He laughed. "Shei-Devil indeed."

Shouting from the house drew their attention. Sheilagh hopped off the steps and he followed. A second later the screen door whipped open with a snap and Erin came marching out. Finn followed a second later.

"Are we still going out tonight?" he called.

"No!" Erin snapped. She got back in her car, turning the key so hard the engine squealed and they all winced. A moment later she peeled out of the driveway leaving them fanning away a cloud of dust.

"Hey, Tristan. What are you doin' here?" Finn asked, coming over to where he and Sheilagh were standing at the truck.

It was remarkable how much he looked like Luke, but there were also differences. Luke had a hard glint to his eyes, where Finn's were soft and easygoing. Finn was slightly smaller as well. Not by much. He'd seen first hand what logging would do to a man's body, but Luke had that extra muscle from training.

"I'm fixing Sheilagh's truck."

He frowned. "Why didn't you ask me to do it, Shei, 'stead of making Tristan come all the way out here?"

Sheilagh's lips parted and she looked up at him, a flash of guilt showing in her green eyes.

Tristan quickly said, "I don't mind. I told her I'd do it."

"You need any help?" Finn asked.

They looked under the hood and Tristan made a few more adjustments. Finn suggested they change the oil while they had everything open. Just as Tristan was tightening a cap, he heard a door close and his neck prickled. He turned and saw Luke, keys in hand, staring at his truck.

Pretending he was still tightening things up, he watched as Luke scanned the yard. Their gazes met and Tristan's breath caught. His heart sped up as Luke strode in their direction.

"What are you guys doing?" he asked. Tristan pulled himself out from under the hood and grabbed a rag to wipe his fingers. "Hey, Tristan."

"Just fixing Shei's car. We got it covered," Finn said and Tristan definitely picked up on his clipped tone.

"Need any help?" Luke offered.

His brother and sister both looked surprised. Sheilagh snorted. "Yeah right. I'm sure you have other stuff to do. Isn't Oscar the Grouch expecting you for your weekly meeting to go over the finer points of being a surly douche muncher?"

Tristan frowned at her and she immediately looked contrite and embarrassed.

"We got it covered," Finn said and turned back to the truck.

He watched as Luke took a deep slow breath, his smile falling. It took everything he had not to go to him. "Okay then," he said in a tight voice.

That was enough. "Actually," Tristan said. "We're doin' a tune up and could use an extra pan. You know where I can get one?"

Luke's eyes met his and he nodded. "Yeah. I'll grab one."

Sheilagh and Finn were involved in a lecture Finn was giving about not abusing her brake pads. Quietly, Tristan slipped away and followed Luke into the big house. The house was quiet and he found him in the kitchen holding three cake pans.

"Hey," he said.

Luke tried for a smile and failed. "Hey. My family's not real happy with me right now, if you couldn't tell."

He didn't comment and Luke shifted. He looked at the door leading to the side porch and asked, "How'd you get here?"

"Drove."

"But why?"

"Sheilagh called me."

He faced him and frowned. "How does she have your number?"

"I gave it to her."

His brow continued to crease. "Why?"

"In case she ever needed anything, like her car fixed. What's the big deal?"

Luke's Adam's apple rolled as he swallowed. "I don't have your number."

Taking a step closer, until they were only a foot apart, he whispered. "I'll give it to you."

Luke's eyes searched his and he wanted so badly to touch him. He took a half step closer and Luke's nostrils flared. His arms extended, passing him the pans. "You can use these."

Tristan took the pans and stilled when Luke's finger intentionally grazed his. "I could come over when we're done with the truck."

"Yeah. That'd be good," Luke whispered.

The front door opened and slammed and they stepped apart. "Tristan?"

He turned as Sheilagh came into the kitchen. "There you are. Finn said to bring out the pans."

"On my way," he said turning and following her out.

Luke helped with the car and Finn and Sheilagh seemed to drop the attitude they'd originally treated him to. Every chance Luke got to brush his hand over any part of Tristan, he did. His expression was always blank, but Tristan recognized the longing banked in those navy blue eyes. He felt it too.

As they finished, Luke mentioned a game on television and Tristan immediately took the hint. The problem was, Finn wanted to watch the game too.

Rather than heading to the barn, the three of them—four, once Frank showed up—wound up in the big house on the couch. It definitely wasn't the plan he and Luke had in mind.

When the game ended, Luke stood and said, "I gotta get ready. I'm going out tonight."

"You going to O'Malley's?" Finn asked.

Luke hesitated and said, "Yeah." His lips compressed the minute Finn jumped up and said he was heading there too since Erin canceled their plans.

It was almost laughable. Tristan would have found it amusing if he wasn't dying to get Luke to himself again. When they got to O'Malley's, things didn't improve. It was bad enough they couldn't sit next to each other or get a second alone, but what was worse was the parade of women that came up to Luke every five minutes.

Luke had the decency to flush, but that didn't make it any easier to bear. These were women he'd slept with, fooled around with, most of them recently. The longer this went on, the more they both got pissed off.

"I think I'm taking off," Tristan said as some girl rubbed up against Luke and insinuated in none too cloudy terms where they'd left off, basically with her mouth full of Luke.

Luke's head snapped up. "You're leaving?"

"Yeah. I think I've had enough."

Luke's shoulders lifted and his eyes moved as if he didn't know what to do. "See ya."

"Byeee," the girl next to Luke cooed. Yeah, he'd definitely had enough.

When he got into his truck his phone buzzed. He read a text from Luke.

INDUSTRIAL PARK by the high school. Ten minutes.

SIGHING, he tossed his phone aside and backed out. He wasn't in the mood for excuses. It was what it was. This, until Luke was ready to open up to those around him, was how it would be. Eventually the barrage of women would ease, but for now there was nothing either of them could do about it.

He waited at the industrial park, feeling like a trespasser, for twenty minutes. It was remote and backed up to the school, which was closed for the weekend. When he finally saw Luke's headlights he climbed out of the truck.

Luke parked next to him and met him halfway. "I'm sorry. That sucked."

"Yeah," Tristan agreed.

Luke stepped close, but didn't touch him. "I didn't know what to do."

He sighed loudly. "Isn't much you can do. It is what it is."

"You're mad."

"No, just irritated. How would you feel if all my ex-lovers showed up and hung all over me?"

"Fuck that," Luke said quickly. "I'll make sure it doesn't happen again."

"It's gonna happen from time to time, Luke. Unless you

want to go announcing to the world that you prefer sucking cock, the girls will continue to come."

His lips thinned and he stepped close, his body heat encroaching on his space. "Only your cock."

"That's right." It was essential Luke knew he wasn't the only one who could be demanding.

Luke's nostrils flared as he stared at him challengingly. His hand snaked out and cupped him through his jeans. Tristan stepped back.

"What's wrong?" Luke asked.

"We're in an industrial park, Luke."

"I want you."

"I want you too, but not here."

"Leave your truck and come back to my place. I'll bring you to get it in the morning."

So clandestine. "Why?"

"Because I want to prove to you you're who I want. No one else matters."

Maybe he would have objected had he not needed the reassurance. Instead, he nodded.

They drove in silence. When they reached Luke's place the big house was dark. Shutting the lights on the truck, he followed Luke into the barn quickly. Luke locked the door and they faced off in the den.

"Tell me what you need," Luke said.

"You."

He came to him in three strides. His mouth crashed over his, needy and giving. Tristan gripped the back of that strong neck and kissed him almost punishingly. He was angry with Luke for sleeping around. He knew it was all an attempt to fuck Tristan out of his life. It hurt like hell seeing so many women he'd touched.

Tristan pulled at Luke's shirt and he lifted his arms as Tristan proceeded to strip him of it and toss it to the ground. "Suck my cock," he said, pressing Luke's shoulder low.

Luke dropped to his knees and undid his pants. Tristan didn't touch him. He folded his hands at his back and waited. Luke grabbed his flesh and tugged.

"I said suck it."

Luke glared at him. "You think I mind sucking your dick?" he asked challengingly.

Tristan shrugged. "Open your mouth and show me."

"All right," Luke answered, a little too calm.

Tristan stepped forward and fed his cock between Luke's lips. He moaned as Tristan thrust deep. "Take all of me. Show me how much you love my cock."

His mouth lowered and Tristan saw him struggle with the fullness at the back of his throat. "Breathe. That's it."

His dick grew wet with Luke's saliva as his mouth tunneled over him, each time getting closer and closer to the base. When he started easing back and dicking around at the tip, Tristan cupped the back of his head and pulled him closer.

"Open for me." He pressed deep and the softness at the back of Luke's throat constricted over him. "Look at me."

Glassy eyes gazed up at him.

"That's my cock you're sucking. Now show me how much you love it."

Luke's eyes flared and he went crazy. His mouth

pumped rapidly over his shaft as his fingers dug into Tristan's flexing thighs. It was messy and hot as hell. He couldn't believe this was only the second time Luke had done this. Holy fuck, his mouth was amazing.

Every time he praised him or gave him direction, Luke showed that initial sign of defiance, but then did exactly as he was asked. It was like watching a wild stallion get broken in.

At first he was fierce. Rebellious blue eyes challenged every demand placed on him, but soon he was gentled, calmed. Luke would never be completely tame. He had too much animal in him. Tristan had no doubt he'd be taking his licks later for demanding the reins. But he needed to make it perfectly clear he was no pushover.

If Luke was truly his man, there would be no room for anyone else. He'd never felt so possessive of another person before. Flirting he could take, but the invitations had to stop. Luke needed to know who buttered his bread just the way he liked it.

"I'm coming," he warned, giving Luke time to pull back.

He didn't. "In my mouth," he rasped falling onto his heels and opening wide.

The invitation excited him and quickened his release. Tristan jerked his cock and his climax spilled onto Luke's tongue and chin. His skin prickled as his body tightened. Incredible.

When he finished, Luke grinned, blinding him with that devastating dimple, licking his lips, moaning, satisfied. "You're the only person I'll ever let boss me around like that," Luke said. "And now, I'm gonna fuck the shit out of you."

"That so?"

"On your back, cowboy."

His heart raced. "Should we go to the bed?"

"You can try. Doubt you'll make it."

Tristan felt the side of his mouth kick up in a grin. He only made it half a step when Luke had him on his back. They wrestled and laughed and when Luke filled him, Tristan took it as his due, handing back the control he'd borrowed. He didn't need the control like Luke did.

Besides, there was nothing better than being completely possessed by this man and knowing his desire was enough to push him to the brink of madness. When they made it to the bed, it was well past midnight.

They set the alarm for four and snuggled into each other's arms. Yes, they had to exist in secret. And yes, it wasn't always gonna be easy. But nothing—*nothing*—could make either one of them walk away at this point.

"Baby, did you see what I did with the shampoo I bought?" Tristan asked as he sifted through the things on the counter.

Luke's mug of coffee clicked as he set it on the granite counter top. His arms wrapped around Tristan's torso, the stubble of his unshaven jaw abrading his shoulder.

"I already put it in the bathroom."

Tristan picked up his mug and stole a sip, puckering at the amount of sugar Luke always doused his first cup with. Turning, he grinned and kissed Luke's cheek as he headed toward the bathroom.

He went to his drawer and withdrew a thermal and jeans.

"We should call out today," Luke said, watching him from the door of the bedroom.

Tristan gave him a doubtful look. It had been six weeks and they'd finally found their way. Never before had

Tristan been this happy. Things were far from perfect, but he was hopelessly and irrevocably in love with this devastating man.

"You know we can't do that. We're clearing out the 300ᵗʰ Acre today. Your dad'll be pissed if we don't show up."

Luke sighed. "I know, but it's tempting."

It was. Exceedingly so. He hustled into the bathroom, tossing his clothes on the wide vanity sink—right next to the little jar holding both their toothbrushes—and turned on the shower. "You better get the lead out if you don't want to be late."

They showered and dressed. Luke drove them to work as he usually did. Luckily they left before dawn so no one really noticed they always arrived together.

They'd worked out a bit of a routine. Every night, after ten, Tristan would slip out of the house and walk around the block where Luke's truck awaited. They'd return to the barn, have a late night snack, and head off to bed together. It helped that they worked at the same place, because most assumed Luke picked Tristan up each morning.

Ryan was the only one that knew what was actually going on. This made Luke incredible uncomfortable and he'd yet to confront his cousin's knowledge of the situation.

When Tristan told Luke that Ryan knew they were a couple, they'd had their first fight.

. . .

"You had no right to tell my relative something so personal about me without asking!" Luke had stormed slamming the fridge after grabbing a beer.

Tristan calmly folded his arms over his chest. "He may be your cousin, but he's my best friend."

"Well, so am I!"

"Stop shouting."

"No. I'm fucking pissed off and I'd rather shout than break something."

"Luke, he won't tell anyone. If anything, this will work in our favor. Ryan knows how private you like to keep your business and he knows this isn't something we want to broadcast to the family or the locals. He'll cover for us when things get sketchy. I'm staying here every night. We arrive at work together every morning. Rosemarie and Liam wonder why they never pass me on the way to the bathroom anymore or see one less cup of coffee in the pot after I've supposedly gone."

"I don't want people in our business."

"And they're not. You're overreacting. Ryan's known I'm gay for four years now and he's never betrayed my trust or made me feel like anything less than anyone else."

"He works with us, Tristan. I can feel him judging me."

Tristan tried to force a calming breath as he bristled at Luke's use of the word 'me'. When he became so single mindedly self-involved and forgot they were an 'us' it really pissed him off. "No one is judging you."

"Bullshit."

"What's he judging, Luke?" he'd finally shouted, throwing up his hands in exasperation. "That you're in love? That I love you back? That two people are in a committed relationship? If you

actually talked *to him, you'd know the only feelings Ryan has about our situation is envy and happiness. He's happy we found each other, happy we're happy. It'd be nice if you could, for once, be happy about it too!"*

"I am happy!"

"Then why are you shouting?"

"Because that information is fucking private!"

Tristan looked at the floor and said in a low voice. "Right. It's always private with you. God forbid you let those that love you get close. They'd never understand. You've got them all figured out. Have their minds made up without even giving them the opportunity of deciding for themselves." He'd grabbed his keys off the counter. "They're my friends too, Luke. And they're not a bunch of assholes. The only person passing judgment here is you. I'll see you at work tomorrow."

AFTER THAT FIGHT, their relationship had been strained. Tristan had stayed away from the barn for four long and lonely nights until Luke eventually apologized. Tristan knew this was difficult for Luke. It wasn't always a picnic for him either, but it was utterly impossible to keep everyone in the dark. He lived with Ryan. He was his best friend. He simply couldn't lie to him about something as big as what he felt for Luke.

Since then, Luke had made a good effort to not seem so ashamed of who and what they were, but Tristan saw through the act. It was one thing to appear quietly indifferent about homosexuality. It was something altogether different to change the channel whenever a gay man came on TV, which Luke had done in the den at the big house.

As if he wasn't already man enough, Luke had to put out an aura that he didn't want anything slightly feminine around him. The channel swap thing, Tristan may have overanalyzed, but then, in the weeks that followed there were other little comments that grated.

When Braydon came home from college for a weekend, Luke had indulged in a long, intoxicated conversation about how hot some girl was. He slept alone that night. Then there were the references about tits and what a nice set of legs could do to a man.

Luke had four brothers and Tristan was glad they were finally rediscovering Luke's better side, but when guy talk broke out it was never enough for Luke just to sit there. He had to constantly make a point to the others that he liked women. It wouldn't be so aggravating if it was all bullshit, but the underlying truth was, Luke wasn't gay. He was bi.

They talked about it often, and only sometimes argued. Luke didn't understand how his cover was any different than having Ryan cover for them with lies about where Tristan frequently disappeared.

Tristan accepted his argument as a valid point. Maybe it was wise, in a place like Center County for them to cover their tracks. But he preferred simple discretion to muddying things up with lies.

It seemed a consistent bone of contention between them and Tristan hoped it worked itself out. No secrets stayed buried forever. He'd learned that the hard way. He could only hope, that when their lifestyle was eventually exposed, Luke would be prepared to deal with it.

By the time October rolled in, Tristan's southern blood was missing the warmth. Center County was colder than a witch's tit and his truck straight up objected to driving in the frigid weather.

When Halloween arrived, Luke and Tristan decided to join the others and go to the big blowout at O'Malley's. It was a good break to the usual and Tristan had found the perfect costume.

Snapping his old wranglers and clasping his largest belt buckle in place, he did up his flannel and grabbed his hat. Luke was gonna get himself a real cowboy tonight.

They met in the parking lot of O'Malley's. The bar was packed. Women scampered through the cold lot in little more than stockings and lingerie. Shutting off his truck—which was really fighting the nip in the air—Tristan waited until Luke's truck pulled up.

Climbing out, he headed to where he parked. Luke's lights shut off, the door creaked open and down stepped two black boots, long, tapered blue pants, and a fitted midnight blue shirt. "Arrest my heart," Tristan said quietly. "You're the sexiest police officer I've ever seen." Luke turned with a smile, fitting his shiny brimmed police hat on his head. "You got cuffs on that belt we can play with later?"

As Luke looked at Tristan's costume his eyes flared with desire then his smile turned to a scowl. "Jesus Christ, we're the fucking Village People."

These were the moments Tristan envied gay men that

had partners who embraced the lifestyle. He'd never get Luke anywhere close to a gay cruise ship. Even there, he'd be too uptight to unclench.

He made light of the comment. "Mmm…and they want you as a new recruit."

Luke's scowl darkened. He turned and tossed his hat back in his truck. "I'm not going in there like this."

For the love of fuck. "Will you knock it off? I'm sure you're not the only man in uniform tonight. Do you think everyone will suspect I'm fucking every sailor, biker, and native inside? You're being ridiculous."

"Lower your voice," Luke hissed.

That was it. Tristan yanked off his own hat and snapped, "I'll make it easy for you. I'm going in. You can follow or leave. I won't even look at you so no one accidently mistakes you for anything but straight, because we all know what a travesty that would be for big man Luke McCullough."

He turned and shoved his way into the bar. Kelly was slammed behind the counter and Sheilagh was hustling drinks out to the tables. Her red hair was down and curled under, tucked behind one ear. He noticed her right away because it was kind of impossible to miss the full length, ruby sequined gown catching reflections from every flickering light in the bar.

Tristan hovered by the corner of a bistro table in the back where people had left purses and glasses to go dance. When Sheilagh saw him, she smiled. "Hey, cowboy! You look great!"

Deciding not to let Luke ruin his night, he hugged her. "Thanks. And what are you supposed to be?"

"I'm Jessica Rabbit," she said, then posed shooting her leg out of the slit that traveled all the way up to the top of her thigh. *"I'm not bad. I'm just drawn that way."*

He laughed at her perfect pout and purr. Dragging a finger up her leg he whistled. "Better not let your brothers catch you showin' off all that leg, baby girl."

Her smile fell and her bare shoulders slowly shifted as she drew in a long breath. Her eyes locked with his and he frowned.

"What's wrong, Shei?"

It took her a second, but eventually she shook her head. "Nothin'," she rasped. Pressing her painted lips together, she cleared her throat. "Listen, I gotta get back to work. What are you drinking? Soon as I have a sec I'll bring it right over."

He handed her a ten. "I'll take a bottle of Bud."

Once Sheilagh took off, Tristan settled into one of the chairs. He watched the door for Luke, but didn't see him come in. Checking his phone, he saw no missed texts or calls. He didn't know if he left or came in while he was talking to Sheilagh.

A band played and the dance floor was packed. Sheilagh kept his drinks coming and whenever she had a second she kept him company. He was about to call it a night when he saw a familiar police uniform on the dance floor.

"You gotta be fucking kidding me." Luke's hands were all over Dorothy's hips as he danced between her and the

Wicked Witch of the West. "Motherfucker," he hissed and finished his beer.

"Need another one?" Sheilagh said from his left, sneaking up on him.

He shouldn't. It was obviously time for him to go and he didn't want to put himself over the legal limit.

"It's my break soon, so I'll grab you one first," she said and took off.

When she returned, Tristan's mood had soured and his temper had flared beyond his tolerance. "You wanna dance, Shei-Devil?"

She stilled. Her lips parted and she stared up at him wide eyed. Quietly, without expression, she rasped, "Okay."

He led her to the dance floor, far away from Luke and the cast of Oz. The song changed to *The Time Warp* and the band was killing it with a cool punk version. Rocky Horror he could do.

"What is this?" Sheilagh laughed.

"It's *The Time Warp!*" he shouted, astounded she didn't know it. "Oh, baby girl, you're makin' me feel my age. Listen to the words. It goes just like they say."

He jumped to the left, stepped to the right, threw his hands on his hips, drew his knees in tight, and thrust his pelvis. Sheilagh was hysterical. Her face came to life as she watched him and followed his lead.

In that moment, he was so grateful for her friendship, because she made him forget about Luke for a few minutes and remember what it was to simply have fun and not worry about what anyone else thought.

When Magenta's solo started he grabbed Sheilagh's little hand and twirled her around in a sort of mamba tango, spinning and circling her on cue. As he arched over her, dipping her low, her small hand gripped his shoulder and her green eyes flashed. She was breathless, suspended in his arms only inches from the floor, but smiling as though having the time of her life. At least someone appreciated him.

He sprung them back to their feet as the song picked back up and they jumped right into the line dance. It was awesome and perfect and something inside of him recalled what it felt like to simply exist freely.

Like in the musical, the last note of the song dove into a drowning blend of keys and everyone melted and cheered. The band announced they would be taking a break for a few minutes and Tristan caught his breath.

"Hey, Luke," Sheilagh said, grinning widely.

Tristan tensed and turned to find Luke's gaze hard on him, his expression otherwise blank. "Hey, Shei," he said, in a monotone voice. "Tristan."

"Luke."

They glared at each other challengingly for another moment. The stereo kicked on and Sheilagh grabbed Tristan's arm. "I love this song! Dance with me, Tristan."

He was pulled away from her brother as Christina Aguilera's voice belted out an opening line about not being able to keep a good girl down. This was not a Time Warp line dance. *Show Me How to Burlesque* was probably one of the sexiest songs he'd ever heard. It was fast, sultry, dirty, and Sheilagh owned it in her glitter dress.

As she crouched and dipped her bedazzled booty low, Tristan's eyes flared. Men around the bar watched her longingly as she gyrated with quick, seductive moves and he frowned. She was seventeen!

Her fingers spread wide as she dragged her hands down her open thighs, pulling the slit of her gown open. Jesus. Was she nuts? Her brothers were probably watching and having a coronary. Men started crowding around her and Tristan panicked.

He caught her wrist and drew her close to his chest, shooting a territorial glare over her bare shoulder. "Take a hike," he snapped at the leering perv dressed as Clark Kent.

Holding her inside the shelter of his body didn't seem to slow her motions. Didn't she know what she was doing to the men watching her? She certainly was showing everyone how she burlesqued. When the song stopped abruptly he was beyond relieved. Another song came on and she made as if she was going to dance some more.

Keeping hold of her wrist he dragged her back to his table.

"Don't you want to dance some more?" she called, trailing after him in her high heels.

"I think you danced enough for one night, baby girl. You got the whole male population ogling you."

They made it to the table and he grabbed his beer. Sheilagh was out of breath and watching him. Over her shoulder he spotted Luke, Kelly, Braydon, and Finn, all scowling at them.

"What about you?" she asked.

"What?" he pulled his eyes away from the angry Irish mob.

"Were you ogling me?"

He frowned. "Of course not. I was trying to block others from undressing you with their eyes."

Her expression wilted. "Oh."

"They don't all know you're only a teenager, Sheilagh. It's a bar. If they don't recognize you as the waitress, they'll assume you're fair game. You can't tempt trouble like that."

Her brow creased. "Maybe I wanted them to look."

That pissed him off. "Why? So they recognize your body and not your brains? Don't be that sort of girl, Shei. You're better than that."

Her face tightened and he knew he'd upset her. Angrily, she said, "I won't be a teenager forever. I'll be an adult soon and then maybe all of you will stop treating me like a baby."

She was angry, but by the end of her little edict she'd gotten herself upset. Her eyes blinked and she turned to walk away. He grabbed her wrist. "Baby girl—"

She pivoted, sharp emerald eyes cutting off his words. "Stop calling me that! I'm not a baby! At first I thought it was sweet, but now I get it's just how you all see me."

She stormed off and he was speechless. The brothers walked like a wall of fury toward him.

"What the fuck was that?" Finn demanded.

"Not cool, Tristan," Braydon snapped.

Luke said nothing, but his scowl was so harsh no words were needed.

Kelly simply added, "She better be coming back or you're hustling drinks the rest of the night."

He shook his head. "I didn't make her dance like that! I was trying to keep the creeps away from her." Tristan sighed when their expressions failed to lighten. "I'll go talk to her."

When he made it to the back of the bar he couldn't find her. He asked a woman to check in the ladies room, but she wasn't there either. Or the woman had lied to him. He pushed through the fire exit and found the back lot empty. Then he heard sniffles. Shit.

He quietly stepped out and followed the low whimpers coming from the other side of the building. "Sheilagh?"

"Go away."

He did the opposite and stepped in front of her. "Please don't cry."

Her fingers chased tears away from her lashes as if their presence was offensive.

"Jesus, Tristan, will you just leave!"

He jerked back. She'd never talked to him like that before. "No! What the fuck is it with you McCulloughs? Someone cares and you all freak out."

She scoffed. "You don't care."

"Of course I care. I love you, baby girl—I mean, Sheilagh. I hate seeing you upset."

Her hand paused as she rubbed her nose and her head tilted. "What?"

"What do you mean what?"

"You *love* me?"

"Of course I do. You're my friend, Sheilagh. I'd never do anything to intentionally hurt you."

She sniffled. In a small voice she admitted, "I love you too."

He smiled and tucked her hair behind her ear. "I'm glad. I'm sorry I hurt your feelings. I was only trying to look out for you."

She shrugged it off. "It's okay. I'm being overly sensitive. I just hate being treated like I'm younger than everyone else."

"But you are younger."

Her lashes lowered. "Will you make me a promise?"

"Anything."

"Once I turn eighteen, will you treat me like an adult and start seeing my age as just a number?"

He'd probably always see her as younger. He had this unfamiliar need to take care of her, watch out for her. She was beautiful and he worried one day that devious streak of hers would land her in a heap of trouble. Sighing, he said, "How about this, you always be honest with me and let me look out for you and I promise after your eighteenth birthday I'll never treat you as anything other than an adult."

She grinned. "I like that deal."

"Good. Now let's go inside before your brothers come out here."

"Tristan?" He stopped from turning and faced her. "You can still call me baby girl. If you want, I mean."

Smiling, he pinched her chin. "You got it, baby girl."

When they went inside Finn was dancing with Erin,

Braydon had himself between two nurses and Kelly was back behind the bar. Sheilagh said a quick goodbye and reported back to her tables.

Scanning the bar, Tristan gave up without really looking too hard for Luke. He'd probably left anyway. Without stopping to say goodnight, he headed out to his truck.

The lot was still packed. He slid his key into his door and popped the lock.

"Thanks for talking to my sister."

He stilled and turned to find Luke in the shadows. The fake badge he wore reflected the light cast over the lot. He braced himself for more drama. "Just being a friend."

"She could use a good friend. She's going through a rough time lately, feeling sort of unnoticed and different. She doesn't have a lot of people to talk to."

He frowned. "Why?"

Luke shrugged. "Sheilagh's always been off the charts smart. She's in a lot of AP classes with upperclassmen and that sort of makes it hard to fit in with peers her age. Some of her classes are also independent, which makes things more difficult. She didn't even go to the dance last month because she said no one asked her. How a girl that looks like my sister doesn't get asked to a dance is beyond me."

Tristan hadn't known any of that, but it explained a lot. "Well, I think she'll be all right now."

Luke nodded. "She looks up to you."

"I think she'd look up to the rest of you too, if ya'll stopped looking down on her."

"She's still a kid."

"Won't be for long. Maybe it's time ya'll start treatin' her like the rest of you wanted to be treated at seventeen. Help her adjust into adulthood gracefully."

"Yeah."

They stood in silence for a beat. Tristan shifted and said, "I'm gonna take off."

Luke's head tilted, his eyes scrutinizing. "I'm sorry I freaked out earlier."

"That all you're sorry for?"

Luke had to know he was pissed about him groping those girls on the dance floor and pretending it was just dancing. When he didn't say anything, Tristan sighed. "How about this, Luke? How about, when you're ready to really treat this thing like an equal and committed relationship, you call me? I'm not asking you to put a rainbow sticker on your truck or go parading around Center County on a crusade. I'm just asking that you show me you want what we have enough to stop feeling ashamed of it in private."

Luke's brows synched tight. "You're breaking up with me?"

"No. I'm asking you to take some time and think about what you want. I can do discreet, but I can't do this ongoing shame like we're doin' something wrong when we aren't hurtin' anyone. You need to either deal with who you are and let yourself be happy, or go find yourself someone you ain't ashamed of loving, because I *love you*, Luke. And I'm tired of feeling like some dirty habit you can't quit."

"You're not a dirty habit," he whispered.

"Just think about what I said."

Climbing into his truck and driving away from Luke was one of the hardest things he'd ever done. He was terrified, after taking some time, Luke would convince himself it was just too hard to love him and do exactly what Tristan suggested and find someone he wasn't ashamed of loving.

As he drove home his mouth pursed tight and the road blurred under the sheen of tears. No one else compared to Luke. He was enigmatic yet loving and when he loved he did so with a fierceness impossible to ignore. Tristan had never felt so owned by another person as he did when Luke possessed his body. There were absolutely no complaints in that department, aside from the fact that Tristan gave him everything and Luke still held a part of himself away.

The truck slid in beside Ryan's and he shut off the engine, lacking the energy to drag himself into the house. Blinking at the sagging material of the roof, he let a tear slip past his lashes and fall to his ear. "Fuck."

He had to do this. He had to make Luke decide what he wanted or this would never work. He couldn't go on, one week blissfully happy the next week fighting over the same old shit. He had insecurities too, but he never made Luke feel responsible for them. It was getting so bad, sometimes he almost had the urge to apologize for stuff that wasn't his shit. *I'm sorry I love you and make you face a side of yourself you don't like.* Fuck that.

The sensor light at the back door kicked on and

Tristan wiped his palms roughly down his face. It was Ryan taking out the trash.

He climbed out of the truck and went to give his friend a hand dragging the cans to the curb.

"Hey. How was O'Malley's?"

"Packed," Tristan said, grabbing a can. "How was your date?"

"Awesome. I just dropped her off."

"That's good."

Ryan turned. "You okay?"

"Luke and I had a fight."

"Wanna talk about it?"

"I'm not even sure how to explain it. It started because he said we looked like The Village People."

Ryan looked over his costume. "What are you supposed to be?"

"I'm a cowboy. Come on, man. See the belt?"

"You look like you always do."

"Well, my hat's in the truck."

"Oh. What was Luke dressed as?"

"A cop."

Ryan snorted. "Damn, I was hoping he dressed as the sub-looking biker. That would have been funny as hell."

"Yeah, right. That'd be a little too gay for your cousin."

Ryan smiled sympathetically. "I'm sorry he's like that. I honestly don't know why. My Aunt Maureen and Uncle Frank wouldn't give a shit who he loved as long as he was happy. You shouldn't have to deal with partiality, especially from your own partner."

"Yup."

They headed into the kitchen and Tristan grabbed himself a glass and the pitcher of tea on the counter. "You wanna watch a movie or somethin'? I need to stop thinking for a while."

"Sure." And that was why Ryan was one of his closest friends. He never judged him or drew lines between them, thinking Tristan was any less deserving of happiness in this world than anyone else. He just accepted him the way he was and shared in his ups and downs without preconceptions. He was—plain and simple—a true friend.

CHAPTER 8

Luke's knee was gonna snap if he didn't chill. Breath hissed out between his teeth as he braced himself and tightened his fingers on the handles of the leg press machine. Sweat burned his eyes as he tensed and shook with exertion. A roar cut from his chest as he pressed the weights forward again. They came down with a clank and he panted.

"Jesus, Luke, take it easy," Finn said as he messed with the free weights a few feet away.

"Fuck that." Luke grit his teeth and forced out another rep. Pain shot up his quad and he nearly passed out.

When he opened his eyes Finn was standing over him. "What the hell are you doing?"

Grabbing his sweat rag, he forced himself to stand. His legs quaked, but he refused to stop. "I'm working out. What the fuck does it look like?"

"It looks like you're trying to kill yourself. Why don't you tone it down a bit?"

"Why don't you mind your own business? There's a nice girly machine over there that makes you feel like you're at the gyno. How 'bout you go play with that and leave me alone?"

Finn threw up his hands. "Fine. Asshole."

His brother turned and hit the showers. Luke went to the row machine and put it on the maximum resistance. He was freaking out and needed to blow off some steam before he killed someone.

It had been a week and Tristan had yet to call, text, or even look at him at work. A fucking week! He was pissed. Pissed at himself, pissed at Tristan, and pissed off at the fucking world. This was bullshit.

When he finished the rower, he jumped on the elliptical and stuffed the ear buds of his iPod in his ears, cranking up the volume and setting it to shuffle. He'd been hitting the gym hard these last seven days, spending at least three hours blowing off steam, but it still wasn't enough. Something had to give and it would be either his knee or his stubbornness. He was sort of hoping for the knee.

He wasn't ashamed of Tristan. That was a bunch of shit. He fucking loved the guy. He needed him and then he'd gone and pulled this shit and Luke didn't know what to do.

He missed him. He missed his clothes showing up in his laundry, missed the scent of him on his sheets, missed his face. Enough time had passed, enough thinking. This was who he was. He couldn't make himself be anything else and it wasn't fair for Tristan to demand otherwise.

At five miles his legs went numb, but he kept going, kept pushing himself closer to that breaking point he couldn't seem to reach. His steps faltered as heavy metal cut to soft piano notes.

He frowned. Fucking Tristan was always stealing his iPod and slipping songs into his playlist. He glanced at the screen and read *Your Song,* by Elton John. Jesus.

His legs rolled over the pedals as he approached seven miles. His thoughts grew distracted with each softly sung lyric. When the chorus about life being wonderful while the other was in the world kicked in, a strange tightness stole into Luke's chest.

His brow tightened and he sped up, clearing his throat in an attempt to dislodge whatever was choking him. The piano picked up and his eyes burned from more than sweat. *What the fuck?*

He grabbed his sweat rag and wiped down his face, but he couldn't stop blinking and the pinching in his heart got tighter the more the song carried on. Was he fucking crying? Jesus. He shook it off, but as each word filled his ears, images of Tristan and the pain of missing him seemed to multiply with each syllable.

He glanced around the gym, glad no one was really looking at him. Panicked, he killed the machine, not having the time to wipe it down. He left his shit and fled to the locker room. As soon as he closed himself in a bathroom stall, he yanked out his ear buds and braced his arm on the door, breathing hard past the lump clogging his throat.

He couldn't stop the throbbing in his heart. Shoving the heel of his palm into the socket of his eye, he wiped hard at his face. *It's sweat. It's fucking sweat.* He turned and his head fell back against the metal divider. Screwing his eyes tight, his lips pulled wide and he silently forced down a harsh breath through his teeth. The muscles in his neck bulged as he tried to fight back the tears, but he wasn't strong enough.

You fucking pussy. You're crying over a guy in the fucking locker room.

His fingers closed into a fist and he slammed it into the thigh of his bad leg.

Fuck you! I fucking hate you! You loser! He mentally berated himself, using every harsh word he could think of, but nothing helped. It hurt. Physically hurt. Not like a cut. Not even like when his knee snapped. No, this was something lethal, a malignancy inside his heart he couldn't push out. He fucking loved him. Loved him like he'd never loved anyone.

He didn't want to be happy with anyone else. He only wanted Tristan. He wanted the fear to go away, wanted the courage to love him like he deserved, embrace what they were and be someone Tristan would be proud to call his own.

But he was a pile of worthless shit, too worried about labels and titles and rank to let go and surrender. If only he could give in, let go, and trust Tristan to know when enough was enough, to know when to keep quiet and when it was okay to let down their guard. He was terrified Tristan would expose them to the wrong people and there'd be hell to pay and he hated that Tristan worked through this fear without him years ago.

He needed him. He needed his boy to help him through this. It might never be all right, but if Tristan was at least there with him, it would be doable. Nothing worked without him and he wanted him back.

THE FOLLOWING NIGHT, Luke paced his den and waited for the sound of Tristan's truck. He hadn't answered Luke's text so Luke wasn't sure if he was coming. Looking over the table one last time, he checked to make sure everything was perfect.

Candles. Check. Tristan's favorite beer. Check. Mood music. Check. Burnt chicken because he fucking sucked at cooking. Check. The only thing missing was the man of the hour.

He looked at his watch and waited anxiously. It was ten after seven and he still wasn't there. *He's not coming.*

Yes, he is. Give him a few minutes.

Shit. He was freaking out. He'd sent Tristan a text that day while at work. He'd actually watched as it went through and Tristan pulled out his phone and read it. Nothing fancy. He'd simply written, *Dinner at my place at seven? We'll talk.*

Tristan's expression remained inscrutable as he'd read the text and slipped the phone back in his pocket without responding. Luke had scowled at him, but when Tristan's eyes remained focused on Ryan who was telling some story about a girl he'd been seeing, Luke stomped away.

Once he'd cooled off and convinced himself Tristan avoided replying because he was only trying to be discreet, he figured he'd get a response after work. That didn't happen. He made up one excuse after another, talking himself into setting the table, prepping the meal, and lighting the candles—Jesus, he really was gay—and all without a single word back from Tristan.

Pissed that it was now quarter after, he whipped out his phone and punched out a text. *You could have at least let me know you weren't fucking coming!* His thumb hovered over the send for only a second before clicking the message off into Gspace. A second later there was a knock at the door.

He didn't hear a truck. Maybe it was someone from the big house. He looked back at the table. Fuck. Well, they didn't know who he was expecting. He opened the door and stilled.

Tristan's head was tipped down as he read his phone. His mouth pursed acerbically as his lashes lifted, pinning Luke with an unimpressed stare. "I was parking the truck out of sight. It took me a while to walk here."

"Sorry. I thought you weren't coming and reacted. Come in."

He slid his phone into his pocket and followed Luke inside. Luke walked to the table and turned.

All signs of exasperation left Tristan's face as he took in the scene Luke had created. "You did this?"

Uncomfortable with scrutiny that resembled praise, he quickly said, "It's nothing special. The chicken's burnt and the beers probably warm by now. It's just dinner."

"*You* did this," Tristan repeated. "Why?"

Because I'm an asshole and you deserve someone so much better and I'm hoping you never realize that and leave me for good. "Because I wanted to talk."

Tristan walked over to the table. His finger dragged over the cloth Luke had stolen from his mum's pantry. He raised a brow and strolled to the iPod dock on the counter, reading the artist playing. It was U2, *With or Without You.*

When Tristan finally faced him, Luke wasn't sure what he was thinking, if he was inwardly laughing at him or thought his attempt at getting him back was pathetic. He licked his lips, waiting for him to say something.

Tristan rounded the table slowly. When he stood only a few inches away, Luke's breath caught. He'd missed his eyes, missed his scent, wanted to pull him close and breathe him in, never let go.

"What did you want to talk about?" Tristan asked quietly.

Bono crooned in the background and all his words fell away. He had so much to say but couldn't form a single syllable. Struggling to keep it together, he took Tristan's hand and paused when he flinched. Luke met his eyes and pulled those tense fingers apart, splaying them wide and placing them on his chest.

"This hurts," Luke whispered, pressing Tristan's hand

over his heart. "When you're not with me, it hurts and I want the pain to stop."

Tristan looked at him, his eyes creased with apprehension. His lips parted and he swallowed. "Oh, Luke."

"Please. Please come back to me. I love you. I love us. I don't want to be here if you're not by my side."

Tristan's head tilted. His eyes shimmered with unshed tears. Everything inside of Luke tightened waiting for his rejection. He wasn't a prize. He was a fucking mess half the time, always in a prickly mood and worried about shit he had no control over. He got no peace aside from the moments Tristan was there, making him laugh, making him smile. He didn't want any part of this life if Tristan wasn't there to walk through it with him.

When Tristan's fingers brushed over his ear and down the side of his neck he moaned, the sound almost a whimper.

"I love you, you big stupid jerk. I was coming here tonight whether you invited me or not."

Luke blinked at him in shock. "You were?"

"Yeah. I missed you like crazy these past few days and if you couldn't see that we're right together I was gonna come here and make you see. I don't want to fight anymore. We have something too special to waste our time worrying about the rest of the world."

He let out a huge sigh of relief. "Thank fucking God."

Tristan laughed and pulled him into a hard hug. Luke's hand curved around the back of his head and held him tight. Their mouths found each other's and they smiled as they kissed.

"I can't believe you did all this," Tristan said. "I feel so unprepared."

"I burnt dinner."

"That's okay. That's how I like my steak."

"It's chicken."

"Oh." They laughed.

"Want a beer?"

"Sure."

They settled into the table and ate the sides. Tristan made an effort to cut the chicken, but it was hopeless. The tension eased and they slowly began talking about the things that needed to be addressed.

Luke confessed he was angry and told Tristan about his breakdown at the gym. Tristan was empathetic, but quiet and Luke knew he had to put more on the table than burnt chicken and promises to behave better.

After a few beers and giving themselves time to digest, he took Tristan's hand. "I want to be with you tonight." Tristan squeezed his fingers affectionately, but Luke knew he wasn't getting what he was saying. "I want you to make love to me, Tristan."

His eyes cut to Luke's, questioningly. "What are you saying?"

"I won't stop you this time. I'm ready."

Tristan's face was blank, his eyes searching Luke's as his shoulders lifted with each steady breath. "You're sure?"

He swallowed. "Yeah. Just… be gentle."

He stood and held out a hand to Luke. "Come with me."

He let Tristan lead him to the bedroom and watched as

he pulled back the covers. Tristan knew where everything was. He reached into the nightstand drawer and pulled out a condom and the oil, placing it carefully on the bedside table.

When he approached Luke, he gently cupped his face and traced his lips over his. "I love you."

"I love you too."

Tristan slowly stripped him and Luke let him. He didn't want the lead tonight. He needed to feel Tristan's arms around him, know he would always be safe in his keeping.

When they reached the bed they were both naked. They touched and kissed, but nothing was rushed. Hands caressed over flesh in slow, sultry exploration. Their legs coiled around each other and their mouths sucked on every bit of skin they could find. Luke's fingers dragged through Tristan's soft hair, loving the feel of it between his fingers. His body shivered, reveling at his lover's presence in his life once again.

When it was time, Luke's stomach constricted with excitement. He wanted this. It scared him. They were opening a new door to their relationship and he wasn't sure he'd ever be the same once he crossed that threshold, but this was what he wanted because this was him and Tristan.

Rolling onto his knees, he braced his weight on his forearms. Tristan's hand roamed over his backside, cupped his front, and Luke shut his eyes, savoring the sensations of such sweet caresses.

Need built inside of him until he was rocking into

Tristan's thighs. Then the first touch came. Luke's skin was warm from the oil. His body clenched as one little finger tried to press past the entrance nothing had ever traversed.

"Relax. I won't hurt you. You need to relax and let me in," Tristan said, his other hand petting over Luke's back.

Luke drew in a deep breath and forced his muscles to unclench.

"That's it, baby." Pressure pinched his hole and then there was an unfamiliar presence in his body as Tristan's finger breached him.

It didn't hurt. The motions were slow, calm. They opened up sensations inside of him Luke had never experienced before. The deeper Tristan probed the harder Luke breathed. When his finger sank all the way in Luke grunted.

"You feel that, baby? That's just one finger. Imagine how good it will be to finally have my cock there."

Luke's body tightened and hardened as Tristan began to pump his finger in and out. Untried nerve endings came alive and his body grew so sensitized he broke out in a sweat. It felt incredible—deep, sensual, maddening.

More pressure came as Tristan slid another finger inside. Warm licks of his tongue teased around his hole and Luke slowly unraveled, falling into a dark world of pleasure.

His shoulders bunched as Tristan reached deep. "Open for me. You feel that? That's your prostate." He teased the sensitive pocket and Luke nearly came.

Breathing hard through his teeth, it was impossible to

concentrate. Tristan's fingers withdrew, replaced by the blunt head of his cock.

"You're body's ready for me. Are you?"

"Yes," he rasped, needing to feel him inside of him.

The heat of Tristan's body slowly blanketed him as a kiss was pressed into his shoulder. "I love you, Luke."

His response was cut off as Tristan's cock breached his entrance. Luke's fists knotted in the sheets. His teeth clenched as his body accommodated all that girth and length.

"Fuck."

"You okay?"

"Yeah," Luke rasped. "Just…fuck."

"I'm only half in. Should I keep going?"

Half in? Holy hell, he was going to split in two. His body seemed to catch fire as it stretched to accommodate Tristan's suddenly mammoth cock. Drawing in a determined breath, Luke nodded.

Tristan pressed deeper and when he was seated fully inside of Luke, emotion tunneled through him hard. He breathed raggedly trying to grasp what was happening. Never had he felt so cherished, so looked after, so loved. Tristan's possession was immeasurable, comparable to nothing else he'd known.

The sound of Tristan's breathing met his ears as it beat slowly over his back. His hands ran over Luke's arms, followed by tender presses of his lips. "You okay, baby? You feel incredible."

Even Tristan's voice was ragged and it occurred to Luke that this was not only huge for him. It was huge for his lover as well. Sweat beaded on his brow as he swallowed hard. "It's…I don't have words for it."

"Let me show you how good it can be."

His cock slowly withdrew and glided back in, gently pulling on every nerve ending of all that soft tissue. With slow strokes, Tristan made love to him and Luke realized how stupid he was for putting this off. It was magnificent. Better than being on top. Better than anything any woman's body could give him. *This* was what he'd needed and only Tristan could provide it so perfectly.

As their pace picked up, Luke began to lose himself a little more. It didn't matter what day it was or even what tomorrow would bring. All that mattered was the two of them, here and now, making love in the most straightforward way two men could.

His cock filled and jerked sending his body into spasms of what was the most earth-shattering climax of his life. But that was second to the passion, third to the love. This was his partner. This was whom he was meant to be with. He never wanted to let him go and somehow, no matter what came, they'd figure out a way to be together forever.

PART II
THEM

CHAPTER 9

*E*ight months later...

LUKE ENTERED the barn and placed the stash of sausage and eggs he'd stolen from his mum's on the counter. Heading to the bedroom he kicked off his boots and climbed into bed. Tristan stretched and smiled under his kiss.

"Good morning, beautiful."

"Mmm... you taste like syrup," Tristan said, touching the brim of Luke's Jeff cap. "This looks good on you. I'm glad I bought it for you."

Luke held his upper body suspended over Tristan and rubbed his hips through the sheets. "I brought you breakfast."

"Thank you. Did Braydon get in okay?"

"Yup *and* he brought home a girl."

Tristan's brows lifted. "No shit? Someone from school?"

"Yup. Cute little thing. Freckles, sort of shy. Not exactly what I'd consider Bray's type, but she seems nice."

"What's her name?"

"Samantha."

"Is she coming to the game today?"

It was their open season game they had every year when all the college relatives returned home for the summer. Luke hadn't played last year because he hadn't been in the best place. Things were different this year and he couldn't wait to show off his skills in front of Tristan. "I'm pretty sure they'll make her play. No one gets to sit out unless they're over fifty or pregnant."

"Cool. I wanna meet her."

Luke dipped his face low and nestled Tristan's neck. "I love the way you're beard feels against mine in the morning."

"Do you?"

"Mmm-hm. Why don't we warm up before the big game?"

Tristan's hands cupped his ass. "You gonna wear those tight little baseball pants?"

"If you want me to. I think I have a pair around here somewhere," Luke said, nibbling his shoulder.

"Mmm... I want, baby. I want."

They made love for the better part of the morning before Tristan got to eat his breakfast. When Tristan left, Luke showered and found an old pair of his baseball pants from high school. They were small to begin with, but he'd gotten a lot bigger since he'd last worn them.

Looking at his reflection in the mirror, he mumbled, "The things I'll do for that boy." Grabbing the cooler of beer, his bat and glove, Luke drove over to the field.

When he got there the majority of his family was already filling the stands. He grabbed the extra equipment out of his truck and carried it to the dug-out. Luke felt Tristan's eyes zeroing in on his ass the moment he stepped on the sand.

Hiding a smirk, Luke gave him a little show, tightening it up as he unloaded the spare bats and gloves.

A shadow fell over him as he was bending to retrieve the last few items in the bag. "Need a hand?" Tristan's voice cut through him and he shivered.

"Yeah. A big strong set."

"I think I got what you need."

Standing, he smiled. They didn't crowd one another, but the others were far enough away that no one could hear their words. "That so?" Luke asked, a knowing glint in his eyes.

Tristan let out a slow growl. "All I can say is it's a good thing I wore my loose jeans. Fuck, you look good."

His sister's voice had them turning, her words laced with laughter. "Oh, my God, Luke! The T-ball team called. They want their uniforms back."

Tristan snickered and Luke shot him a look. "See what I do for you?" Turning to Sheilagh, he smiled. "What? These are my baseball pants."

She skidded to a stop a few feet away. "They're a little

small."

"That's how they're supposed to be."

She snorted. "Oh, okay." Casting her smile on Tristan, she said, "I want you on my team today."

"Sounds good, baby girl. Who's pickin'?"

"Me and Miller are captains."

Luke cursed. "Shit. She's gonna put me on her team."

Tristan frowned. "Who's Miller?"

"Braydon's ex. Sort of waspish. You wouldn't like her," Sheilagh provided.

"I like everyone," Tristan said.

Luke slapped his shoulder casually. "Trust Sheilagh. You won't like her." He'd try to keep his distance. Jen Miller hung on him and his brothers like a cat in heat. Hopefully his sister picked him for her team before Jen got the chance.

The three of them sauntered over to the others and waited for Braydon and his new girl to arrive. Luke took more ribbing for his wardrobe, but seeing how Tristan kept uncomfortably shifting in his pants, it was all worth it.

Bray came through the fence with his little friend, Samantha, by his side. She looked sort of terrified and mouse-like. Sheilagh yelled, "Finally, we can pick teams. Jen and I are captains."

Everyone gathered around home plate. A second later, Jen shouted, "I get first pick! Luke!"

"Fuck," Luke cursed under his breath. His sister's first pick would be Tristan since they were like The Skipper and Gilligan together.

"Kelly."

Luke turned, surprised she hadn't picked Tristan. *Please pick Tristan. Please pick Tristan.*

Kelly joined his sister while Jen surveyed the players. Bray's girlfriend fidgeted and worried her lip. Luke hoped she wasn't picked last. That was always a shitty feeling, especially when you didn't really know anyone.

"Bray," Jen called. *Who didn't know that was coming?*

Braydon left Samantha's side and joined their team. Everyone turned toward Sheilagh. Kelly whispered something in her ear. His sister smiled. "Samantha."

Awesome. Maybe Jen would pick Tristan next.

"Me?" Samantha asked.

"Yeah, you. Come on. Welcome to the winning team," Sheilagh said tugging Sam between her and Kelly.

"Finn," Jen picked again.

Sheilagh's mouth curved into a smile. "Tristan."

Luke sighed. He knew Tristan would wind up on Shei's team. That girl could be the biggest cock blocker.

The choosing carried on and their team took to the field. Sheilagh batted first, then Colin, and so it went.

Luke stood on the pitcher's mound and checked if his team was ready. He sent out a sharp whistle when he saw Jen in right field groping Bray. That was so not cool with Samantha sitting there. "Yo! Break it up! We got a game to win."

Colin stepped up to the plate and pointed his bat toward the outfield. "Settle down, Babe," Luke teased.

It was nice having his eldest brother home for a change. Once Colin made his vows at the end of summer,

Luke worried things would never be the same between them. He would be a *priest.*

He pitched the ball and Colin nailed it. Everyone went nuts. The outfielders dispersed as Colin rounded first and Sheilagh slid home. By the time Colin was passing second, the other team earned another run. The ball was fumbled from player to player and took forever to make it back to the infield.

"Come on, guys! Throw the damn ball!" Luke shouted. Jen was distracting Braydon again. He growled. He was competitive and his team was dicking around. Colin slid home, a cocky grin on his face.

Samantha stepped up to the plate. Great. It wasn't like he could strike out the new girl. The bat looked like a foreign object in her hands.

"Helmet," Luke yelled.

"What?"

Did this girl never play baseball before? "You need a helmet."

"Oh." She turned and grabbed the helmet Colin had just tossed aside.

Luke wound up.

"Eeeeeasy out!"

He turned and scowled. Why *wouldn't* Jen taunt the new girl? What a fucking bitch. His gaze snapped to Bray who went over and told Jen to can it.

Luke threw out a slow pitch. Samantha swung with the enthusiasm and determination of a major leaguer, but missed completely.

Jen's laugh echoed across the field.

"Take your time, love," Kelly yelled from the dugout.

Luke threw another slow ball and Samantha swung again, this time without as much zeal.

"Strike two!"

Colin yelled, "Come on, Sammy. You can do it!"

Luke opted for an underhand pitch this time, which wasn't allowed, but no one seemed to complain. When the bat connected with the ball Samantha stared as it bounced across the field.

"Run!" the team in the dugout shouted all at once.

Samantha gave a startled yelp, dropped the bat, and hauled ass toward first base. Luke grabbed the ball and hurled it toward Finn, who purposefully missed the catch and spent time chasing after it. Braydon was manning first base and when Finn threw him the ball with ridiculously obvious bad aim, Bray ran in almost slow motion to retrieve it.

"Get the ball!" Jen shrilled.

By the time Braydon had the ball in hand Sam was safe at first. Bray slapped Sam on the ass and Jen grumbled something from the outfield.

Next up was Kelly. He whacked the ball and when he got to first Sam was still standing there.

"Jesus," Luke muttered, rubbing his head.

Kelly whispered in Sam's ear and she bolted. Luke squinted to the outfield to find the ball. Everyone was soon safe at their bases and the batter he'd been waiting for was up.

Tristan dusted off the plate with his shoe and gave the bat a slow practice swing. Their eyes met and he smiled.

God damn, he was sexy. Luke preened and strutted over the mound, putting on quite the show as the pitcher. When he snapped back and let it fly, Tristan swung. The crack echoed around them and off he went, running in all his glory. His boy.

Samantha made it across home plate only to be trampled moments later by Kelly. But she took it in good spirit and laughed as Kelly spun her around.

"I did it!" she shouted, holding Kelly by the shoulders, still bouncing like a child. "I did it! I got a home run!"

Next came Tristan in a flash, crossing the plate. He turned and pointed at Luke. "Us cowboys are *real* good at baseball." He winked and Luke bit his lip so not to grin too noticeably.

The game continued for nine innings. Jen had moved on from Bray to Finn and then made her way to Luke. When they switched she went after Tristan, and Luke nearly cracked a tooth his jaw locked so tight. Luckily, Sheilagh didn't much care for the girl and got right in her face. He wasn't sure what Sheilagh said to Jen, but she backed off right away.

The game ended when Luke cracked it out of the park with bases loaded. They won by two runs.

"You bring the cooler?" Kelly yelled as he slapped Bray's girl right on the rump, causing her to jump. "Way to go, slugger!"

Luke loaded up the equipment. "In the truck. Grab a bag on your way."

They walked to the lot and Finn tossed him a beer. "Good game."

"Thanks," Luke said, taking a long sip. "We going to O'Malley's?"

"Does a bear shit in the woods?" Finn shot back.

He shot Tristan a glance and caught his quick nod that he wanted to join the others. "Sounds like a plan," Luke said. He frowned when he saw Bray. "Hey, where's Samantha?"

His stupid brother looked around as if just realizing she wasn't there. Jen shot Luke an evil glare for pointing out her absence.

Luke rolled his eyes. "Better go find her."

WHEN THEY ARRIVED at O'Malley's everyone was ready to let loose. Even the aunts came out. His mum, Aunt Colleen, and Aunt Rosemarie wasted no time getting pissed. Luke loved how Tristan looked at Aunt Rosemarie as a surrogate mother since he didn't really have parents.

The women cackled, regaling Tristan and Samantha with stories the rest of them had heard a hundred times.

"He shot him right in the arse, our daddy did!" Colleen laughed.

"It was not his bloody arse," Rosemarie objected. "It was his balls." She leaned close to Samantha and whispered, "I heard he only has one left."

Samantha blushed a deep shade of red and Luke's dad interjected. "You've all got it wrong. I've got two balls! He shot and missed me, but I'd let him fill me with bullets if it meant I still got to marry his prettiest daughter." His dad smiled at his mum and she batted him away.

"Ah, now see. You've gone and filled him full of whiskey and he's already trying to get me knickers off!" Maureen squeaked. "Frank! The children!"

Luke rolled his eyes. That was his parents.

"Did your grandfather really shoot your dad for eloping with your mother?" Sam asked. Poor little mouse probably felt like she was in the loony bin.

Luke smiled and shook his head. "Nah, he might of taken a swing at him for not marrying my mum right and proper in a church, but he never shot him. The story gets more exaggerated every time it's told."

"You see," Kelly cut in, sliding Luke a fresh beer. "Our mum was seven years younger than our dad. Our grandfather waited on the porch of the house until they returned from their honeymoon. Aimed his colt right between his legs and pulled the trigger. It's the God's honest truth, love. I've seen the scar." His brother was so full of shit, but Samantha watched as Kelly stepped back and pointed to his crotch. "On a McCullough that's the biggest target. We're all hung well enough to make a Clydesdale jealous."

"Jesus, Kelly, you're scaring the poor girl!" Luke reprimanded, but couldn't stop laughing.

Braydon came up beside Sam. "What are we drinking?"

"Let's do a car bomb," Finn suggested.

Luke looked for Tristan who was still talking with the aunts. Kelly passed out pints of black beer and the four brothers dropped in their shots, hooting as each glass was emptied.

Tristan didn't join them at the bar until the parents were making their goodbyes. They moved to a large round table and more drinks and shots were poured.

Tristan and Sheilagh sat across from him and Luke continuously caught his sidelong glances. It was hard, in mixed company, not being able to talk as much as they wanted or touch each other freely, but they'd gotten used to it.

Colin and Samantha were at the bar. Probably because Braydon had once again forgotten he had a guest to look after. Jen Miller was still there and taking turns hanging on Finn and Bray. She was such a twit.

When he glanced back at Tristan he was leaning close to Sheilagh. He whispered something Luke couldn't make out and then she laughed. Tristan put his arm around her and squeezed her shoulders, rocking her from side to side.

Luke frowned. He liked that Tristan got along with all his siblings. Loved that they all seemed to love Tristan. Sheilagh and Tristan had been close since he first moved to Center County, but something about the way Sheilagh laughed had Luke's hackles rising.

His little sister had turned eighteen and Luke had yet to see her bring home a boyfriend. He recalled last summer when she mentioned liking someone, but he supposed that never panned out.

Maybe she likes Tristan.

He tossed the thought away. No. They were friends. Tristan looked at Shei like a little sister. No one, aside from Ryan, knew Tristan was in a relationship. They all assumed he was single. If she liked him, Tristan would have said something. Sheilagh wasn't shy about things like that. Was she?

As they continued to whisper and laugh, Luke repetitiously studied them. There were little things he suddenly noticed that he hadn't seen before. Like when Tristan talked, Sheilagh stared at his mouth, her motions suspended as if she breathlessly hung on his every word.

Luke frowned.

His sister went to the bar to get another soda. She returned and handed Tristan a fresh bottle of beer, but she didn't just hand it to him. She dangled it over his shoulder and Tristan playfully traced his fingers up her arm.

What the fuck?

Noticing other similar gestures over the better part of an hour, Luke's temper flared. He wasn't sure if he was pissed because that was his little sister or because he'd never really seen Tristan flirt with a woman before. This was definitely flirting.

When Tristan pulled the cherry out of her soda and fed it to her, Luke had seen enough. Abandoning his beer, he walked to the front door and left.

The door of the bar slammed behind him only to open a second later. The lot was mostly filled with family cars and vacant of any patrons. He went to his truck parked in the shadows, knowing Tristan was right behind him.

"Luke. Luke, stop damn it!"

Luke stopped, rigidly faced Tristan, fisting his hands on his hips. "What?"

"Don't leave. I'm sorry." He stepped close.

He was sorry, because it was obvious what was

happening in there. He looked in Tristan's eyes and saw he hadn't meant any real harm. Letting out a deep breath, he dropped his hands and said as calmly as he could manage, "I'm not gonna stand there while you're flirting with my sister. It's misleading and you know it. You wanna play mind games with some girl, pick someone other than Sheilagh."

Tristan frowned. "I was just having fun with her. I wasn't leading her on."

"You were, and you damn well know it. If you like her, fine, that's a whole other argument we can have. But you and I both know she's not your type."

Tristan stepped closer and Luke's body reacted. All day he'd watched him and his desire had built.

In a hushed voice Tristan said, "No, she's not my type."

Luke breathed in Tristan's heady scent. Meeting his gaze, he whispered, "Then don't lead her on. She's my sister. She doesn't deserve to get her feelings hurt. She's young."

Tristan's hand reached out and captured the fingers hanging at Luke's side. "I'll be more careful. I'm sorry. Please don't leave."

Luke nodded. "I don't like seeing you flirt with women. I'm not used to it."

"I wasn't flirting. I only do that with you."

His lip twitched. "Damn right." They were very close, their voices hushed in the quiet night. He looked around to make sure they were alone. Unable to resist another minute, Luke ran his fingers through Tristan's hair and pulled his face close.

Their breath mingled and he said, "You looked so good today on the field."

Tristan chuckled. "You should have seen my view." His hand touched his ass. "Love these pants. I could see *all* of you."

Luke brushed his lips over his. "You owe me. Do you know how much I got my balls broken for wearing these?"

"Game's over. Why you still wearing them?"

"Because I love when I catch you watching me and get that look in your eyes like you can't wait to fuck me."

Tristan's hand gripped the back of Luke's neck yanking him close. His mouth closed over his in an aggressive kiss. They didn't have much time, but he needed to feel his lips on him, just a taste to hold him off until later.

Tristan jerked back. "Did you hear something?"

Luke listened, quieting his breathing. "Probably just a deer in the woods."

Tristan kissed him one last time. "Love you."

Yeah. That's what he needed to hear.

"Come on. Let's head back in. You go first. I'll follow in a few."

He watched as Tristan headed back in and gave himself a minute to collect his head and cool his body. There was definitely something nosing around in the woods. His scalp prickled as he had the strange sense that he wasn't alone. Frowning, he turned and looked around the lot one last time. He didn't see anyone. All the cars were dark.

Shaking off the eerie feeling that he was being watched, he went back inside.

CHAPTER 10

uke saw Sheilagh climb out of his parents' car and went after her. He wanted to get her alone for a few seconds to feel her out about Tristan. If she had feelings for his lover, she needed to curb them. He couldn't explain to her why that wouldn't work, but she really needed to set her sights on someone else if that was the case.

His father grabbed a sack of groceries out of the car and trailed his mother. Luke jogged over to the open tailgate and scooped up a bag. "Hey."

Sheilagh jumped as if she hadn't seen him approaching. "Hey."

He followed her into the house.

Snatching an apple out of a basket, she wiped it on her shoulder. Luke placed the bag of groceries on the counter and frowned when he saw they weren't alone. This was why he moved out. People were always everywhere in the big house.

Sheilagh bit into her plundered apple and slid onto a chair at the table beside Bray, Kelly, and Sam. "Luke, you wanna go to the lake today? Pat and Ry are going."

"So really," Kelly butted in, "you're planning on displaying your jiggly bits in a bikini for Tristan, is what you're saying."

Luke frowned. Shit. Did they all see it?

Sheilagh lobbed her half eaten apple at Kelly who laughed, caught it, and took an appreciative bite.

Luke needed to think. He couldn't talk to his sister with everyone around. "I think I'll hang back today. I have some stuff to get done."

Sheilagh shrugged, his presence obviously not that important to her. "How about you, Samantha? Wanna come to the lake?"

He only half listened and his siblings discussed their plans. Braydon seemed to want to take the boat out. Luke could get into some fishing, but he'd just told Sheilagh he had stuff to do. She didn't seem to really give a shit. Maybe he'd spend some time with Bray since he wasn't always home.

The kitchen door swung open and Colin stepped in. Luke slipped out to check what Tristan had planned. He was still in bed fighting a hangover.

When Luke returned to the barn, he nudged him. "Hey."

Tristan grumbled.

"Listen, Bray's taking the boat out, but some of the others are going to the lake. You feel like fishing?"

"I feel seasick enough. No boat."

"Do you care if I go?"

Tristan peeked his eye out from the pillow. "Will you be all day?"

"Probably a few hours at least."

"No, you go ahead. I need sleep. If I feel better maybe I'll head to the lake with the others."

Luke wanted to warn him to stay away from Sheilagh, but he didn't want to be dramatic. "Okay. I'm gonna get ready." He placed a kiss on his shoulder. "Sweet dreams."

Twenty minutes later he had the truck packed with his gear and was waiting for Bray.

TRISTAN DIDN'T GET out of bed until noon. He showered and cleaned himself up and went to the lake to find the others. When he arrived, he found Samantha, Shei, and Pat, Ryan's brother, playing cards on the sand. He'd sort of regretted not going with Luke on the boat that morning, but his gut was rotted from too much whiskey and he needed the sleep.

He dropped his things on Sheilagh's towel and walked into the lake. The water was warm and felt great. He dove through the surface and swam about fifty feet out to where the floating dock sat. Pulling his body out, he lay down on the planks and let the sun bake the booze out of his system. He was never drinking again.

He could hear the radio from the beach, but not enough to fully make out the song. Drifting off, he enjoyed the peace for about twenty minutes. Then he heard Sheilagh's mouth as she raced Pat into the water.

They swam to the dock and he smiled as she splashed him. "Devil!" he teased, splashing her back.

She spun her hand over the surface and propelled a deluge over Tristan. Her laughter carried over the lake, echoing off the trees in the distance.

"You're gonna get it if you keep it up."

"Oh, am I, Tristan?" she purred. "Are you gonna give it to me?"

He shook his head, resting his face back in the shadowed pocket of his folded arms. She swam away only to return a few minutes later, splashing him again.

"That's it." He stood. "Cannonball!" Throwing himself off the dock, Sheilagh screamed as he landed next to her, propelling water everywhere in his wake.

She laughed and climbed out of the lake. Her bikini bottom slurped back as she raced up the ladder of the dock.

"I see your hiney," he called in a sing-song voice.

She shot him a devious look over her shoulder and flashed him a butt cheek. He laughed and she cannonballed into the water. When she popped through the surface, he splashed and dunked her.

They horsed around, racing from the water to the dock. Eventually they fell into a contest of who could do the most creative dive. Pat waded in the distance shouting out scores.

As Tristan stretched, preparing to do his ultimate corkscrew swan dive, Sheilagh shoved him. He tensed as his body nearly toppled into the lake. Turning, he grabbed her by the waist and tickled all that skin showing.

She squealed and called mercy. He made her really beg for it. They were all laughing and, when he let go, she lost her balance. He laughed ruthlessly as her arms pin wheeled out and she fell backwards, plunging into the water.

Pat clapped and called, "A perfect ten!"

They played in the water for most of the afternoon. When they heard the boat buzzing nearby, Tristan's ears perked up. Finn, Luke, and Bray waved and killed the motor, the boat rocking close to the dock.

Tristan asked about their success and Luke was being his quiet, observant self. When Sheilagh climbed up on the dock, her brother said, "Bathing suits a little small, isn't it, Shei?"

She frowned at him. Finn and Bray didn't comment outwardly on their sister's teeny bikini.

"You guys done for the day?" Tristan asked.

"About," Bray said. "Kelly texted me. He wants to do a bonfire tonight."

"Sounds good," Tristan said. "I'll see you guys then. I'm gonna head home for a while." He met Luke's gaze. They were fairly good at reading each other's subtle looks. Tristan would see him a bit before the bonfire and then they'd head over together. He'd text him when he got back to his belongings on the beach just to make sure they were on the same page.

When Tristan finished getting ready that night, he grabbed a sweatshirt and headed downstairs. Ryan was sitting in the living room watching TV. "Hey, we're all having a bonfire at the lake tonight if you wanna come," Tristan invited.

"Nah, Sarah's coming over soon. I think we're just gonna hang out here since we won't be here for most of the summer."

That was right, they were all going on their family vacation, something Tristan had been invited to, but politely declined. He loved them for letting him stay in their house, but he didn't want to intrude on their family moments.

"How come you didn't ask her to go?"

"Not there yet," Ryan said. "Maybe as it gets closer."

Tristan hoped Sarah was a decent girl. Ryan wanted to be in love and he didn't blame him. Life was so much easier when you had a loving partner to share it with.

He grabbed his sweater. "Well, have fun tonight."

"You too."

When he reached Luke's he parked on the other side of the windy road where trees blocked anyone at the big house from seeing his truck. So many trips through the bramble and woods had cut a beaten path directly to the barn.

He let himself in and heard the shower running. Dropping his keys and sweater on the counter, he went to the master bath. Ah, there was the sexiest bum in the entire universe. It was tempting to strip and join him, but Tristan held strong. "Hey."

Luke turned. Water cascaded over his curved, toned shoulders. His body could have been cut from stone it was such a piece of fine art. "Hey. Missed you today."

No matter how much time passed, hearing a man like Luke openly share his feelings always did extraordinary things to him. "Missed you too, baby."

Luke reached back and killed the water. Tristan tossed him a towel and he ambled out of the shower alcove, grazing his lips with a kiss. "I'll be ready in ten."

He watched as Luke dressed methodically in jeans and a t-shirt. His feet slid into a pair of Reefs. They'd come so far over the last year. "You know," Tristan said reminiscently. "We've known each other a year now."

Luke's smile was telling. His dimple winked as he grinned with bashful charm. "I know. Do you consider our anniversary when we first kissed or when we first decided we were a couple?"

"I think we should celebrate all of it. All the firsts mean something to me."

Luke stuffed his wallet and keys in his pocket and swaggered over. He met Tristan's gaze and whispered, "Me too. It's all special."

Leaning in, Tristan pressed his lips to his. "I love you."

"Love you too, cowboy. You ready?"

They took Luke's truck to the lake and parked. "I told Ryan I'd take his truck down to the body shop tomorrow. I think they can buff out that dent fairly quick."

"What about going to Wells County? I thought we were gonna pick up the new flooring for the guestroom."

"If we're gonna turn it into a computer room, you should start calling it that."

"Whatever. Are you not going to be able to go with me?" Luke asked as they strolled through the grassy path toward the lake.

"I told you I would, babe. I'll head to town tomorrow and pick up the truck and we'll get it done this week."

Luke squeezed his hand. "Thanks. I'd do it myself, but I gotta get—"

All words cut off as they spotted Colin standing in the shadows by the dunes.

Luke released his hand. "Oh hey, Colin. I didn't see you standing there. What are you doing?"

Colin shifted awkwardly, which was strange. Of all the McCulloughs, he was probably the least flawed. He was becoming a priest and, while he drank with them on occasion, his life and priorities were elsewhere. "I was just heading down there. Hey, Tristan. How ya' doing?"

Tristan nodded. "Good, man. You?"

"Good."

He felt Luke's paranoia and tried to remain calm. It was always tricky when they ran across someone and their guard was down.

Colin must have noticed Luke's change in demeanor. "What's up, Luke? You look like you're about to be sick."

A hollow laugh rolled out of Luke's mouth. "Uh, nothing. I'm gonna head down to say hi to the others. I'll catch you later, Tristan. Colin." He took off.

Colin frowned. "Is he all right?"

Tristan shook his head, but continued to watch Luke go. "Yeah, he's just…Luke."

Colin shrugged and they headed toward the fire.

Tristan sat next to Colin who was talking with Kelly. Luke was across the fire from him, next to Bray who was cuddling Samantha on his lap. He didn't really know the girl, but she didn't seem Bray's type. Sheilagh sat by his side roasting marshmallows, which really meant she was being lazy and catching them on fire. After she blew out each cindered sugar torch, she offered it to him.

Colin seemed down and Tristan tried to keep conversation going with Sheilagh to give him and Kelly privacy as they whispered back and forth. Finn and Erin were another strange couple. They looked good together, but that was it. Erin was always in a pissy mood and the group of them rarely acknowledged her. She and Finn had dated since high school and everyone believed they'd eventually marry. It was odd that Samantha, who just showed up a few days ago, seemed to fit in better than Erin who'd been around longer than him.

They drank and laughed and told stories. It was a peaceful night, the kind Tristan liked. He loved this family and couldn't imagine how dull his life would have been without them.

Snagging Luke's gaze across the flames that licked into the black sky, he tipped up the corner of his mouth and winked. Luke winked back and Tristan savored the realization that life was pretty good.

A while later Colin stood and announced he was calling it a night. Tristan wasn't really paying attention, but he turned at Colin's offer to take Sammy home so Bray could stay.

The whole thing was casual, but there was something strange happening. Sam was there as Bray's girlfriend, but for some reason Tristan had an easier time seeing her with a guy like Colin. But that couldn't happen. Colin was three months from becoming a priest, something he'd wanted to do since he was a teenager, according to Luke.

He shook off his suspicions and went back to whatever the rest of the group was laughing about. All in all it had been a fantastic weekend. Summer had officially begun and once Ryan's family was gone on vacation, Tristan and Luke would get a change of scenery.

THEY DECIDED to take the following Friday off for a little them time. Friday morning, they'd been packing up the truck with supplies for a day on the boat, just the two of them, when all hell broke loose.

The door to the big house whipped open and Colin stormed out. McCulloughs were always loud and rowdy, but never Colin. Luke frowned at Tristan who was loading the cooler into the truck bed. Colin marched into the yard and let out a frustrated roar.

"What the fuck?" Luke muttered under his breath, confusion clear on his face.

"Should you go talk to him?"

Before Luke could answer, Kelly came out of the house and walked straight to Colin. They watched from the barn as the two talked. Kelly appeared calm, but Colin was anything but.

Tristan stood, unsure what to do as their voices carried. Their words weren't clear enough to make out, but the two brothers were definitely arguing.

The door swung open again and Braydon stormed out, a dark scowl on his face. Luke's posture tensed. "What the hell's going on?"

"I don't know. Maybe you should go see," Tristan suggested under his breath so their presence remained unobtrusive.

Bray marched directly to Colin. "Yo, Colin! I need to have a word with you." He didn't stop until he was in Colin's face, hands on his chest, shoving him hard. "What the fuck do you think you're doing?"

"I think you should go over there," Tristan said. "This is bad."

Luke took a step forward as Bray shouted, "I ought to kick your sorry ass! What the fuck did you think would happen? It would all just go away?" No one ever talked to Colin like that.

Kelly said something and Bray turned and snapped, "Stay out of it."

Tristan watched as Kelly stiffened. Things were getting ugly. "Fuck you, Bray. And fuck you too, Colin."

Braydon turned back to Colin and pushed him again. "She's up there about to cry, and it's all your fault."

"Shit," Tristan cursed. "Go break them up before they kill each other, Luke. This isn't good." He knew he saw something the other night he shouldn't have. He wasn't sure what happened, but this definitely had to do with Samantha.

Luke walked over to the three of them, but kept his distance. If anything actually shook down he was the muscle capable of putting a stop to it. They continued to argue. Things were chaotic and they each shouted over the other. Luke closed in like a jungle cat prepared to pounce at any moment.

Braydon shoved Colin a third time. "You had no right to play with a girl like her knowing you were never going to change your plans! She fucking loves you, asshole. And you're so God damn pigheaded you're going to let her go so you can go play monk and take vows of poverty and celibacy and any other sacrifice that makes your pompous ass feel more like a righteous martyr."

What happened next was something Tristan never expected to see. Colin turned on Braydon, his arm snapping back with shocking speed, fist tight, and slammed a jab square in Bray's face.

"Holy shit," Tristan hissed and absolute mayhem erupted.

Punches flew and the sickening whack of knuckles collided with flesh. Kelly dove into the melee just a second before Luke ran at the group, shouting and ripping them all apart.

"What the bloody fuck is going on?" Luke roared, gripping Colin and Bray by the scruff of their necks.

Colin's shoulders heaved as he glared at Bray who had blood smeared from his nose to his cheek. Kelly swaggered back a few feet appearing completely unharmed.

"What the fuck?" Luke shouted again.

"Sorry," Colin said to the three of them.

"What the hell happened?" Luke demanded.

"Nothing," Braydon snapped, averting his gaze as he wiped his face on his shirt.

Luke cut his hard glare to Kelly who held up his hands. "Don't look at me. I was dragged into this."

Colin turned on his heel and stormed off. What the hell happened? As he marched toward the woods, he passed Tristan standing by the truck and he snapped, "If you're looking for Luke, he's that way."

Bray threw up his hands, got in his car and took off. That left Kelly. When the coast was clear, Tristan slowly walked over to them. "What was that all about?"

"Nothin'," Kelly said, shaking out the grass in his hair. "Sammy had an anxiety attack and apparently her and Bray aren't all they're chalked up to be."

Luke frowned. "What's Colin got to do with it?"

"Everything," Kelly said.

"Whoa. What are you saying?" Luke asked. "He's making his vows in August."

"Exactly," Kelly said, his irritation clear. "I'm gonna go check on Sam. Two fucking men sniffing around her and they both take off like pussies when she needs them."

Kelly headed back to the house and Tristan looked at Luke. "Colin and Sammy?"

Luke shook his head as if it simply didn't compute. "No. That's impossible. He's gonna be a priest and she's Bray's girlfriend. Colin wouldn't do that."

"I'm of the belief that people can shock the shit out of you when it comes to love," Tristan said.

Luke caught his meaningful look. "True. Let's get out of here. I need a break from all the crazy hospitality."

The day on the lake was the escape they needed. They brought rods to fish, but ended up simply lounging in the sun as the boat floated calmly over the lake. They talked about what happened that morning and neither of them could make a bit of sense out of it. It was impossible to imagine Colin as anything but a priest.

The following weeks rolled by with little drama compared to how explosive the summer had started. Samantha eventually went back to wherever she lived and Braydon apparently moved on. Colin buried himself in community service for the church and everyone was chugging along as usual.

Finn and Erin broke up, but got back together two weeks later, which was the norm. Kelly was booking new bands at the pub where everyone frequently passed time. And Sheilagh had been accepted into three top-notch colleges, each one offering her a full scholarship. She had her pick of the litter, but had yet to decide.

There wasn't anything spectacular that happened, but Tristan recognized those warm months as the best time of his life. He'd never been more settled or content. He and Luke rarely fought. Sure they argued, but they'd learned how to talk things through without letting their emotions take the lead. They discussed their feelings easily and every heart to heart confirmed Luke was the only man for him.

He wanted to marry Luke, but that wasn't an option. Still, he sometimes daydreamed about committing their lives to one another in front of those they loved. He didn't know if they'd ever get there or if Luke wanted such things, but it was a private fantasy Tristan entertained often.

Early August was hot. The days at the lumberyard were brutal and their nights usually resulted in laying around in the air conditioning at the house. Ryan's family would be back from the Outer Banks soon and Tristan was sad to let their little haven at the empty house go. He liked having Luke there, in his bed, around his things.

They'd each hinted around a desire to live together, but both seemed to think it was too soon. Tristan would do it in a heartbeat, but that would definitely lead to questions and explanations would be necessary, explanations Luke was not ready to give.

They talked about setting up the guest room at the barn and saying they were simply roommates, but Tristan didn't like that idea. They could carry that lie forever. It would be too easy for Luke to go on acting like they were never anything more than roommates. Tristan was selfish enough to say no, hoping that eventually they'd come clean with the McCulloughs and be able to live, as they wanted, openly, with no lies.

It was the last weekend before Ryan's family returned and they decided to spend it locked away from the world at the quiet house. They had a peaceful dinner, watched some television, and relaxed, leaving the rest of the world behind.

Luke snuggled into the crook of his arm and sighed. Tristan pressed his lips to his hair. "Tired?"

"No. Just comfortable. This is nice."

It was nice. Even though they had Luke's place, they were always conscious of others nearby. He ran his fingers over Luke's arm and burrowed closer. "I had a nice day with you."

Luke turned and smiled at him. "Me too." Their gazes held as he slowly leaned over and placed his lips to his. "Wanna go to bed?"

Tristan ran his tongue over those full lips. "Yes, but I don't want to sleep." His hand traveled over Luke's chest to the crotch of his jeans. He rubbed and Luke stretched back on the couch, giving him room.

Tristan lowered himself to the floor and glanced shyly up at Luke as he undid his pants. Luke got comfortable, reclining on the couch and watched as Tristan slowly withdrew his cock.

Leaning forward, Tristan licked over the tip and slowly took him to the back of his throat. There was no rush. They had all the time in the world. He worked his mouth over Luke's flesh as he sighed with pleasure, softly running his hands through Tristan's hair.

Tristan leaned back and pulled Luke's jeans all the way off.

"Take yours off too," he rasped and Tristan did as he said.

They lay on the floor, hands pulling, caressing, mouths kissing, and soon they were twisted on top of each other, each pleasuring the other with their mouth. Tristan's body arched as Luke sucked him with long, slow strokes of his tongue.

It was languid and sensual and divine. He loved the soft tease of Luke's hair at his thighs. When they were each close, things became a bit hasty. Luke pulled at Tristan's sack, causing him to moan, long and hard as he deep throated Luke's cock.

Their bodies rocked and tensed as they closed in on their finish. When they came, they did so moments apart. It was beautiful and intrepid. They rolled to their backs, head to foot, foot to head, and breathed.

Luke's fingers caught his and rubbed softly over his knuckles. "Let's shower and go to bed."

That sounded perfect. "Okay. You head up. I'll meet you in the shower. I'm just gonna clean up down here real quick."

Luke carried his clothes upstairs and Tristan chuckled at the sight of his naked ass. He gathered their dishes to take to the kitchen and shut out the lights. The shower kicked on, rattling the pipes in the walls of the old house. Tristan returned to the living room to gather his clothes and stilled when the doorbell rang.

He glanced at the clock. It was almost dark, but not as late as he'd thought. Sliding on his jeans he went to the foyer.

He turned the knob and paused. "Sheilagh?" She was the last person he expected to see.

"Hey, Tristan."

She was all gussied up. Her hair was done, but getting mussed by the slight drizzle in the air. She had high sandals on her feet and a tight jean skirt. Why was she there? "What are you doing here? Is everything all right?"

"Everything's fine. I just figured with Pat and the others gone you were probably lonely and I wanted to stop by to see if you needed some company."

Shit. He honed in his hearing to listen that the shower was still running. "Uh, now isn't really a good time."

She took a deep breath and smiled. He needed to get rid of her. Quick.

"Look Tristan, I know you think I'm just Ryan's little old cousin who doesn't know what's good for her, but I'm here to tell you you're wrong. I have feelings, Tristan, and I know you feel them too."

What?

The drizzle was now soaking her shoulders through. She shivered and he stammered trying to think of a reply. This was not good. Not good at all. As a matter of fact, this was completely fucked in the eye bad.

"Why don't you invite me in and we can talk like two adults?" she purred.

That wasn't possible. He swallowed slowly and cursed under his breath. She took a slow step closer to him and he quickly said, "Look, Shei, you're an awesome girl. You're fun and beautiful and someday you're gonna give some lucky guy a run for his money, but I'm afraid that guy ain't me."

He saw the stubborn glint in her jade eyes and feared he might have to actually hurt her feelings to get rid of her, which was the last thing he wanted to do.

"Can we just talk for a minute? You don't need to

invite me in, but…" She glanced down at her breasts where her nipples were pressing through the thin fabric of her shirt. "I'm getting wet."

"Fuck. Here." He stepped back so she could get out of the rain, but still managed to block her way into the house. She crept closer and he shifted uncomfortably. The rain picked up to a fast patter and he could no longer hear if the shower was running or not.

"Look," she said, placing her hand on his arm. "Don't pretend that the two of us haven't been dancing around this for the past several months. I know you think I'm attractive and I know you're aware of what I think of you."

This was so bad. "Sheilagh—"

She stepped closer until her rain dampened breasts pressed against his bare chest. Her arms looped around his neck and she whispered, "Don't tell me you never thought of just letting it all go, Tristan, and taking what we both know you want."

When she pressed her lips to his he tensed. He gripped her arms in his hands and peeled her off of him, stepping back farther into the house.

"I can't do this, Sheilagh."

"Why?" she asked, letting go of some of that put on maturity and showing the confused—on the cusp of petulant—eighteen year old she hid inside.

He should just be as honest as he possibly could. "Because I'm seeing someone."

She jerked back as if he sucker punched her in the stomach, her posture faltering and her confidence crumbling noticeably. "Who?" Her voice was suddenly strained and raspy.

Tristan winced. The last thing he wanted to do was hurt her. But there was no good that could come out of her misconceived feelings. "It's not important."

"It is to me. You told me it was nothing personal, that you didn't want anyone, so pardon me if I find it imperative to know who was able to persuade you otherwise when I, who was willing to be anything you needed or wanted me to be, could not."

He'd never said that. She'd asked why he was single and he shrugged it off, saying he simply liked being untethered, but she'd never laid herself bare like this before. If she had, he would have shut it down immediately so nothing like this could ever happen.

When he saw her blinking back tears something hard crushed down on his chest. Fuck. Without thinking, he brushed his knuckle over her cheek.

"Don't do this, Sheilagh. When I told you it wasn't anything personal I meant it. You're sweet and one of my friends, but no matter how much you think you can be what I need, you can't."

She whimpered and he didn't miss the protective way her hand fluttered to her stomach as though his confession caused her physical pain. "I…I don't understand."

He looked down. "Look, I can't explain right now—"

She gasped, her fingers rushing to her lips. "Oh my God. You're not alone. She's here now, isn't she?"

Sheilagh stumbled back a step. He stepped forward into the rain to steady her, but she shoved away his hands.

"Babe? Where'd you go? I thought you were going to join me in the shower."

Fuck!

He tensed and so did Sheilagh. His panicked gaze rushed to hers and he saw recognition take form on her pale face in the shape of horror.

"Sheilagh, it isn't what you think," he quickly rushed out.

Her shoulders quaked as she stepped back another pace. "Luke? You and Luke?"

He rapidly shook his head. "You're misinterpreting the whole thing, Shei—"

But his false words fell on deaf ears as Luke opened the door. Everything stilled, as no one seemed to breathe. Tristan panicked. There was no mistaking the situation. He was half dressed and Luke was in a God damn towel. This was bad. This was so bad.

Luke's easygoing expression shriveled, the blood rushing from his face as his mouth opened in shock. "Sheilagh?"

"Luke?" Her face was devoid of anything other than shock.

Luke's mouth opened and closed as he floundered for an excuse. "I...I was doing some renovations at the guest house and I needed to shower so I stopped here to get cleaned up." That didn't even make sense.

It was hopeless. Shutting his eyes and pulling in a much needed breath, Tristan quietly said, "Don't bother, Luke. She heard you."

Luke stiffened as if Tristan were lying. He actually did

a pretty good job of looking offended at what Tristan was 'apparently' implying. But it wasn't going to work. Sheilagh wasn't stupid and no matter how unprepared she was for this, she knew exactly what it was.

Luke gave him a hard look, which he knew was all a performance. If he acted indignant he could pretend he was blameless. Tristan understood the knee jerk reaction, but it hurt all the same, especially since Luke wasn't the first lover of his to play that hand.

There wasn't time to do the damage control needed. Sheilagh turned and ran through the rain to her truck.

"Sheilagh!" Tristan shouted, but she peeled away, sending puddles spewing into the dark.

He faced Luke who was white as a sheet. Stepping inside he shut and locked the door. Luke didn't move.

Tristan flicked on the lights. "Should we go after her?"

Luke was catatonic.

"Luke! I need you to be present right now. What the fuck do we do? She's really upset and she shouldn't be driving."

Luke blinked. "What the hell just happened?"

Jesus Christ. They didn't have time for baby steps. "Your sister just showed up offering me quite the proposition when she discovered I couldn't possibly be with her because I'm fucking her brother!"

Luke's neck twisted as his blinking gaze cut to Tristan. "She doesn't know that."

"Yes, she does. She's not stupid. And why would you come here to shower if you were working at your house?"

"I just said the first thing that popped in my head!" he snapped. "Fuck! What are we going to do?"

"There's nothing we can do unless you want to go find her and explain everything. I don't think she wants to see me right now. She's hurt and embarrassed."

"I can't face her."

Tristan shook his head. "You're gonna eventually have to. She knows about us. If you don't want her to say anything, you need to talk to her."

Luke's chest heaved. He seemed to be hyperventilating. Tristan went to him, but he kept pacing and he couldn't get close enough to calm him down.

"What if she tells everyone?" Luke suddenly blurted.

Tristan rubbed his palms over his face. If she told everyone, then she told everyone. It had never been his intention to live his life forever in the closet, but Luke was different. He knew Center County wasn't the place to host a gay pride parade, but Tristan truly believed if the family knew, they'd be okay with it.

"Then she tells them," he said quietly. "It's been a year, Luke. I can't act like I regret any part of it. You're my partner. I love you. I want a life with you. Forever. People are going to learn about us eventually and we need to figure out how to deal with that as time goes on."

Luke's blue eyes wavered behind a sheen of tears. "I'm scared." He dropped into a chair and Tristan went to him.

Dropping to his knees and cupping the back of Luke's head, he pressed his forehead to his. "I know, baby, but this is your family. They love you. I think you should call

Sheilagh and try to explain the delicacy of the situation. Ask her to respect our privacy."

"I don't know if I can do that."

"You can. It'll be hard, but I'll be right here when you make the call." He slipped his phone out of his pocket and handed it to Luke. It took him over a minute to take it. When Luke held it in his hands, he stared at it as if he didn't know what it was. "Her numbers under Devil."

Luke nodded and pressed send. He clicked off a moment later. "It went to voicemail."

Shit. "Why don't you just say what you need to say and she'll listen to the message when she's ready. Maybe that's the best way to deal with this."

Luke pressed send again and drew in a deep, shaky breath. "Sheilagh. It's Luke. Listen… I know you're upset right now and I'm sorry." His voice cracked and his face dropped to his palm as he silently started to cry. Tristan rubbed his back as he went on.

"I'm so sorry. I know you're mad and hurt. I never meant to hurt you. I don't want to hurt or disappoint anyone. I can't help it. I…love him." He drew in a jagged breath. "Please. Please, just… this is the happiest I've ever been. Please don't take that away from me. I'm not ready for the world to know."

His arm dropped and his thumb slid over the screen, ending the call. Tristan took the phone and slid it back in his pocket. His hands cupped Luke's shoulders. "Look at me, baby." Luke's mouth was a tight line, his expression tense with the effort to hold all his emotions inside. He blinked at him and Tristan said, "You did good."

CHAPTER 11

The recovery from that night didn't come for some time. As autumn arrived, Sheilagh stuck around rather than head off to college as expected. Tristan hated the way her smile no longer greeted him whenever they crossed paths. Luke was pissed she didn't leave for college when she should have. He saw it as a complete waste to turn down so many scholarships and his relationship with his sister only grew more strained as time went on.

Sheilagh never told the others about what she'd seen. Luke, knowing this, still couldn't seem to trust that she'd hold their secret forever. That winter, over the holidays, Tristan ate with Luke's family. No one seemed to mind his presence aside from Sheilagh who no longer spoke to him beyond when it was absolutely necessary.

Things had changed. Colin was a totally different man and Samantha was back. She was also pregnant which was an entirely unpredicted drama. Bray was often in Philadelphia finishing his degree and Kelly was Kelly. Finn was still with Erin on Tuesdays and random Thursdays, but their relationship followed a continuous pattern of quarrels and juvenile breakups the rest of them couldn't keep track of.

When Finn wasn't distracted by Erin's high maintenance presence, Tristan sensed him observing him and Luke. He suspected Finn was realizing things about his twin the others had yet to pick up on.

He kept his hunch about Finn's suspicions to himself, not seeing the point in stressing Luke out about the inevitable. They carried on in their clandestine relationship and with each passing month their guard grew a bit more lax.

When their two year anniversary arrived the following June, they went to the cabin in the woods and made love for seven days straight. Tristan told the family he was returning to Texas to visit old friends and Luke made up some bullshit about possibly returning to college and having to take an entrance exam out of state. No one found out they were lying, but they also didn't look too hard to see the truth.

It was a blurred line, wondering who knew the truth and who was in the dark. Samantha was another person he suspected knew their secret. She was always the first to suggest Luke ask Tristan to come to family functions. This made their lives easier, but stressed Luke out all the same.

July rolled into August and they were moving along as

always, steadily getting older, but marking their days with little more than quiet celebrations between him and Luke.

They were at the market one day, arguing over cinnamon bagels versus the kind with raisins that Luke liked, when something strange happened.

"You could just pick the raisins out," Luke argued. "I'd pick them out for you."

"You can't pick raisins out of a bagel. They're buried inside."

"Just buy both kinds then. I'm done arguing over fucking raisins," Luke said tossing both bags in their cart.

They turned and stilled as a girl Tristan didn't recognize was standing in front of them smiling up at Luke. He frowned and looked to Luke to see if he knew her. His face was blank.

"Hi." The girl said. "Remember me? Mallory."

"Uh…" Luke shot him a guilty look. Great. Who was she? Someone he'd slept with? She didn't look like Luke's prior type. This girl had a stout little build and quite a bit of curves. She was pretty, just not in the long legged willowy way most of Luke's exes were.

"Sorry?" Luke said. Maybe he didn't know her.

"We met in the woods. You gave me a ride back to my car…"

What?

Tristan scowled at Luke. When was he in the woods picking up strange women?

Luke cleared his throat. "You must have me confused—"

The girl's eyes turned apprehensive. She glanced at

Tristan as if second guessing her statement. "My mistake." She quickly said. "I thought you were someone else." And just like that she turned and fled toward the dairy aisle.

Tristan glared at the back of Luke's head as he watched her go. When Luke turned he drew back. "What? I have no freaking idea who she was."

Narrowing his eyes, he asked, "You haven't given any girls rides in the woods?"

"Why the fuck would I be driving around the woods picking up strangers?"

He believed him, but that didn't explain what the hell just happened. They didn't discover who the girl was until a few weeks later.

Braydon was leaving for his senior year of college and, as usual, they were going to make him vomit to help him remember them. Everyone was meeting at O'Malley's that night.

Tristan and Luke were getting out of the truck when Bray's Jetta pulled in. They paused when they noticed he had a passenger. The side door opened the same time as Bray's driver door and Sheilagh's glistening red head popped out.

"What's she doing here?" Luke asked under his breath.

"Look who I found," Bray called.

Luke noticeably tensed as he always did in his sister's presence, but played it off. "Hey, Shei-Devil."

"Well, hello, boys!" she said with more expression than Tristan had seen her hold in months. Something was different.

They went into the bar and headed in Kelly's direction.

Sheilagh was almost twenty, but still under the legal drinking age and he didn't like her in the bar on weekend nights. She definitely wasn't a kid anymore as she seemed to frequently go out on dates, but she was still too young to be at a bar doing more than waitressing.

He protectively stuck by her side and for once she didn't seem to shoulder him off. They approached the bar and she reached in her purse, slapping something down on the lacquered counter.

"I'll take a shot of Tully," she said, lifting her chin and grinning proudly.

Her fingers lifted and a fake ID showed. Kelly snatched it up. "Where'd you get this?"

"Braydon," she purred. "He's the new favorite, so all you ass clowns better up your game."

Tristan frowned and Kelly shot Bray a look. "You got her a fake ID?"

"Like she doesn't drink at home," Bray argued.

"That's different. She's safe there." Kelly tucked the ID next to the register. "I'll serve you, but I'm keeping the ID. You drink here or home. Nowhere else."

Sheilagh accepted his conditions. "Line 'em up!"

Kelly set the shots up like good little soldiers and they each threw one back. Sheilagh hooted as her empty glass returned to the counter and Tristan smiled. He missed seeing her happy and was glad she was enjoying herself.

Erin suddenly appeared and Sheilagh rolled her eyes. "You're drinking?" Finn's girlfriend asked.

"Problem?" Sheilagh snapped, raising a sharp red brow. She was back. The feisty Shei-Devil was back.

Erin huffed and turned to order a drink. The bell above the door rang and Finn came in. "Finally," Erin hissed.

The first round of beers was passed out and Tristan rolled his eyes as Erin shrugged off Finn's greeting. God, she was such a bitch. Finn took his beer and disappeared. Erin scowled after him and Sheilagh didn't miss a single beat.

"Hey, who's that pretty girl over there Finn's talking to?" the devil taunted, earning an evil look from Erin.

Tristan turned. "It's the girl from the woods."

"The woods?" Sheilagh asked.

"Long story," he mumbled, shooting Luke a look.

Luke's head tipped to the side as he observed the girl talking to his twin. Sheilagh said, "I'm gonna go see who she is." And off she went.

They hung at the bar and a while later, Pat and Ryan showed up. Tristan sidled up to Luke and whispered, "Your brother seems to know her. Case of mistaken identity?"

"That's what I'm thinking," Luke said back, sipping his beer.

Finn, Sheilagh, and the bagel aisle girl came over to the bar and another round of shots was poured. It was gonna be a long night.

Luke held his shot high and said, "To our golden boy, Braydon. May his last year of school be the best he's seen yet!"

They raised their glasses and shouted, "To Braydon!"

"Solute!"

The bagel girl slammed down her glass and gasped. "What was that?"

"'Tis the best Irish whiskey O'Malley's has to offer," Finn said.

"It tastes like shit," she grumbled, wiping her lips with the back of her hand.

Tristan laughed. He sent Luke a look telling him he wanted to meet this newcomer. Luke strolled over. "Hey, I know you."

Finn chuckled. "Yeah, I heard you two met at the market."

Tristan caught the slight tensing of Luke's expression, but he quickly covered his obvious nervousness that Finn might have heard they'd been grocery shopping together.

"You thought I was Finn, didn't you?" Luke asked the girl.

"Sorry about that," she said, her face flushing.

Luke smiled. "No problem. So, where'd you come from?"

Turns out, the girl, Mallory—or otherwise called Philly—had recently moved from Philadelphia to Center County and was starting a job at the high school. What a strange small world.

Mallory was actually pretty cool. She was funny as hell and everyone seemed to like her. Everyone except for Erin, but she didn't like anyone.

Tristan saw Luke was stressing and assumed it was over Finn's comment about them being in the market. Finn hadn't mentioned knowing Tristan had been there, but he probably knew.

Erin was acting all sorts of affectionate and sweet to Luke's twin, which was such a pathetic act. It didn't last long. Tristan watched as she whispered something to Finn and his easygoing expression turned to a scowl. A minute later he was dragging her out of the bar for what was likely their usual weekend brawl.

Bray was teasing Samantha about being a school-teacher. "Bet those boys love it when you wear those pencil skirts and write stuff on the chalk board."

"Schools haven't had chalkboards in years, Bray. And I don't wear skirts."

"You should. I always paid more attention to the sexy teachers. Remember that teacher who used to work at the high school, the hot one with the long pipes?" Bray asked Colin and Luke.

Luke, of course, jumped all over the topic. "Oh, yeah, what was her name? She had a great body."

Tristan sighed. This was par for the course whenever Luke felt the least bit threatened by exposure. Looking away, he caught Sheilagh's look of confusion.

Finn returned and Luke yelled loud enough for the entire bar to hear, "Hey, Finn!"

Finn looked irritated but pasted on a smile. "Yeah?"

"What was that teacher's name who always wore the lacy slip we'd peek at in middle school?"

"Ms. Fitzpatrick."

Luke clapped his hands. "That's it! She had a set of legs on her."

Finn paused then gave a hollow chuckle, glancing over at Tristan. Yeah. He knew. Tristan met his confused stare, saw the sympathy in his eyes. It was bad enough dealing with a lover who refused to come out. It was a whole different mess when others began discovering their relationship and said lover exploited every opportunity to act straight. It was embarrassing.

Tristan lifted his shoulder in a negligent shrug, telling Finn Luke would always be Luke.

As the night carried on, everyone got plastered. Luke made an ass out of himself, but only to the three of them who were aware of the man he really was. At the end of the night, Ryan called his mom to come pick them up. Tristan was glad for the audience. It gave him an excuse to go back to Ryan's alone.

He couldn't deal with Luke when he got like that. It was insulting on so many levels, and set them back at start. Sometimes he wondered why he even put up with his attitude. There were days he wanted to scream for the world to hear that he was gay. Not to expose Luke, but to see if Luke would stop acting like they were just friends.

In the end, he did nothing. He loved him. He loved a man who hated the fact that he couldn't help but love him back.

AS WINTER SETTLED IN, Luke realized something about himself. He was a jealous person. Not in the territorial sense like he was with Tristan. If anyone tried to touch his boy he'd go on a rampage. That was that. But this sort of jealousy was different. This was envy.

Finn and Erin had broken up and this time it seemed to be for good. Luke's twin seemed incredibly happy with the turn his life had suddenly taken and Mallory was a new important part of it. His brother was going to marry the girl and made no effort to hide how hard he'd fallen.

Once Luke realized this, something hollow and uncomfortable took shape in him. He wanted what Finn had. He wanted a spouse.

It took him a while to pinpoint exactly what was eating him, but when he did he was sure of it. Samantha's little girl, Tallulah, was another new and coveted thing in Luke's life.

His niece, Lula, was a handful, but all she had to do was look up at him with those dark blue McCullough eyes and he'd give her the moon. He realized he wanted children someday too.

All of these things, marriage, family, were part of the normal procession of life. But his life with Tristan didn't allow for those gifts. They'd never have children together and with the back and forth way the senate worked, they'd never have a marriage—at least not the way a man and a woman could, unanimously accepted by the world.

He wanted Tristan and he wanted those things, but he still didn't want the world to know he was gay. As time went on, it became less and less about his family's opinions. Tristan's importance in his life lapsed theirs sometime over the past two and a half years.

Still, he had this instinctive feeling that so long as they lived in Center County they had to keep their personal life private.

He feared if they came out something bad would happen. The world was a fucked up place and whenever there was news about hate crimes on TV he mourned how horrible people could truly be.

Tristan had picked up on his surly mood. Luke didn't want to talk about what was bothering him, because there was really nothing Tristan could do. He could promise everything would be fine, but there was no guarantee in that. It was all just words.

He reached a point where he thought he might be fine with telling his family, but what if word got around and someone started shit with Tristan and he wasn't there to protect him? His biggest fear was seeing Tristan hurt for only being who he'd always been.

Tristan accepted his excuses not to talk about what was bothering him and eventually stopped asking. When Mallory gifted them with more little McCulloughs the following year, all Luke's feelings came hurtling back.

He couldn't breathe in his own skin and he needed to escape. His breaking point came when Kelly announced he was getting married. Fucking Kelly!

Of all the McCulloughs everyone expected Kelly to remain single the longest. Luke knew his rogue brother was changing after he ended up in jail one night. Kelly didn't go into much detail about the situation, but it all had to do with a girl that had wrapped herself up in Kelly's head and now they were getting married.

Everything was happening around them and he and Tristan seemed stuck in the same place. Birthdays passed, babies were born, and anniversaries accumulated. It was hard seeing everyone get together to celebrate another year gone by when he and Tristan never did more than share a toast in the solitude that was their life.

He was happy, but not. He was lonely, lonely for all the small joys the others got to share along the way. It had been years since that first kiss. His home was no longer new. Tristan's belongings mixed with his. Everything was theirs. But it wasn't.

On their fifth anniversary Luke decided to do something different. He needed to commemorate how far they'd come together. On a whim, he ordered tickets to Ireland and told Tristan to take the last week of July off.

"Why?"

Luke left the home office with their ticket vouchers, fresh from the printer, in his hand. "I'm taking you away."

Tristan smiled. "Where?"

"Ireland. I've always wanted to go and I want you to come with me. We can get the hell out of here and be ourselves for a while."

"I'm always myself, Luke."

"We can be together. I rented a little cottage in a village. We can visit pubs and not worry about others seeing us."

Tristan drew in a slow breath, his smile fading. "I see."

"You don't seem excited."

"It sounds like a great trip. But you know we don't need to travel halfway around the world to enjoy all those things."

Luke dropped into the chair beside him. "I know.

Just…will you do this for me? I need to get away from here for a while."

Tristan's hand rubbed over his back. "Okay. But since we're giving anniversary presents early, I have one for you."

Luke turned and grinned. "You do?"

"Of course. You're my ball and chain. I would never forget an anniversary." Tristan stood and went to their bedroom. He returned a moment later with a small box.

"Here. Open it."

It was little and the corners of the paper were taped tight. Luke fumbled with the wrapping and unearthed a small satin box. He snapped it open and frowned. "What is this?"

Tristan removed the ring and lowered to the floor in front of him. He met his gaze and smiled nervously. "They passed the vote in Delaware. Eventually it'll come here. I know it will. It has to." He licked his lips and took Luke's hand. "I want to marry you, Luke. I know we can't right now, but some day we will. Even if the senate dicks around until we're in our sixties, I want to still be with you then. Whether it happens next year or when we're two old farts who can barely get it up anymore, you're who I want to marry."

Luke's heart raced. Holy shit. He was proposing? That was his job. He was pissed off he hadn't had the brains—or the balls—to do it first. Why hadn't he done that?

A coldness settled in his stomach. Because proposing to Tristan would mean accepting he'd never have a family like his siblings.

"Will you marry me?"

Luke's brow puckered as he sadly accepted that this was the best option life could give him at this time. Not that Tristan wasn't an amazing partner. He was! But that their love would have to hold on until the world became a more accepting place. Pushing aside the injustice of their limitations and embracing his blessings, he said, "Fucking right I'll marry you. You're the love of my life."

Tristan sucked in a breath and Luke realized how unsure he'd been of his answer. "You will?"

He nodded. "Tristan, I don't want to live if it isn't with you. If Pennsylvania recognized gay marriage I'd marry you tomorrow. I hope one day they do. For right now, though, I'll wear your ring and the two of us will know that means as much as any piece of paper."

Tristan shot up and kissed him hard. "I love you, Luke McCullough."

The ring slid onto his finger. It was pretty. Brushed steel, manly, but nice. He smiled. It looked right on his finger. "I'm getting you one too."

Tristan's face split with a wide grin. "All right."

That night when they made love it was earth shattering. Tristan covered Luke like a blanket, filling him with such tenderness, such need. When Luke took Tristan, he was not as refined.

He possessed him completely, for the first time knowing there would never again be another. This was his soul mate, his partner. His everything.

PART III
US

CHAPTER 12

"Luke!"

Tristan turned as Kelly shouted across the bar. The easy mannered guy looked frazzled as he said something to Sue, the barmaid. He rushed to their table. "Come on, get in the car. We have to go."

Luke stood, his face hard. "What's happening?"

"Just come on. I'll explain once we're on our way. Tristan, you come too."

They followed Kelly to the door of O'Malley's and jumped in his SUV. Tristan took the front and Luke climbed in the back. Their doors were barely closed when Kelly spun the wheel and peeled out of the parking lot.

Tristan's stomach tightened. Something was majorly wrong. Did someone die? Fuck.

"What's happening?" Luke shouted over the seat.

"Fucking Sheilagh is what's happening!" Kelly stormed, as he barreled down Main Street.

Oh God. His heart raced. Sheilagh had gone a bit off the deep end in the past few years. She was twenty-four and her own person, but that didn't make it any easier to watch her destroy her life. Every weekend he watched her go home with some piece of shit. Fuck! Maybe someone hadn't died, but if anyone hurt her he'd kill them.

"What do you mean Sheilagh? Is she hurt?"

"She's gonna be," Kelly growled.

"Use fucking words we can understand, Kelly. What the fuck happened to Sheilagh?"

Kelly yanked the wheel and they all slid with the momentum of the speeding car. "I was serving up drinks when I heard Tim say to Russ he was heading over to Puss n' Boots tonight."

Tristan frowned. "What's Puss n' Boots?"

Kelly didn't answer because Luke snapped, "Get to the point!"

"They were all going to see the newest act. Some hot number with red hair. Then the fucker turned to me and said, *Yeah, Kelly, you probably know her. Little devil named Sheilagh.*"

Luke shouted, "Are you fucking serious?"

"What the fuck is Puss n' Boots?" Tristan yelled.

Luke's expression was nothing but hard lines. "A fucking strip club!"

"*What?*"

"Exactly," Kelly growled. "I'm gonna kill her."

Tristan's mind reeled as they peeled into the lot of Puss n' Boots. The place looked disgusting even from the outside. Jesus. This was what she'd turned to? What was she thinking? She had everything and turned her back on all of it. *For this?*

He fumed silently as they climbed out of the car. "Are you coming?" he asked Luke as he opened his door.

"No. I'll go ballistic if I see her in there traipsing around naked."

"Come on!" Kelly snapped.

Tristan slammed the door and followed Kelly. The place smelled dank, like old booze and perverts. They went through the back and Kelly stopped dead in his tracks. "Jesus motherfucking Christ. I'm going to kill you."

Tristan couldn't see past the door Kelly was blocking, but maybe that was a good thing. He heard Sheilagh's startled voice.

"Kelly! What the hell are you doing here?"

"Cover yourself."

"You have to leave," she snapped.

Kelly covered his eyes and growled, "When I heard you were here, I nearly maimed a guy for spreading rumors. Then we called around and no one knew where the hell you were. Never in my life did I think you could be this stupid. Get your shit and get in the fucking car. We're leaving."

"You're not my father, Kelly."

Kelly's shoulders shook in front of him as he snarled, "Should I go get Dad? Will that make you leave?"

Sheilagh's voice was suddenly small. "You wouldn't."

"Try me, Sheilagh. I am this close to losing it. Get in the fucking car."

"No. I'm next."

Was she out of her God damn mind? Before Tristan could say anything, Kelly stomped into the room. "You're not getting on a stage and jiggling your lady bits for every pervert in Center County. Now move!"

"Get off me!" she screamed and Tristan had heard enough.

He stepped into the room. "Kelly."

They both stilled and looked toward the door. Sheilagh's face turned deep crimson. He kept his expression calm and looked only into her eyes. His jaw locked. He wasn't looking, but he was certain she had little covering her.

Kelly released his hold on her arm. "You try talking some sense into her," he snapped and marched to the door.

Sheilagh looked like a frightened cat ready to bolt. Choosing his words carefully, he pronounced each measured syllable with a calmness he didn't feel. "You're not doing this, Shei."

"You don't get a say in what I do, Tristan. My days of hero worship are over." The venom of her words could not disguise the hurt in her voice.

He was in front of her in two strides. In a menacingly soft voice he said, "Don't do this, Sheilagh. We won't let you. You're better than this. Your other brother's in the car. Don't make him see you like this. Let's go."

Her body trembled. He didn't need to clarify that the other brother was Luke.

Gritting her teeth, she met his cold stare and said, "Tough."

He was done arguing with her. He plucked her up off the ground, hoisted her over his shoulder, and marched her little ass out to the car. The door slammed and she punched his back. "Put me down! I'm up next!"

He opened the back door of Kelly's SUV and tossed her inside. She scrambled to an upright position and he slammed the door in her face. The second he was in, Kelly threw the car into reverse and they took off.

Luke shouted a curse and tossed a blanket at her.

Completely enraged, Sheilagh sat up and shrieked, "You have no right!"

"Shut up!" the three of them shouted at once.

Tristan had no idea where Kelly was taking them. He was too pissed to ask. Sheilagh kicked the back of his seat like a little brat and he'd about had it with her shit.

"Where are we going?" she asked. No one answered.

When they hit the highway just outside of town the SUV jerked as Kelly veered off the road. Gravel spewed under the tires as the vehicle tore onto the shoulder and he threw the SUV in park.

No one said a word for about a minute. Tristan flinched when Luke shouted, "Are you out of your God damn mind?"

"Oh, shut up Luke! *You* have no right to pass judgment on me!"

Kelly swiveled in his seat, his blue eyes shining in the dark. "What did you suspect people would do after you bared your titties for the town? Praise you? Christ, Sheilagh, use your fucking head!"

"Like you have any room to talk, Kelly! There isn't a woman in Center County who hasn't seen your wank!"

"And do you think I didn't pay a price for my actions, Sheilagh?" Kelly stormed. "It's like the sheep fucker!" her brother snarled and turned toward the windshield.

What? Who was fucking sheep?

Sheilagh's voice echoed his thoughts. "What?"

"Shamus the sheep fucker!" Kelly snapped. "The old Irishman in the bar that built the church and sailed the sea, but no one remembers that because he fucked *one* sheep."

"No one's fucking a sheep, you moron!" she growled and kicked the seat again.

"Well, what do you think people would say if you started stripping? You wouldn't be Sheilagh the beautiful McCullough or Sheilagh the genius. No, you'd only be Sheilagh the stripper. Do you want that kind of reputation?"

That was enough. Tristan turned. "Why would you do this, Shei?"

She blinked repeatedly and he could tell by the tight set of her jaw she was ready to cry. He waited. Her stubborn chin jutted out and she snidely asked, "Why not?"

He wasn't going to let her bait him. "You're better than that. You know you are."

Luke sat, seething, as he glared out the window and growled, "This is bullshit. When are you going to grow up?"

She pivoted and shrilled at her brother, "Me? How about you, *Luke*? When are you going to grow up? You have an awful lot to say about how everyone lives their life, when you don't have the balls to let the world see who you really are!"

Fuck.

The car grew deathly silent. Kelly said her name in warning, "Sheilagh."

"No! I'm sick of it! Just say it! Say it!"

"What do you want me to say?" Luke turned and roared.

Tristan's stare cut to her and it took everything he had not to freak out like the rest of them. This was about her, not them! With deadly calm he had no idea how he was maintaining, he said, "This isn't about Luke. It never was. I'm sorry, Sheilagh. I know this isn't what you asked for, but sometimes life is unfair."

She glared back at him. "I wanna go home."

No one said anything for several seconds. "You're going away," Kelly finally announced.

"What?" she snapped, panic in her voice.

They'd all sat by and watched her blow her potential over the last six years. Kelly was right. It was time for her to leave.

"You're going to college. There's nothing for you here

and you know it. It's time for you to get on with your life and make something of yourself."

"You don't get to decide for me, Kelly."

Luke turned to her. "Stop being a brat. Do you have any idea what kind of opportunities you have? You don't know what it's like to have such potential snatched away."

"I really don't care what any of you think. This is my life—"

"Then do something with it!" Luke snarled. "You haven't done shit since you graduated. What are you waiting for?"

Kelly stared out at the road and quietly said, "Here's how this is going to roll. You're going to get dressed and we're going to take you home. Tomorrow, you're going to fill out applications and this fall you *will* be enrolling in college. You either agree to that, here and now, or we drive your ass right to Dad."

When she didn't reply, Kelly barked, "Do we have a deal?"

Tristan continued to watch her. She was obviously using all the strength she had not to break in front of them. "Sheilagh, do this for yourself. You deserve better than the life you've been leading. Go be something amazing, because the rest of us don't have the gifts you have."

A tear tumbled past her lashes and she batted it away.

"We're all scared, Sheilagh," Luke softly said and Tristan's heart pinched. He hadn't let her get to him with head games and that was huge. "No one ever truly gets what they want in life. You need to do this. You need to get out of here and make something of yourself."

There was no more talking after that. Sheilagh turned

her stare out the window. Luke did the same. Kelly drove. And Tristan wondered at the words his partner had just used. *No one ever truly gets what they want in life.*

He convinced himself Luke had been referring to their inability to marry and *not* their relationship in general.

When they pulled up at the big house Sheilagh ran out of the car. Kelly took several deep breaths and Luke unlocked the car door. "Wait," Kelly said.

Tristan turned. Kelly didn't look at either of them. In a low voice he said, "For the record, you don't have to justify anything. It's okay."

Yeah. Tristan swallowed.

Luke's hand hesitantly lifted and clapped over Kelly's shoulder. He didn't look at his brother, but there was no mistaking the gesture as anything less than the first acknowledgment Luke had willingly made in the history of their relationship. "Thanks."

His door shut and Kelly let out a slow breath. Tristan looked at Kelly. "Thanks for telling him that."

"He's my brother. I love him. I just want him to be happy."

Tristan nodded. "How long have you known?"

Kelly shrugged. "I always knew you were gay."

His eyes widened in the darkness. "You did?"

"Yeah. Before I was married, I got a lot of the girls you flirted with. Stories started adding up. You never hooked up with any of them. It took me a while longer to figure out about Luke. I just thought you guys were tight. But... then I noticed the rings last year and it all made sense. How long?"

"Next month will be our sixth anniversary."

He let out a slow whistle. "That's a long time to keep a secret."

"You have no idea."

Kelly turned. "Can I ask you something?"

"Sure."

"Why doesn't he trust the family enough to tell everyone?"

Tristan shook his head, wishing he had the answer. "I think he's scared. He's afraid if one person knows, the world will know and as much as he loves you guys, there aren't enough of you to protect us from all the nasty people out there."

Kelly nodded, accepting his answer. "Well, for the record, I've looked at you as another brother for a long time, Tristan." He held out a hand. "Welcome to the family."

Tristan blinked back tears. Kelly couldn't know how much his words meant. It was the closest he'd ever come to knowing what it was to have in-laws. He shook his hand and rasped, "Thank you."

When he reached the barn, Luke was sitting at the table, staring at nothing. He didn't look angry, like Tristan had assumed he'd find him. His expression was...contemplative.

"You okay?"

Luke sighed. "Yeah. I think I am."

Tristan laughed. "You don't seem too sure."

"I'd like to crucify Sheilagh, but with Kelly...I'm okay with that."

"Kelly's a good guy."

"You'll get no argument from me."

OVER THE NEXT WHILE, Sheilagh sent away applications and settled on a school. When she left the following fall, Tristan was sad.

He'd been worrying about her since he met her. He loved her like a little sister and now he feared she hated him beyond redemption. With her gone and the rest of McCulloughs gone off and married, the big house was, for the first time, quiet.

She'd come home for Christmas and smiled at him a few times, but it never reached her eyes. He worried he might have broken the delicate closeness they'd always shared.

It wasn't something Luke was good at talking about. He had never liked the fact that his little sister had a crush on Tristan or the fact she knew things about them they wanted kept private. Kelly was fine with Sheilagh and told Tristan she called him often. It wasn't the assurance he was hoping for, but it was enough to get him through.

As time traveled on, their isolated existence from the rest of the family seemed to grate on both of them. Luke fluctuated. Sometimes Tristan found him turning the ring on his finger with a sweet smile on his face. And other times he found the ring forgotten next to the sink in the bathroom.

Tristan never took off his ring and didn't understand

why Luke did. They'd had a couple incidences with Luke laying it on thick with the guys at work. He mostly talked about women like most guys did when those locker room moments came up, but then he'd started keeping company with a few men Tristan didn't approve of. The new guys working the yard liked to break balls and use words like homo and faggot. Tristan hated them, but Luke never seemed to mention them outside of work.

Tristan often thought about bringing the topic up when they were alone, but those moments were so rare he hated the idea of dragging the world's ugliness into their little sanctuary. He supposed if Luke were hanging out with these men outside of work it would be more of an issue, but since they were only co-workers and every job had idiots hidden somewhere among the staff, Tristan tried to get over it. He learned to ignore the guys at work and eventually tuned them out.

That March, Sheilagh was due to return home again. Tristan was anxious and determined to make sure everything was going okay with her. He'd paced all night waiting for her car to arrive that Sunday, but it never did.

Monday morning he sent Luke to the big house to see what changed.

"What do you mean she's not coming until Wednesday?"

Luke shrugged. "Hell if I know. She told my mum something about staying to help one of her teachers."

Tristan stepped back and frowned. He'd wanted to see her, but Luke was being his normal emotionally stunted self and already putting up walls at the first mention of his sister.

The next two days dragged. He hung out at Luke's all day Wednesday waiting for her to arrive. As he heard a car pulling up he left Luke alone where he was playing on the computer and rushed to the door.

When he opened the door he stilled. That wasn't Sheilagh's truck. It was a BMW. Who the hell was this bozo?

The front door of the big house opened and Maureen stepped out. "Oh shit," he muttered as she lifted a rifle and aimed it at the fancy car.

Then he heard Sheilagh's familiar voice. "Ma! It's me! Put the gun back!"

"Sheilagh? Oh! I thought it was some lost drug lord in that fancy car." She lowered the weapon. "Who's with you?"

The doors of the car opened and Sheilagh and the driver stepped out. Maureen holstered the gun in her apron and went to greet them. Tristan held back. The guy with her was old. Older than Tristan.

He turned and went to find Luke. "Luke!"

"Yo!"

He was still in the office. "Sheilagh's here."

Luke's eyes stayed on the computer screen, focused on whatever he was doing. "Okay. You going over there?"

"No. She's with someone."

He turned. "Who? A guy?"

"Yeah. An *old* guy."

Luke frowned. "What?"

"I think we should go check it out."

Luke pursed his lips to the side. "I can hold off."

Tristan huffed and went to the window. "Oh, good. Your dad's back." He pulled out his phone as it buzzed. "Speak of the devil."

He read the text from Frank. *There's some putz here with Shei.*

He looked over and saw Luke got the same text. It must have gone out to all the guys.

"See!" Tristan snapped. "Your dad doesn't like him either."

Luke rolled his eyes. "The guy's been here for five seconds. You don't know anything about him."

His eyes went back to the window. "Oh, there he is. I'm gonna go mess with him."

As he left Luke yelled, "Stop acting like a girl!"

Tristan ignored him and rolled up his sleeves. Steeling his face with his hardest I'm—a—mean—motherfucker—from—Texas scowl, he meandered over to the BMW. He didn't know why, but he was really bothered by the fact that Sheilagh was close enough to someone to bring him home and no one knew who the fuck he was.

Tristan crossed his arms, showing off his tattoos, and purposefully crushed a twig under his boot to get the guy's attention. The guy turned and Tristan drawled, "You here with Sheilagh?"

"Are you one of Sheilagh's brothers?" He spoke with a British accent, which Tristan wasn't expecting. Must be one of those fancy college types. He narrowed his eyes. "She ain't my sister."

Placing the overnight bag he'd retrieved from the car onto the ground, he extended his hand. "I'm Alec Devereux, a friend of Sheilagh's from Princeton."

Tristan eyed his hand, but made no move to shake it. This guy was definitely too old for Sheilagh. He was handsome and that voice was sexy as hell, but Sheilagh was twenty-four. This guy looked close to forty. Too old for college and too old for Sheilagh. "What kind'a friend?"

He dropped his hand and seemed put out. Hopefully Frank gave him a hard time as well. "A good friend. Who are you?"

"Just another keeper. You'll want to watch yourself."

The Brit frowned. "Pardon?"

Tristan twisted his head slowly, cracking various vertebrae in the process. "Shei ain't ever brought a man home. You look a bit...old...to be her *friend*."

The door to the barn opened and Tristan grinned. If he was intimidating this guy, wait until he met Luke.

Luke stepped to his side. He'd removed his shirt and probably done about fifty push-up's real quick so his muscles appeared more defined. "Who's this?" he said, tipping his chin. Tristan almost laughed. He knew Luke wouldn't be able to resist playing with this guy.

Tristan glanced at him. He was wearing the Jeff cap he'd bought him years ago. He could gobble him up in that hat. In a monotone voice, he said, "Sheilagh's friend."

"Sheilagh doesn't have friends we don't know."

The Brit arched a brow. "I'm Alec."

"Alec," Luke said, testing the word. "Shei brought you here?"

The guy nodded.

Luke chuckled and shouted, "Sheilagh! Get your ass out here before we string up your 'friend'!"

The door on the porch whipped open and Sheilagh came barreling out. "Don't you come up here trying to intimidate my company. Take your sorry asses on home and come back when you've found some manners. Alec, come inside. You don't need to bother with them."

Tristan grinned. *I'll be damned.* There was the fire that had been missing around here.

Luke laughed and said, "Take a McCullough out of Center County, but you'll never get the McCullough out of her. I can see that prep school of yours still has its work cut out for them, Shei-Devil."

Shei smiled, the expression slow and full of hidden affection. "No fancy neighborhood's gonna change me, Luke. You should have known better if you were hoping to send me away and get some debutant back."

Luke laughed. "Pretty brazen bringing a friend back with you, Shei-Devil."

"Well, you know me. I like to shake things up."

She didn't look at Tristan. As a matter of fact she remained on the porch, keeping her distance. Tristan didn't like that, especially when he sensed the new guy taking his measure. Had she told him about them?

"How come you didn't come home on Saturday?" Tristan finally asked.

Sheilagh shrugged. "I had things I wanted to do."

His gaze cut to Alec's who was indeed studying him. Tristan glanced back in her direction. "I'll bet.

Tomorrow night we're hitting O'Malley's. You like whiskey, *friend?*"

"When it suits."

What kind of answer was that? Tristan nodded. "Good. I'll have your shots ready."

The door to the house opened and Maureen came out. "Oh, I didn't know you boys were here. Well, come and eat. The food's getting' cold and I didn't cook for nothin'."

Tristan stepped toward the house without waiting to see what Luke did. He didn't make room for Alec the old Brit and the man had to step aside to let him pass. *That's right. This is my family and no stranger's gonna come sniffin' around without our permission.*

When they settled in at the table Tristan started his inquisition. "How long are you staying, Shei?"

"We have to go back early Sunday morning."

"What are you majoring in, Alec?" Tristan asked, his tone suspicious.

Alec cleared his throat. "My concentration is philosophy."

Sheilagh drew in a breath. "Actually, Alec's a—"

Alec interrupted. "Pass the salt, sweetheart."

Everyone stilled. Sweetheart?

Frank stood and cleared his plate. The man lingered at the sink, giving them his back. Tristan and Luke eyed Sheilagh's *sweetheart* challengingly. Maureen, who was still chatting around them, slipped in a quick prompt for Sheilagh to slide over the salt, but then went back to her abridgment of the current McCullough events and doings.

After dinner Tristan still wasn't at ease. As they lay in

bed he texted Finn. He kept it short and to the point. *Devil brought a guy home. I don't like him. Bring your torches and pitchforks to O'Malley's tomorrow.*

Finn texted back a minute later. *Lol. I'll have the wife polish the gun.*

Tristan laughed.

"What's so funny?" Luke asked.

"Finn. I told him about Sheilagh's *sweetheart.*"

Luke's expression was not amused. "Why do you care so much?"

Tristan shrugged. "I dunno. I just do. Don't you think it's goofy the way she looks at him all cow-eyed?"

"No different than the way she looked at you for years."

"That's not true."

"Uh…yeah, it is."

Tristan bristled as a thought occurred to him. "Do you think he knows about us?"

Luke rolled over and faced him. "Would it bother you if he did?"

"No. Not really. I just don't think Sheilagh should go spreading around shit that isn't her business to people we don't know."

Luke studied him for a moment. "Oh, my God. You don't want him to know you're gay. You're embarrassed."

"No, I'm not!"

Luke laughed, but not with humor. "Then what? Are you afraid he'll think you're a pussy if he knows? The guy was wearing slacks for Christ's sake, Tristan. I'm pretty sure you're tougher than he is."

"I know I am."

"Then what is it—" Luke's words cut off. His eyes moved in the shadows and then he said, "You're jealous."

Tristan scoffed. "Of what?"

"Sheilagh. You're all bent out of shape, because she's finally over you."

"She was never under me."

"Yeah, she was, maybe not the way she hoped to be, but you still let her get under your skin. She's had a crush on you since you fixed her truck when she was a kid. Now she shows up with some guy in a fancy car with a fancy accent and it's making you crazy."

"That's bullshit."

Luke chuckled. "I didn't know a gay man could get jealous over women."

"I'm not fucking jealous." He wasn't. It wasn't anything sexual. It was just strange. Sheilagh had always been there. He feared she didn't need him anymore and he didn't like that.

"Whatever," Luke muttered turning back to his stomach. "All I know is that this guy better not say shit tomorrow night about *us*. I don't know him and I'll have no problem kicking his ass if he starts spreading rumors."

Tristan glanced at the ceiling. For some reason he cared that Alec might know they were gay. Would this be what it felt like if they were open about their personal life? He didn't like the paranoid worry running through him. He felt…insecure and distrustful that he was being falsely judged before he was given a chance.

Wait. Who was that prick to judge him? He was the

new guy. Tristan had been around for years. Why was he so bent out of shape over this?

He'd always been cautious, but this was the first time he ever really understood how Luke might feel. It was the first time he ever experienced the actual awkward sensation of wanting to deny who he was, like he was ashamed of it or something. That didn't make any sense.

Luke fell asleep and Tristan's mind wandered. Maybe it wasn't so much that he was ashamed of it, but that Sheilagh was yet another McCullough moving forward in a traditional sense. If she moved on, who would he have to fall back on?

Jesus. That was a fucked up thought. Why did he need a fallback person? A fallback *girl* for that matter. He wasn't into having a beard in his life, but was that what she'd become? His safety net? The one guarantee that if Luke ever stopped loving him she'd keep him breathing?

God, he was fucked in the head.

Luke wasn't going anywhere. Sure, they still had issues from time to time, but who didn't? Yes, Luke occasionally still flirted with women in public and it pissed him off, especially when he drank, but they were engaged. Things were different now. Someday they'd make vows like the rest of them. He was being ridiculous.

His mind went back to Sheilagh. What if this guy was using her? And why was he so much older? Sheilagh was older than most college students. She should have brought home some veal, not this guy.

❧

THE FOLLOWING night he went home and showered then headed to O'Malley's. He wasn't even sure why he was going after the day he had. Chad and Dalton, the new guys, had worked with him and Luke that day and since then he'd been in a bad mood.

Luke was pissed at him because he called him out on being a pussy. They'd all been loading up the chipper when Dalton said something derogatory about gays. Tristan stilled and apparently didn't do a good enough job hiding his irritation.

"What's the matter, Tristan?" Dalton had sneered. "You ain't no faggot lover, are you?"

Luke made a sound that said *not likely* "Yeah right. Tristan's a lady-killer. You should have seen the girl he went home with last week."

Tristan's gaze narrowed as he eyed Luke, but his lover played it off, going on about all the hot chicks Tristan bagged on a regular basis.

"Why don't you shut the fuck up and work, Dalton?" Finn said. Tristan looked at Luke's brother, surprised he'd stepped in. Finn, usually a mellow guy, looked pissed.

"Whatever," Dalton muttered and mumbled something under his breath.

"What was that?" Finn got right in the guy's face.

Luke stopped what he was doing and watched as his twin did what he should have done.

"You got a problem with me, McCullcugh?" Dalton said, tossing down the branch he'd been lugging.

Dalton was a big guy, but Finn didn't back down.

"Yeah I got a problem. I got a problem with you running your mouth when you should be workin'."

Dalton stiffened. "You ain't my boss."

"Wanna bet? It's my name on your check. So from now on, how about you save all your little comments, save us all a headache, and do your fucking job. Can't work with that? Work somewhere else." And with that Finn got in his truck and left.

"What's his problem?" Dalton said, but no one commented.

Tristan had steamed the rest of the day until Luke finally caught up with him in the locker room.

"Hey, you all right?" Luke asked.

Tristan looked around and tossed his gloves in his locker. "No, I'm not fucking all right. What the fuck, Luke?" he hissed.

"What did you expect me to do?"

"Well, being as you just stood there when your brother came to my defense, I'm guessin' I shouldn't expect much."

"I did stick up for you—"

"No!" Tristan hissed, getting right in his grill. "You mocked me."

"I covered your ass."

"To a guy like Dalton Thorndale? Like I give a fuck. I'd rather let that prick know exactly what I am and deal with the consequences then have him think I agree with his little *fags* should die crusade."

Luke grabbed him by the shirt. "Lower your fucking voice before someone hears you."

He smacked his hand away. "Why? Because they might know what I am? What you are?"

Luke shoved his face close. "No, because those guys are big and they got friends. I don't want to have to worry about you when I'm not there because your damn foolish pride got you on their hit list."

Tristan stepped back and glared at him. "You're bigger than all of them, Luke. You could have stood up to him, but you didn't. Once again you lied because you're too much of a pussy to stand up for what you believe in." He grabbed his keys. "I'll see you tonight."

As he drove to O'Malley's he wondered why he was even bothering to go. He noticed Luke's truck the minute he pulled up and thought about bailing. Then he noticed the BMW. "Fuck."

He'd go and check out this guy Sheilagh was with then he'd leave unless he got a bad feeling about him. Tristan strode to their usual table, meeting Luke's eyes and then Sheilagh's. Luke still wore a surly puss on his face.

Like always, Luke made no gesture of acknowledgement at his arrival. The others greeted him and he nodded. He shouldn't have come. He was in no mood for social bullshit.

The first round of shots was delivered and he picked his mark. Sliding one to Sheilagh's date, Tristan mumbled, "Drink up, old man. You're going down tonight."

Alec twitched, obviously hearing his comment, but he made no outward reply. Sheilagh slowly tipped back her shot. No one else seemed to notice Tristan's mood.

As the night carried on and the booze saturated their

brains, everyone was laughing and shouting over each other. When Sheilagh stood to use the restroom Tristan casually abandoned his beer and headed to the back.

She came out of the restroom smiling and staggered to an abrupt halt when she found Tristan waiting outside the door for her.

"Having fun?" he asked.

She frowned. "As a matter of fact, yes."

"I see you moved from the kiddie table to the grown-up section."

Her brow tightened. "What's that supposed to mean?"

"He's a little old for you, don't you think?"

"I think a lot of things, Tristan. Lately I've been thinking about what an asshole you've been."

His eyes narrowed. "What are you doing with this guy, Shei?"

"Wouldn't you like to know?"

He took a menacing step closer. "He's old enough to be your father."

She laughed, tauntingly. "Oh, trust me, he treats me nothing like a child."

Tristan's jaw locked. "Don't say shit like that. It makes you sound like…"

"What? A whore? Funny, when I walked right out of this bar—numerous times—with other men, right under your nose, you didn't seem to object."

His lips thinned. "Did you bring him here to piss me off?"

She gaped at him, fire in her jade eyes. "Believe it or not, Tristan, I brought him here because he makes me happy. Your reaction never crossed my mind. Now, why don't you go find my brother and get the fuck out of my way?"

She brushed past him and he caught her arm. "I don't like him."

She jerked her arm away and glared up at him. "I don't really give a shit what you like. For the past six years you've made it clear you didn't like *me*, so as far as what or who I'm doing, you don't get a say."

He towered over her and growled, "You're not a slut. Don't act like one."

"Get away from her."

Tristan stiffened. Turning slowly, he found Alec standing in the hall, his glare drilling into him. "You got a problem?"

Alec took a slow step forward and pulled Sheilagh to his side, never once taking his eyes off Tristan. "I ever hear you use that word around her again and *you* will be the one with a problem. I'm not interested in some pissing match with some kid struggling with his identity. My understanding is you made your choice years ago. Whatever you think you're doing, think again. She isn't a game you get to play when you want to feel macho. I see you approach her again or manipulate her, you and I are going to have to talk."

It was amazing how much it tore him apart hearing this guy come to Sheilagh's defense. What was happening to him? He would never hurt Sheilagh. This guy didn't know their past. It also hurt like hell to admit that he'd spent six years with Luke, who didn't come to his defense, yet this guy that Sheilagh had met recently came to hers. Didn't *anyone* love him?

Rather than have some sort of life crisis, he snapped, "You looking for a fight, old man?"

Nothing changed in Alec's cold expression, but he slowly shook his head. "I need not raise a hand to you in order to prove you are beaten."

Tristan scrunched up his nose. "What?"

"She's not yours," Alec stated a bit more clearly. "She's mine. Don't disrespect her again." With that he took Sheilagh's hand and left, leaving Tristan standing there like a fool. He was a fool.

God damn it.

CHAPTER 13

Tristan eventually made his way back to the table. Sheilagh and the old guy were nowhere to be found. Everyone was talking quietly which meant they were talking about someone.

Tristan slipped into his seat and picked up his beer. "What'd I miss?"

Finn slid back in his chair and whistled. "Do you think he blackmailed her?"

"Who?" Tristan asked.

"The professor," Mallory said then turned to whisper to Sam.

"What professor?" What the hell were they talking about?

"Alec!" They all said at once.

Tristan stilled. "He's her fucking professor?"

"That's what she told me," Kelly said, but he didn't seem to think it was a big deal.

Tristan looked at Luke who was frowning. "That fucking asshole. We're definitely kicking his ass now."

"Oh, give it a rest, Tristan!" Luke snapped and Tristan froze.

"No, I won't give it a rest. It's unethical. He's taking advantage of your sister. Man up, *Luke.*"

Everyone stilled and silently turned, staring at him.

The door opened. "Shh. Here they come," Colin said.

Finn—again—was the first to speak up. "You're her fucking professor?" he barked.

The couple froze and Sheilagh scowled. Alec's gaze traveled slowly over their faces. If he was looking for an ally, he wouldn't find one there. Luke shifted like a tiger tethered with a very thin leash. Even Colin had his big brother scowl on.

"Why don't you start by telling us how it is our gifted sister nearly flunked your class, and finish by explaining how you're now sharing her bed?" Luke growled.

What? That was news to Tristan.

"Hey!" Sheilagh snapped. "Get out of your glass houses and I'll give you some rocks, but unless you can claim to have never seduced the town virgin, turned your back on a commitment to God, or never hid who you are out of shame, you can all shut the fuck up."

A chair slowly dragged against the floor as Finn stood. "I didn't do any of that shit so I'll be the first to say, we don't take kindly to someone coercing our baby sister. Nor do we take kindly to some outsider coming in and starting shit with our friends."

Tristan's mouth dropped. Finn looked so much like

Luke. How he wished those were actually his lover's words, but they weren't. Once again, Luke was quiet.

He'd deal with his partner later. For now Tristan turned his anger on the professor. "I think it's time you returned to Princeton, *professor.*"

"All right, everyone just chill," Kelly said, standing from his seat and stepping between the couple and the group. "Sheilagh's an adult."

"Fuck that," Luke growled. "This entire situation reeks of unethical shit."

Finally!

The girls glanced at each other nervously and Samantha suggested, "Why don't you guys ask Sheilagh how she feels instead of jumping to conclusions?"

"Yeah!" Mallory snapped.

Tristan glared at them. Whose team were they on?

Finn cut his wife a look then turned his scowl back on his sister. "All right. Sheilagh, did this asshole threaten to flunk you if you didn't sleep with him?"

"That's it!" Alec snapped. "The entire lot of you can go to hell. Sheilagh is an adult, god damn it. She and I resisted what we—and I said *we*—felt for each other as long as we possibly could. Her grades and her personal life are none of your business. It may not seem ethical, but I assure you my intentions are nothing short of honorable. I love this woman and if you love her as well you'll all back off of her for a change, without judging her, or trying to decide for her. She can decide for her God damn self!"

Holy fuck.

Thank God Tristan was sitting down. Was it really that easy for straight people? They said it was love and everything was suddenly justified? His gaze cut to Sheilagh. Her expression was blank.

The professor turned. "Sheilagh—"

Before he could get another syllable out, she snatched a set of keys off the table and darted for the door.

"Hey! They're my keys!" Mallory shouted.

"You can't drive anyway," Finn told his wife.

Alec turned back to them. "Where the hell is she going?"

Tristan left his beer and slipped away while they argued. He went to his truck as Mallory's little car peeled out of the lot and he didn't look back.

He followed her taillights for about ten minutes until they finally reached McCullough property and Sheilagh pulled over. When he parked behind her, she came tearing out of the little car. "What the fuck do you want?"

Tristan climbed out of his truck and crossed his arms over his chest. "Are you all right?"

"No, I'm not all right! I just stole a car and I'm fucking upset. How the hell does that get confused with bloody all right?"

Gravel crunched as he took three lengthy strides and gathered her in his arms. He was such an asshole. He was dealing with his own issues and he'd pushed her buttons, because for once she wasn't feeding his ego. When had he turned into such a needy, selfish prick?

She fought him for a second then melted into his

unbreakable hold and cried. He held her tight. "I'm sorry, baby girl. I didn't mean what I said."

"I can't take anymore," she rasped.

"Shh. It's okay."

"Nothing's okay!" she argued. "Everything is wrong. Why is everything so damn hard?"

God, he wished he had an explanation for her. "I don't know." He continued stroking her back. "Do you love him?"

"I don't know," she admitted quietly. "He makes me feel things, but I've spent the last few years convincing myself I felt something else. Nothing makes sense now."

Yes, since she was eighteen she'd been aware of the truth, but he was a prick. On the days that Luke couldn't handle what they were, Sheilagh was always there, making him feel good enough. He'd done this to her, confused her when he knew it was wrong, all so he could feel better about himself.

It was time to end it. She deserved to be happy. "Shei, we have to stop. You have to stop expecting me to be something I'm not."

"But sometimes you act like…"

He sighed. "Maybe because it's easier to pretend. Sometimes I'm just a kid again, trying to be what my family expected. Pretending I'm not gay is something I've always done, but I never did it well. Eventually everyone sees through me, sees that I'm hiding something. And when they do, they're angry I wasn't honest or angry I'm not straight and then they all go away. That's how I lost my family in Texas. That's how I lost my childhood best friend. And that's why I fear losing all of you."

He thought about his fight with Luke earlier that day. Dalton was a big bastard and, while Luke could easily destroy him, Tristan couldn't. He was wrong to expect something from Luke he couldn't expect from himself. And Luke wouldn't always be there to protect him. This was all part of their reality, whether he liked it or not.

"I love your brother, but he isn't ready to come out and honestly, neither am I. Center County isn't the most liberal place. I'm afraid if I push him I'll lose him."

"But why do you screw with my head? I know I'm not imagining it. You say things and do things that any woman would take as suggestive."

He sighed. *Because I'm a bastard.* "I just want the best for you. I'm fucked up. You're gorgeous, sweet, and since I met you, you looked at me with those hopeful green eyes. Some days I wish I could be what you wanted. Some days it's so much easier looking in your eyes than his. Do you have any idea what it feels like to look into your lover's eyes, see utter adoration only to have it banked by swift regret, because part of him will always hate that he loves you? It fucking hurts."

"Doesn't he know none of us care if he's straight or gay? We love him. We love you."

He wasn't sure who was hugging who anymore. God, admitting these things hurt. "It's not a question of his family's love. That's a given. Luke has to first love himself."

They were quiet for a few minutes, both thinking on

things that were better left to contemplate sober. After a while, she asked, "Why are you being so nasty to Alec?"

He sighed and stepped back. "It's hard seeing you with him. I never saw you look at someone the way you look at him. Those looks have been solely mine for so long, I don't like you giving them to some guy I don't know. I have no idea if he's just some piece of shit taking advantage of you. My instincts tell me to protect you, because… I feel sort of responsible for the sadness I sometimes see in your eyes. You look at him and I can tell you're really into him. He has the ability to hurt you and I want to prevent that from happening."

She lowered her head. "But there have been others."

"None like him." Tristan walked to the front of his truck, brushed a leaf off the hood and leaned against the bumper. He wished he could sit down. He was suddenly very tired of it all. "He's different. You're different around him. In some selfish way I feel like he's taking you from us. You'll hate me for saying this, but knowing you were always there gave me hope that if things didn't work out—"

"Don't." Her shoulders stiffened. "I'm not your fallback girl. You're gay, Tristan. *Gay.* You have a habit of making your issues mine and I can't deal with it anymore."

He knew that, but…"But what if I'm bi?" Some days were so hard he wished he could simply turn it off and be like everybody else.

"You're in love with Luke."

Luke.

God, what would eventually happen to him and Luke?

He'd been so happy the day Luke agreed to marry him, but part of Tristan worried that day might never come. Part of him suspected Luke hoped the senate dicked around until they were dead so he'd never have to face who he really was.

Tristan was so sick and tired of the same uphill battle. "I've never been with a woman. There have been other men, but…"

"He's my brother," she said quietly.

"And I love him more than I've ever loved any man."

Tristan stepped close and brushed a tear from her cheek. Sheilagh looked up at him with those big eyes and he simply couldn't walk away without knowing. He leaned in and slowly traced his lips over hers. She sucked in a breath as he tilted his head closer.

Her lips were warm, just like Luke's, but different. Softer.

She jerked away, her fingers covering her mouth. "Why did you do that?"

Fuck! What had he just done? He looked away and mumbled the truth. "I needed to see."

"See what?" she snapped.

He was pathetic. "If it would change anything."

"When will you come to terms with who you are?"

"I've been asking myself that since I was a boy. It's hard. My parents hate what I am. There are vicious people in the world, Shei. It's scary being something others hate. You have no idea how easy your life is, being hetero."

They couldn't look at each other. Jesus, how could he

have done that? He hadn't kissed anyone but Luke in over half a decade and he just kissed his fucking sister.

"Did it change anything?"

He turned and faced her. Clearing his throat, he shifted through the guilt and tried to analyze any other feelings. "It felt dirty, like I was kissing my sister."

She laughed without humor. "Are you going to tell Luke?"

God, Luke. He should, but Luke would freak. He didn't want that. Not for him, not for Luke, and certainly not for Sheilagh. "No."

She nodded.

After a while he said, "Let's go back to the bar. Your guy looked a little stunned when you took off. He's probably worried about you. God knows what they've done to him."

"I'll follow you back."

He gently caught her arm. "Are we okay, Shei? I do love you. I'm sorry for being a jerk."

She nodded. "We're okay."

When they reached the pub, Tristan opened her door. They walked in silence and were greeted by loud voices. Sheilagh tensed and increased her strides. "This isn't good."

Tristan chuckled behind her, but his laughter died when he saw Luke's face. He was angry. Lines of apprehension bracketed his eyes and mouth. His stomach sank. Tonight was going to be a long night.

～

LUKE SLAMMED the barn door and threw his keys on the table. Tristan came in a moment later.

"Luke, will you please stop."

Luke drew in a steady breath, looking anything but steady. He fisted his hands at his hips and seethed. "What happened?"

"Nothing."

He turned and pinned Tristan with a skeptical glare. "You're fucking lying and you know it!"

Tristan flinched. "We talked."

"Why is that your job? She has a fucking boyfriend. He could have gone after her!"

"He doesn't know his way around here. She'd been drinking. I just reacted."

"Because it's Sheilagh. For six years she's been a thorn in our side and I'm fucking sick of it. Her feelings for you are childish and stupid, yet you antagonize her and provoke them."

"I just worry about her!" he shouted, again coming to Sheilagh's defense.

Luke's eyes narrowed. In a viciously low voice, he asked, "And when do you worry about me?"

Tristan scoffed. "I worry about you all the fucking time!" How could he even imply he didn't worry? "You have some nerve. How about you, Luke? Twice today Finn came to my defense while you just sat there with your thumb up your ass."

"If I get involved people will suspect things."

Tristan threw his keys. "Stop using that as an excuse! I'm not asking you to blow me in public! I'm asking you to take my side, be a fucking friend! I deserve it, God damn it!"

"And what do I deserve, Tristan? I sat there looking like a fucking bitch while you ran off after my sister like she's the most important thing in your life."

"This has nothing to do with Sheilagh."

"It has *everything* to do with Sheilagh!" Luke roared.

"Why? Because she knows about us? Who cares?"

Luke was breathing heavily. In a nearly silent voice, he said, "Because if you said the word she'd betray me."

Tristan paused, maybe a second too long. "No, she wouldn't."

Luke met his stare and Tristan felt like he could see all his secrets. Guilt had him shifting uncomfortably.

"What happened tonight?"

"Nothing."

"Don't fucking lie to me!" His shoulders jerked back as Luke's voice rattled the rafters.

"Fine! I followed her to the mountain and we talked. She was really upset. I told her she had to stop hoping I'd change. Sheilagh didn't do anything wrong."

The room was silent for a moment. "Did you?"

Tristan twisted and forked his fingers through his hair. He gave Luke a pleading look. "Don't do this, Luke. Don't make this about her. We have enough problems of our own without bringing her into it."

"Did. You. Do. Something. Wrong?"

He sighed. If he didn't come clean Luke would never let it go. In a sad voice he confessed, "You make it so hard, Luke. I just want to love you, but sometimes you make it impossible, because me loving you only adds to the things you hate about yourself. I've put up with it for six long years, and it hasn't gotten better. I know you could leave me at any minute and go find a normal life. I don't have that option. And…sometimes I wish I did. For both of our sakes."

Luke's expression was tight. "You didn't answer my question."

Tristan shut his eyes. "I just wanted to see if I could change."

"What does that mean?" His question came to his ears, hushed rage, livid enough that he didn't need to shout.

"I kissed her, but it—"

"Get out."

Tristan stilled. "Luke—"

"I said get out!"

He couldn't breathe. This wasn't happening. It would be so easy to pin the blame, but he couldn't. He'd done this. He'd crossed that line. He bent and picked up his keys. Swallowing tightly he walked to the door. Without turning around, he said, "For the record, Sheilagh was innocent in all this."

THE DOOR CLOSED and Luke roared. His hands gripped the edge of the dining room table, flipping it on end, sending the chairs crashing to the floor. He turned and slammed his fist into the wall, puncturing the sheetrock.

He couldn't breathe. How could they have done this to

him? Tristan and his own sister? He punched the wall again and when his knuckle split, he turned and slid to the floor.

Tristan was supposed to be his. Forever. His head fell back with a thump. He knocked it back again and again and again until the pain was enough to distract from the vise choking his heart.

Glancing dispassionately at his hand, he noted blood from his knuckle crusted his nails. Twisting off his ring, he lobbed it toward the kitchen, not caring where it landed as it pinged off the oven and rattled over the tile floor. It was all bullshit. They were never going to get married, not in this world or this lifetime. Everything they ever had suddenly seemed superficial.

His hand went to his chest and clawed at his shirt. Why did it have to hurt so much? Staring at the ceiling, his temples wet with runaway tears, he trembled through the pain. Never in a million years had he thought Tristan would cheat on him.

Since the day Sheilagh had discovered their secret, he had an uneasy feeling. She'd made it perfectly clear she wanted Tristan and while Tristan continuously dismissed her efforts, he'd never been stern enough to truly stop them. He could be cruel and fierce with Luke, but he coddled his sister.

He was so tired. Tired of trying to be a man. Tired of trying to please everyone. Tired of life. Something had to give, because this misery was eating him alive.

Luke sat on the floor until dawn, holding his phone, waiting for it to ring, but Tristan never called. Early that morning he heard a car door slam in the distance and thought it might be Tristan. He ran to the front door and opened it. Disappointment immediately swamped him when no one was there. Then he saw Sheilagh and Alec putting bags in the BMW.

He didn't think. He only reacted. Slamming the barn door, Luke barreled over to the Beamer and got right in his sister's face as she was about to get in the car. He shoved her, knocking her bag out of her out of her hand. *"What the fuck, Sheilagh?"*

The driver side door opened, but Luke didn't back off.

She swallowed and looked at him, too much pride in her eyes, even if it was mixed with shame. In a steady, but low voice she said, "I'm sorry. I'm a terrible person. I know."

Luke's nostrils flared. If she was a guy he'd have knocked her out by now. It took every bit of self-control he had left not to hit her.

He panted, emotion clogging his throat. Furious and disgusted, he snapped, "When is enough ever enough with you? I'm sick and tired of feeling guilty over some bullshit childhood crush you have! He's mine. Do you fucking get that? *Mine.* We've been committed as much as society allows for over five years and never has shit like this happened before. I'm your fucking brother!"

Her eyes blinked repeatedly. "I'm sorry."

He shook his head, his eyes narrowing. "Are you? Are you ever really sorry? When are you going to start thinking about someone other than yourself?"

"That's enough," Alec quietly said and Luke turned his scowl on him.

The front door of the big house opened and their father stepped out. "Luke? What's going on?"

Glancing over his shoulder at his father, he returned his glare to his sister, hissing so only she could hear. "I'm done with you." With that he marched back to the barn and slammed the door.

CHAPTER 14

$\mathcal{B}$y Wednesday, Tristan's insides were tighter than a taut fiddle string. Work was torture. Luke wouldn't look at him. If he said his name, he turned away like he didn't hear him. Tristan was dying on the inside and Luke didn't seem to care.

On Friday, he waited for him in the locker room where Luke usually went after collecting his check. When Luke turned the corner Tristan stood from the bench he'd been waiting on and Luke stilled. After a second he went to his locker as if Tristan were only a ghost of his past.

"Luke." He stepped behind him, but Luke acted like he didn't hear him. "Luke, can we please talk?"

He shoved his gloves into the locker and slammed it shut. When he made to walk away Tristan tried to clutch his arm, but Luke stepped out of his reach. He looked hard at the opposing wall, not meeting Tristan's eyes. "Your shit's boxed up. I'd appreciate it if you sent Ryan or Kelly over to get it." With that he turned and walked away.

Tristan sucked in a breath, every speck of oxygen like a hot blade cutting through his lungs. His chest seized, as he couldn't breathe. Gripping the wall, he let out a moan. A harsh sob ripped from his throat as everything inside of him turned to ash.

"Tristan?"

Screwing his face tight and cursing himself, his fingers pinched the tears from his eyes and turned. "Hey, Ry."

Ryan's face was riddled with concern. "What happened?"

He drew in a tight breath. "Nothin'." There had never been a less convincing word to pass his lips.

Ryan came to him and pulled him into a hug. "Hey. Breathe. It's okay."

His arms tightened around him as he silently sobbed into his best friend's shoulder. His face dampened with tears and the heat of his jagged breath. "He hates me."

"No, he doesn't."

But he did. Tristan hadn't told Ryan what happened because he'd thought they'd work through it like everything else. That wasn't going to happen though. Luke had packed him up like a shameful secret in his past and they were done.

"What the fuck's goin' on here?"

Ryan tensed and Tristan quickly pivoted, collecting himself and rubbing away all traces of emotion.

"Go away, Dalton," Ryan snapped.

"Aw, this is a real Kodak moment. Come see what I

found, Chad. Ryan and Tristan sharin' a firm embrace after a hard day workin' in the yard."

"Shut the fuck up, Dalton," Ryan snapped. "Come on, Tristan."

He followed Ryan out and Dalton called, "Bunch a' fuckin' faggots around here. Take it to the theater you fuckin' Mary's."

"Ignore them," Ryan said as they left the hanger.

Tristan had barely heard what Dalton had said, but he was sure it was something offensive.

The following week Ryan had gone to collect his belongings from Luke. Six years accumulated a lot of shit. Ryan carried the last box into Tristan's room and hung by the door. Tristan was useless. He'd stayed in his room staring blindly at the television for six days straight.

"You okay?" Ryan asked.

"Sure," Tristan said unconvincingly.

"Why don't we go out, grab a beer?"

"How did he seem?" He wasn't going anywhere.

Ryan sighed. "Not good. He wouldn't talk about it. Maybe you guys just need some time."

Yeah. Time.

The following week Ryan dragged him out of the house. They walked into O'Malley's and Tristan froze the second he saw Luke sitting across from some willowy creature, smiling and handing her a drink.

Tristan pivoted and left. Ryan came out after him. "Tristan, wait! We can go somewhere else."

Fuck. It hurt! It fucking hurt so bad. He slammed his

palms into his truck and breathed through the pain. He couldn't do this. "I gotta get out of here."

"Where are you going?"

"I don't know," Tristan answered, holding it together by a thread. "Away."

He drove and wound up somewhere in Wells County sitting at some hole in the wall dive. That night he checked into a motel and proceeded to drink the next ten days away, only seeing daylight when he ran out of beer and ventured to find more.

He would never survive living in Center County if Luke moved on. On day eleven he'd contemplated killing himself. Without Luke, who would miss him?

He sat in the dingy motel room and dialed his phone. He was grasping, but someone had to help him.

"Hello?"

"Mom?"

The line was quiet. "Tristan?"

God, he hadn't heard her voice in so long he'd forgotten what it sounded like. "Yeah."

"Why are you calling? Is something wrong?"

Everything. One would think after not hearing her child's voice for ten years she'd sound a little more relieved. Instead she sounded suspicious. "I just wanted to say hi."

"Val, who's on the phone?"

His blood ran could as he heard his father's deep voice.

"It's Tristan."

"Why's he calling?"

The phone muffled like her fingers were covering the

receiver, but he still heard them. "I don't know. I'll be off in a second."

A second, that's all the time they had for him? He dropped the phone at his side and went to the bathroom. He had no one.

When he returned to Center County he went with the mindset that he wouldn't be staying long. His first day back to work landed him in Frank's office.

"Where you been, son?"

"I had some things I needed to take care of."

Frank's gaze studied him. "You back to work?"

Tristan nodded. "I'm not sure how long I'll be hanging around, but I'd like to keep my job until I figure out what's next."

"You know you always have a job here, Tristan. You're family." No he wasn't, but it was kind of him to say.

He didn't see Luke that day or the next. He was stuck on a shift with Dalton, Chad, and Finn over at the 75th Acre. Finn pulled him aside at lunch. "Tristan, you all right?"

There was no point lying. Finn knew who he was. "I've been better."

His gaze scrutinized him. Finn was not someone who spoke without first considering his words. "A lot of that's been going around."

He was silent for a while. He took a few bites of his sandwich and quietly asked without looking beyond his meal, "How is he?"

Finn sighed. "Not good, but he's trying to convince us all otherwise."

"He'll get better. Just give him time."

Dalton came over to the truck and tossed down his battered lunch box. "You two pussies havin' a heart to heart or are us other guys allowed to join?"

Finn rolled his eyes, bunched up his trash and turned away. "Breaks over in twenty."

LUKE TOSSED on some deodorant and slid on a shirt. Grabbing his gym bag, he headed to his truck. His stomach was unsettled since last night, but this was all part of the healing process he supposed. Thank God he had the gym. It was the only thing that kept him going.

He pulled up at Lisa's house twenty minutes later and waited in the truck for something inside of him to tell him he was ready. After about five minutes he forced himself out and rang the bell.

The door opened and Lisa smiled. "Hey, handsome. Perfect timing. Dinner's on the table."

Luke's mouth curved into something he hoped resembled a grin as he followed her to the kitchen. She'd made mashed potatoes—the buttery kind Tristan liked—and steak. Over dinner they chatted and she asked him about working as a logger.

Once the meal was finished, they settled onto the couch to watch a movie. Luke had already seen the film when it came out last fall. Both he and Tristan thought the plot was predictable and the actors were below par.

Halfway through the movie, Lisa shifted and rested her

head on his shoulder. Her hair smelled too flowery and her earring poked through his shirt. She sighed and snuggled closer.

As though he was a puppeteer pulling a string, he consciously commanded his arm to raise and pull her close. She turned and smiled at him, pressing a kiss on his neck.

A while later her hand found its way to his thigh and rubbed through his jeans. Her nails were painted and it looked strange seeing such dainty fingers against the denim covering his knee.

When the movie was over neither of them seemed to want to move. The credits rolled and the room dimmed. Lisa slowly sat up and climbed to his lap. Her narrow arms wreathed his neck as she straddled his thighs. Her mouth found his and her lip-gloss irritated his lips.

After a while, she took his hand and guided it under her shirt. It had been years since he'd felt a woman's breasts. He'd practically forgotten what to do with them. She sat up and removed her shirt. When her fingers unclasped her bra and dropped it to the floor, he did as she expected and leaned forward, capturing the tiny nipple in his mouth. He sucked, but it all seemed pointless. Her hips rocked and he got no pleasure from the whole act.

A few minutes later she whispered in his ear, "Come on. Let's go to my room."

He followed her like a zombie and watched blindly as she stripped down to nothing. He stood compliantly as she removed his shirt and unbuttoned his jeans. He stepped out of his clothes and she placed a condom in his hand.

He stared at the tiny square of foil and blinked, struggling to recall the last time he'd worn one. With Tristan. In the beginning.

She led him to the bed and did stuff to him. He shut his eyes in order to fight back the repulsion of foreign hands climbing over his skin. He was barely hard and knew if he slipped the condom on at this point he'd lose his erection completely. "Can you get me a glass of water?" he asked.

She stilled. "Sure."

When she slid into her robe and left he curled onto his side. His eyes pinched shut as he gripped the pillow, breathing through the tears that threatened to come. He couldn't do it. He couldn't replace the most meaningful person in his life with a collection of meaningless encounters. But more importantly, he couldn't pretend he wasn't changed. This was no longer him and the reality of who he was seemed inescapable.

When she returned he was pulling on his pants.

"What's wrong?"

He approached her as he slid on his shirt. "I just got out of a relationship and this is going a little too fast for me."

Her soft features turned hard. "Don't you lie to me, Luke McCullough. You've been single for years." She put the glass of water on the bureau with a click and tightened her robe. He gathered his boots and left.

When he got home that night he went straight to bed. His face pressed into the pillows and he moaned through the pain flaying him wide. He'd thought if he could sleep with a woman he'd remember how great it used to be, but he couldn't even manage that.

Everything reminded him of Tristan. It didn't matter that his personal effects were gone. His stamp was on everything he owned, down to the color of his walls, the angle of his kitchen tile, and the shadow of his soul. No matter where he turned there was no escaping the phantom of his past. The reality was there. Tristan owned his heart.

Over the oncoming weeks Luke began to truly question his state of mind. He'd avoided Tristan as much as possible at work. The sight of him never failed to cause physical agony. Luke had gotten quiet. He'd lost interest in everything. All he wanted to do was sleep and never wake up.

Weeks passed and nothing improved. Things only got worse. One afternoon he was sitting in the den with his mom and dad watching the draft pick. He couldn't even muster a care about that.

He hadn't thought about his words. They simply slipped out as he sat on the couch watching the analysts discuss players he didn't know. "I'm gay."

A sort of release came with the quiet confession and it was the first time in months he felt some of the pressure building inside of him ease. He looked at his mom who was knitting booties for the newest McCullough. Did they hear him? She smiled softly as her fingers continued to shape the tiny socks. Letting out a maternal hum of contentment, she said, "I know, love."

Luke stilled. She knew? How? Since when? His heart raced. He looked to his dad. The man placed the remote on the table and sighed. Standing, he left the room.

Crap. Guilt and shame bloomed inside of him like ugly spills of oil bleeding over his last tiny shred of calm. But what was worse was the fear of his father's rejection, the absolute terror that he'd never look at him the same. His dad needed to at least acknowledge his statement. It was cruel to ignore it. His father was a good guy. Why wasn't he—

His dad came back in the room and handed Luke an envelope. Luke took it and glanced up at his father, his eyes questioning. Fear and raw vulnerability tore at his insides so hard his fingers shook. What was in the envelope? If it meant losing his father he'd take it all back. His parents were all he had left.

"Open it," Frank said.

Luke's chest tightened as he struggled with the lip of the seal. He pulled out a sheaf of papers. They looked like legal documents. "What is this?"

"That's the deed for your land. I gave each of the kids their own acreage to build on when they got married. Your portions from the barn and six acres back to the east of the big house. There's a space on the bottom for you to add a name."

His chin quivered. It actually quivered.

His dad cleared his throat and held out his arms. "Let's hug it out."

Luke didn't think he could stand. He wished Tristan was there with him. He'd hand him a pen and have him sign on the dotted line. But he wasn't. Because Luke had thrown him out of his life like yesterday's trash.

They weren't turning their backs on him. They were welcoming him with open arms. Jesus. It should have felt better than this, but all he could focus on was the regret, the years he hadn't had the faith he needed in his family's love to accept him as he was.

Slowly he stood and his dad wrapped him in his burly arms. His father kissed his neck and squeezed him hard. "I love you, son."

"Oh, for the love of Mike," his mum said, tossing the knitting aside. "You aren't supposed to hug without me."

She bustled over and hugged him from behind. Luke laughed as her warm form cocooned him. He'd never forget this moment and again he suffered regret that Tristan wasn't here to share it.

After the hugs and tears concluded his father handed him a beer like nothing out of the ordinary had happened. He felt awkward, acutely aware of himself, and sort of lighter.

The draft picks went on, but they slowly started talking. He wanted to be honest—for once—so he didn't shy away when they asked the hard questions. But their questions never bordered on personal things he didn't want to share. They were merely queries about how Luke wanted to proceed.

"Do your brothers and sisters know, love?" his mother asked.

"Kelly knows and Sheilagh knows. And Tristan."

His mother's smile turned sad. "I miss seeing Tristan around. You should tell him to come by again soon."

He swallowed. If it were only that easy.

"And what about the others?" his father asked. "Will you be announcing yourself to everyone now?" He didn't ask in a way that told Luke he preferred one answer over the other.

"No. It's private, sort of an ask but don't tell thing."

"That's probably wise. There's some crazy bastards around here and you don't want any more trouble than you need."

"Exactly."

His mum smiled. "Well, your secret's safe with me, love. I've known for years. Been waitin' around for you to come fix my drapes and help me redecorate, but I guess you're not that kind of gay, now are you?"

He snorted. "No, Mum, I'm not that kind. I'm just same old Luke."

She grinned and tousled his hair. "That's all right. Got plenty of others to help me decorate and sometimes I think the old stuff's fine just the way it is."

"Tristan told me he may be moving."

Luke turned to his father. *"What?"*

"I'm figuring he's your partner—or was. I thought maybe you'd want to know."

"Where's he going?"

"He didn't say. Just said that he was thinking it might be time for him to move out of Rosemarie's and find a new place to call home."

His mum tsked. "Oh, but that can't happen. Luke,

honey, you need to set him straight." She paused and her cheeks flushed. "I mean…not straight…Oh, you know what I bloody meant! Make him see."

Something dry and hard had lodged in his chest. In a gravelly voice he said, "I can't."

His mother made a sound of exasperation. "Of course you can. That's what marriage is. Your father pisses me off all the time. But I forgive him, because I love him. Say sorry for whatever you did and it will work itself out."

If only it was that simple.

"Do gay men like getting flowers?" she asked.

"No man wants flowers, Maureen," his father said.

"Well, then maybe some nice Godiva chocolates. They always make me a little more rational."

"Woman, you haven't been rational a day in your life."

Luke stood. "I have to go." He needed to find someone who knew more about what was going on with Tristan. Maybe Ryan knew.

He looked back at his parents who were having an argument that looked a lot like foreplay. Gross. "Listen, thanks for…just…thanks."

They each stopped bickering and smiled at him. "That's what family does, Luke. We love. No matter what."

Luke left and texted Ryan. *Where are you?*

The phone buzzed back a second later. *Why?*

He sighed, knowing he wasn't his cousin's favorite person at the moment. *I need to talk to you.*

Ryan replied a minute later. *I'm not the one you need to talk to. I have nothing to say to you.*

Luke glared at his phone and wavered. "Damn it." He punched out another text. *Where is he?*

His cousin's reply was quick. *Are you gonna be a dick?*

No! I need to talk to him. Please, just tell me where he is. Luke hit send and waited.

It took over five minutes for the reply to come through. *He said he'd meet you at O'Malley's.*

He didn't waste time punching out a reply. He grabbed his keys and barely slowed at every stop sign along the way. When he got to the pub, he rushed through the door and scanned the room.

Where was he?

He went to the bar. "Kelly, you seen Tristan?"

His brother turned and arched a brow. "He was just here. A bunch of guys were hassling him. I threw them out. He might of left."

Luke's brow lowered. "What guys? Who?"

"I don't know them. Saw the one around a few times— big burly red head—but I don't know his name."

"Dalton."

"Is that his name? He's an asshole. How do you know him?"

Luke didn't answer. He scanned the bar again. Fuck. "Kelly, where did Tristan go?"

"I told you, he might have left. Check the john."

Luke took off to the bathroom. When he found it empty something horrible coiled in his stomach. He returned to his brother. "How long after you kicked those guys out do you think Tristan left?"

Kelly seemed to finally register his panic. "I'm not sure. Why?"

Luke breathed hard. "They work with us. Dalton hates Tristan." Jesus. He needed to find him. He met his brother's eyes. Fear of something so much worse than his family's disapproval had him panicking. "He hates gay people."

"Fuck. Do you want me to call Sue in so I can help you find him?"

There wasn't time. "No," Luke said pulling his phone out. "I'll call you if I need anything. Hopefully he just went home."

He'd dialed Tristan's number before he reached the truck. It rang four times and went to voicemail. "Fuck!"

He dialed again as he drove, his eyes peeled for signs of Tristan's truck. He went past his aunt's but Tristan's truck wasn't there so he kept driving. Where the hell would he have gone? Thinking back to all the places they'd met up in secret he drove to the industrial park. It was empty.

He'd thought about Murphy's, the Irish pub on the outskirts of town none of them went to because it wasn't O'Malley's. Would he have gone there? It was his last hope.

He cut the wheel and headed that way. It seemed to take forever to get there and Tristan still wasn't answering his phone. "Answer the God damn phone!" He drove slowly past Murphy's. It was small and dingy and there were only a few cars in the lot, which made it easy to spot Tristan's truck.

His relief was short lived as he pulled in the lot and saw Dalton's SUV parked there as well. Luke's jaw locked as he tore into a parking space. When his headlights flashed over the shadows a voice inside of him screamed.

Two guys held Tristan by the arms and three others took turns swinging at him. His blood turned to ice as he rushed out of the truck like an animal possessed. Tristan's head hung low between his shoulders and he didn't move when Luke charged in his direction roaring like a rabid beast just as Dalton was about to swing.

"Don't fucking touch him!"

Dalton turned and a slow reptilian grin climbed over his ugly face. Luke was in too much of a rage to hear whatever he said. He ran to Tristan who still wasn't moving, his knees buckled and body limp.

"Tristan!"

Arms grabbed hold of him and he snapped. His fists swung and collided with flesh and bone as they dragged him back. He was strong, but there were too many of them. Someone's foot caught him hard in the jaw and he tasted blood. "Tristan!"

Hands grabbed at his limbs and dragged him to the ground as he fought and struggled to reach Tristan. *Open your eyes!* "Tristan!" He screamed his name again as his body buckled under the force of his attackers.

Luke's scream was only a wheeze as the wind was kicked out of him again and again. Then someone stepped on his bad knee and he felt a horrible snap and vomited.

Pavement scraped his cheek raw. "That ought to hold him," someone said as Luke spit and blinked through tears and blood.

They walked back over to Tristan and picked him up. "Don't," Luke begged, but no one heard him.

One guy yanked Tristan's head back by his hair. His face was caked with blood. Dalton slapped his cheek. "Wake up, faggot. Your girlfriend's here."

Luke breathed hard as Tristan's eyes slowly opened. When he focused on Luke's broken body being held in place by two of the guys, he tensed and struggled. *"Luke!"*

Dalton punched Tristan in the gut and he buckled. "See what we did to your lover boy over there. You should have heard him crying for you like a little bitch."

Tristan went ballistic, but it only provoked their brutality. Luke struggled as well, but he had bones broken in places he couldn't feel and two of his teeth were now knocked loose.

"Get me a knife," Dalton said and Luke shut his eyes and began to cry. Forcing himself to be strong, he met the panic in Tristan's broken gaze. He'd do anything if they just left him alone. "Tristan! Tristan, look at me. Don't look at them."

Tristan's eyes bore into him. He saw the fear. "I love you, Luke."

No. No goodbyes. They were gonna get married. Be a family. "I love you too, baby."

He sucked in a sharp breath as Dalton shoved the knife in Tristan's side.

Luke fought against the arms holding him down. *"Tristan! Tristan, keep your eyes on me!"*

The amount of effort it took for him to do as he said

was evident. Luke watched as his eyes clouded with tears. "I'm sorry," Tristan mouthed.

"No! *No!* You listen to me! No apologies any more. I told them. I told my parents. I love you…"

The knife glistened crimson under the glare of the streetlights and Luke winced, his stomach roiling again, as the sound of the blade sinking into Tristan's flesh met his ears. Dalton drew back when Tristan grunted and punctured his side again. When Tristan didn't lift his head again, Luke cried and continued to whisper, "I love you. I love you. I love you…"

Pain exploded in the back of his head and the world went black. It was an ugly place anyway.

Sunday.

Monday.

Tuesday.

Wednesday.

Thursday.

295

Friday…

"…Blessed is the fruit of thy womb, Jesus. Holy Mary, Mother of God, pray for us sinners…"

Who was praying?

Luke tried to open his eyes, but could only manage to grunt.

The prayers stopped.

He heard movement and then felt cool fingers touch his arm. "Luke. Luke, darling, are you awake?"

His throat was dry and sore. He swallowed, the action painful. His voice was scratchy and barely existent. "Tristan."

Whoever was with him started to cry. "Oh, thank the Lord. Luke, love, can you hear me? Someone get a nurse!"

"Mum?"

Her cries became too thick for him to make out her words. Other voices arrived and something happened. *Tristan. Tristan. Tristan.*

Everything went dark.

Saturday.

Luke's parched tongue licked over his dry lips and he breathed. Hushed voices whispered in the distance. He cleared his throat and rasped, "Water."

The whispers stopped then voices got louder. A straw was placed between his lips and he sucked. There had never been anything more quenching.

"Luke? Can you open your eyes?"

That was his father's voice.

Luke struggled to open his eyes. Bright. It hurt. His lashes fluttered as a blurry image of his father came into view. Someone was with him. He blinked. Finn.

"Hey," Finn said with a smile.

"Where am I?"

"Hospital," his dad said. "I'm so glad you're awake. The nurses said you'd probably wake up sometime tonight since you woke up yesterday." Luke frowned. He had no recollection of waking. "I'm going to phone your mother."

His dad left, but not before Luke saw the tears slip past his eyes. Seeing his father cry was terrifying. He looked at Finn. He didn't look much better.

"You're gonna be all right," his brother said, but Luke wasn't sure who he was assuring.

"Where's…Tristan?"

His brother's expression shuttered and he hesitated.

"Finn…please. Where is he?"

"You… can't see him right now. You have to get better first."

Fuck that. "I need…*Tristan.*"

"Luke, you've been in a coma for a week. Give it a minute."

Every word hurt, but he needed to make him see. He swallowed and forced each word out syllable by syllable. "If it…were Mallory…would you…wait?"

His twin's lips thinned and he looked away, putting his fist to his lips. He pulled himself together and turned. "No. No, I wouldn't wait. They'd have to kill me to keep me away."

"I love him," Luke whispered.

"I know you do. But right now… Oh, God, Luke…it's bad."

His lungs worked in quick pants. Something was taped around his ribs. He couldn't move his limbs. Panic and a feeling of utter impotence grabbed hold of him. He was dead. Tristan was fucking dead.

A low pitched whimper filled the room and he realized it was coming from him. He shut his eyes and twisted his head away so he could cry privately. "They killed him?"

"What? No!"

He sucked in a breath and faced Finn. "Then what? Why can't I see him?"

Finn's eyes were shot with red. He blinked rapidly. "They did a number on him, Luke. He just woke up Tuesday, but he's been in and out of surgery. He's on a lot of meds. They…mutilated him."

He was gonna vomit. His throat worked to hold it back. Breathing through his teeth, his whole body tense, he asked, "How bad?"

"He lost two fingers and was stabbed six times. His nose was broken and his arm."

He couldn't process. So long as Tristan was alive—*oh, Tristan*—Luke's pain didn't even register. The agony of his battered body coming back to life was second to Tristan's condition. Tristan came first. He'd always come first. Luke would have it no other way.

"We called his parents, but..."

"No...don't call them. We're his family."

Finn nodded. "Yeah. Bray and Colin are with him now. He's been asking for you."

"I need to see him."

Finn sighed. "Let me see what I can do."

Finn was gone for a long time. His father came back and soon his mother arrived. Finn finally returned with Bray at his side. They came to his bed.

"Hey, big guy," Braydon said, looking on the verge of tears. "Glad you're back."

Luke tried to smile, but it hurt. "Hi. Didn't know I was gone."

"Gave us all a scare. Here, someone wants to talk to you..." Bray held up his phone but not to his ear. He realized there was a live picture on the screen. It took him a minute to realize he was looking at Tristan.

He sucked in a breath. His hair was buzzed and there was a long line of stitches from his brow to his battered eye. *Jesus.* "Hey, cowboy."

Tristan turned his face away as his shoulders shook. When he looked back, he choked, "Hi." His lips were cracked, but he bit them anyway. "You look like hell."

"So do you."

"I wish I could touch you right now, know that you're there."

"I'm here," Luke said. "Not going anywhere."

Tristan nodded. "They won't let me out of bed yet."

"Fuckers."

Tristan laughed and his chuckle turned into a sob. "I'm so sorry, baby."

Luke gave up fighting back his tears. "You're alive. That's all that matters."

"I love you."

"I love you too."

His family quietly stepped out of the room to give them privacy. They talked until the battery on the phone died. Then they demanded someone bring them some new phones or a cord to plug it in.

The conversation continued through the night and his family appeared every so often to see if he needed anything. He didn't. The only thing he needed was right there. Tristan.

Apparently, someone had called the cops that night. Dalton and the rest of those monsters were in jail. Dalton was facing charges for attempted murder and terroristic threats involving hate crimes. The local news had covered the story, though they got no statement from the McCulloughs.

The day they finally let Tristan out of bed he had a nurse wheel him right to Luke's bedside, where he stayed. They eventually moved his belongings and allowed him to occupy the other bed in the room.

Luke had four broken ribs, a busted knee, a crushed collarbone, a ruptured eardrum, three broken fingers, three loose teeth, and some other shit the doctors were working on. The thing of it was, none of it bothered him so long as they were both alive and there.

Bruises would heal and bones would mend. Surviving such a brutal attack did something to a person. Luke realized he was fighting the wrong fight all along. So long as he let other's opinions shame him, the bad guys won.

The world was not what it once was. Maybe it was better. Maybe it was uglier. The fact was, no man had a right to take another's freedom to find happiness. Tristan made him happy. Their love was the greatest thing he'd ever known and he wouldn't sacrifice it for anyone.

Dalton deserved to die for what he did. There was too much hate. They only wanted the same rights as everyone else in this world. Luke wanted the freedom to love his spouse, not in fear, but in faith, that someday the good would outnumber the bad and they could all live peacefully.

They didn't let him leave the hospital until June. It was hot and he was staring down a long road of physical therapy and follow-up procedures before he'd be able to walk again. But he would walk and when he did, the first steps he planned to take were down an aisle into Tristan's arms.

Sheilagh had come to the hospital and Luke made his apologies. She apologized too. He no longer held her youth against her. She had her own battles to fight in this life and forgiveness was a liberating thing they both needed.

It took longest for him to forgive himself. He still struggled from time to time with facing his shortcomings, but his affection for Tristan was no longer one of them.

The day they returned home Tristan wheeled him into the barn. It looked different. The hole in the wall had been patched and painted. There were pictures from his phone, printed and hung in frames, pictures of him and Tristan.

The furniture had been arranged to make room for his stupid wheelchair and the fridge was stocked with tons of food—including a freezer full of his mum's chicken casserole—and there was plenty of beer.

Tristan helped him into bed and lay next to him. Luke's fingers found his, his thumb rubbing over the bandaged part where his pinky had been and slowly dragging to the next finger that wore his ring.

They each sighed and Luke shut his eyes as Tristan began to whistle through his teeth. He missed hearing that whistle.

Luke's lips pursed as he slowly whistled along to the tune of *Your Song* by Elton John. When they reached the chorus, they each whispered the line, echoing the sentiment that life was wonderful so long as the other was in their world.

CHAPTER 15

The September wind cut across the lake like a gentle bluff, teasing the tails of Tristan's linen shirt. He didn't expect to be this nervous, but he was. His palms were sweating. Trying not to fidget, he ran his hand over his hair, again reminded that it was still quite short compared to what he was used to.

From his hidden location behind the dunes, he heard the low voices of his family. Yeah, they were his family. All of them.

Sheilagh had changed and the McCulloughs were slowly coming to see she was her own person, no longer the baby or an extension of what she once was, she'd become her own masterpiece.

It was good. She was happy. Not in a put on rambunctious way meant to entertain, but in a soul shifting way everyone experienced only a few times in life if they were lucky. Tristan knew what that was like.

It was the moment one finally gave up all pretenses of pretending to be someone else, gave up trying to please others despite one's innate nature. It's the moment one realizes they're cheating everyone by forsaking the truth. He'd learned this in the weeks that followed their return home from the hospital.

He and Luke had slowly settled into their home. Theirs. The curtains no longer had to remain drawn and the door could, for once, rest unlocked. Those weeks had brought about a world of emotion. The realization they were both lucky to be alive made life a bit more extraordinary.

They had this one life, this one moment in time, to live and they wanted to live happily. Embracing that mindset made all the struggles of their past seem suddenly small and inconsequential. They were tired of wearing masks, and once they took them off for good, their relationship bloomed like a wild garden.

They'd been set free. Of course they'd stumble into an impasse here and there. The world was still a dangerous and flawed place for people like them. The difference was, they now had the love and support of their family. They'd cut out their own little corner of the world and finally made a home.

As their bodies healed so did all the old wounds on their hearts. Trying to compensate for society's shortcomings had taken a toll on both of them. But they'd found their sanctuaries.

O'Malley's was so dominated by McCulloughs that it offered a safe haven. Now, they could smile openly at each other, sit close, and even dance from time to time without worrying about outsiders hassling them. Kelly kept a close eye on the patrons at the bar and anyone who started trouble was no longer welcome there, plain and simple.

It was amazing how much their lives had changed. Tristan was now Uncle Tristan. No, Pennsylvania did not pass the vote, but that was no longer a prerequisite for others to recognize their loving and committed relationship for what it was. If it eventually happened, yes, he and Luke would be one of the first in line. But they'd given up waiting for the world to catch up. The approval of the legislatures offered nothing in forms of validating a couple's love. It was a piece of paper they'd probably always covet, but they no longer *needed it* to move on.

"Tristan? You ready?"

Tristan turned at the sound of Kelly's voice. His throat was suddenly tight. "Yeah. Let's do this." He took a step and paused. "How do I look?"

Kelly grinned and tipped his head to the side. "I'd do ya.'"

He laughed. "I'm sure the wife would have something to say about that."

"You look great. Come on. He's waiting."

Tristan followed Kelly to the edge of the dunes. He wasn't sure what exactly lay ahead. Neither he nor Luke was the frou-frou type, so they'd let the women handle all the details.

Kelly's hand closed over his shoulder, halting his steps. "You wait here. When the music starts, head to the water. He'll meet you in the middle."

Drawing in a deep breath Tristan nodded and Kelly disappeared. He shifted and stilled when he caught the first plunking notes of a piano. He'd expected the sound of canned radio music, but this was live. How the hell had they gotten a piano to the beach?

He slowly took his first step out of the dunes and the song being played by Kate, Luke's eldest sister, took form. Holy shit, it was an actual grand piano, pearl white and open, the soft keystrokes echoing over the still lake and into the distance.

Tristan's jaw dropped as Colin stepped forward and began to sing. His voice was deep and melodic. Beautiful. *"When I find myself in times of trouble, Mother Mary comes to me..."*

Tristan's breath caught. Not only did Colin have a dulcet voice, he was singing *Let It Be,* by the Beatles. Shit. It gave him chills.

When the chorus kicked in he was done for. Every McCullough stood and sang, *"Let it be, let it be. Let it be, let it be..."*

Through a blurry sheen of tears he caught movement in the distance. His heart pinched. There he was. Luke. His love.

Swallowing hard on the lump of emotion clogging his throat all the way to his chest, he smiled. Luke met his grin with the most brilliant smile ever to be bestowed on him.

His burly shoulders were clad in a smart black tuxedo jacket that nipped at his waist. His legs were bare, except for his dress socks and the McCullough tartan that made up his kilt. If it was possible, his smile stretched wider. *Oh, tonight was going to be lots of fun!*

He wanted to rush to him, but took his time. With slow, staggering steps, Luke's hand pressed into his cane as he made his way over the sand to where they would meet in the middle. Partners. Equal.

The table in front of the chairs where their family had congregated was dressed simply in white with a candle surrounded by soft green flowers. This was it.

The song came to a close as Luke took his last step. They each let out a sigh of relief at the same time. The family sat and Colin moved to stand, back to the lake, at the other side of the table.

Colin opened up a bible and Tristan saw he had notes written on a slip of paper. "Marriage is a union, a blending of two souls that are no longer complete without their other half. It is as children that we come into the world, thinking we are the universe. But as we grow, we come to see all of our human traits and know, we are but one piece of a whole. Love is the recognition of that other piece of our soul, and marriage is the binding of two people into one.

"When I asked Tristan about the moment he recognized Luke as the other half of his soul, he told me it was the first time he held Luke in his arms and realized he never wanted to let go. He explained it as an epiphany, that there had always been this hollow part of him only Luke's love could fill. He said it was Luke's heart and he wanted to take it into his keeping and protect him forever.

"I asked Luke the same question and he told me it was

more complicated, noticing something present that hadn't always been. He said he knew Tristan was his soul mate through absence. On the days Tristan wasn't there, the sky seemed a little duller and the sun wasn't quite so bright. Music didn't sound the same without Tristan there to sing beside him. Days lasted too long and time became a company he didn't enjoy if he wasn't with his other half.

"Today we are here to celebrate the binding of these two souls as Tristan and Luke vow before family and friends to love each other completely and irrevocably, for the rest of their lives. They shall forsake nothing as they confirm their true love."

Placing his cane against the altar, Luke took Tristan's hands in his and squeezed. Colin closed the book and turned his gaze to them. "Luke, do you take Tristan to be your husband, from this day forward, in equal love as a reflection of true self, a partner on your path, to honor and to cherish, in sorrow and in joy, until death shall part you?"

Luke met Tristan's gaze. "I do."

"Tristan, do you take Luke to be your husband, from this day forward, in equal love as a reflection of true self, a partner on your path, to honor and to cherish, in sorrow and in joy, until death shall part you?"

Tristan smiled at Luke and tightened his hands around his. "No. I promise to love him from this day forward, in equal love as a reflection of my true self, a partner on my path to honor and to cherish, in sorrow and in joy *far past* my last breath. He will be my husband for all eternity and

I will love him beyond any man made law, any earthily plane, because he *is* the other half of my soul."

Luke's wide grin was more brilliant than any sunset. He quietly said, "Me too. Put that down for me too, Colin."

The family laughed and Colin did the same. "Tristan and Luke, you have proclaimed your commitment to each other, before your family and friends, as a symbol of your undying love and devotion." He folded a strip of tartan over their hands. "In love and in loyalty, now and in all time to come, may you be joined, forever, as one, in a bond so true, no man shall ever have the power to divide you. You may kiss the groom."

Luke gripped the back of his head and pulled him close. "Come here, cowboy."

His firm lips pressed into his, softening and opening as his tongue stole across his mouth. The family stood and cheered and the two of them smiled against each other's lips, laughing, tears of joy in their eyes.

And that was how he became Tristan McCullough, a Texan orphan who loved so boldly and so true, he never would forsake his true self or face the world alone again.

The End

If you enjoyed BROKEN MAN, you will love CONTROLLED CHAOS, the next story in the McCullough Mountain Series. Skip ahead for a sneak peek inside

Paranormal Vampire Romance
Original Sin | Dark Exodus | Prodigal Son

LGBTQ+ & Menage Romance
Broken Man (MM) | Breaking Perfect (MMF) | Forfeit (MMF) | Hurt (Non-Consensual) | Protege

Sexy Nerds & Second Chances
Blind | Untied

Teacher Student, Workplace, and Age-Gap Love Affairs… Oh my!
British Professor | Pining For You | Breaking Perfect | Falling In | Sacrifice of the Pawn

Single Dads & Single Moms
Simple Man | Pining For You | First Comes Love | Controlled Chaos | Intentional Risk

Dark Psychological Thriller & Tortured Hero Romance **(TRIGGER WARNING)**
Hurt

Non-Fiction Books for Writers
Write 10K in a Day: Avoid Burnout

About the Author

Lydia Michaels is the award winning and bestselling author of more than forty titles. She is the consecutive winner of the 2018 & 2019 *Author of the Year Award* from *Happenings Media,* as well as the recipient of the 2014 *Best Author Award* from the *Courier Times.* She has been featured in *USA Today, Romantic Times Magazine, Love & Lace,* and more. As the host and founder of the *East Coast Author Convention,* the *Behind the Keys Author Retreat,* and *Read Between the Wines,* she continues to celebrate her growing love for readers and romance novels around the world.

In 2021, Michaels released the groundbreaking, non-fiction series, **Write 10K in a Day**, to commemorate her career in the publishing industry. She looks forward to many more years of exploring both fiction and non-fiction writing, teaching about the craft, and learning from the others in the author community.

Lydia is happily married to her childhood sweetheart. Some of her favorite things include the scent of paperback books, listening to her husband play piano, escaping to her coastal home at the Jersey Shore, cheap wine, *Game of Thrones,* coffee, and kilts. She hopes to meet you soon at one of her many upcoming events.

You can follow Lydia at www.Facebook.com/LydiaMichaels or on Instagram @lydia_michaels_books

Other Titles by Lydia Michaels
Wake My Heart

The Best Man
Love Me Nots
Pining For You
My Funny Valentine
Falling In: Surrender Trilogy 1
Breaking Out: Surrender Trilogy 2
Coming Home: Surrender Trilogy 3
Sacrifice of the Pawn: Billionaire Romance
Queen of the Knight: Billionaire Romance
Original Sin
Dark Exodus
Calamity Rayne: Gets a Life
Calamity Rayne: Back Again
La Vie en Rose
Breaking Perfect
FREE! - Blind
Untied
Almost Priest
Beautiful Distraction
Irish Rogue
British Professor
Broken Man
Controlled Chaos
Hard Fix
Intentional Risk
Hurt
Sugar
Simple Man
Protégé
Forfeit

SAMPLE CONTROLLED CHAOS

*"Y*ou just march right on over there and say… *Hi. My name's Becca. I'm celebrating the end of a very long and boring marriage to a man who only fucked me on anniversaries and birthdays, always with his socks on—in the missionary position—until he decided to seduce our neighbor, the succubus slut from hell, better known as Beelzebub's Whore. I think you might possibly be the most beautiful man I've ever laid eyes on and I want to offer you one night of wild, swinging from the chandeliers, no strings attached, smurf sex."*

Becca Stevens' lips parted as her insane best friend, Nikki, said all that without taking a single breath. Shaking her head she swallowed and asked, "Is that all?"

Nikki's lips drew at her tiny swizzle straw. "Mmmm! You should also require he make you come—*at least* three times."

"I can't say that!"

Nikki sighed and placed her empty cocktail aside, leveling Becca with an uncompromising stare. "Honey, it's been a decade. A *decade* of sad, unfulfilling, plan your grocery list while he ruts for a grand total of two minute, unceremonious sex. You *need* to come."

Becca rolled her eyes. "I can't say *any of that*, let alone the part about *coming*! And what the heck's smurf sex?"

The waitress passed and Nikki flagged her over. "We'll take another round, please." She spun back to Becca. "Smurf sex is when you fuck until you're blue in the face."

"Oh."

Becca wouldn't know anything about that. If she calculated all the minutes she'd ever spent having sex, she'd probably only reach a grand total of two hundred. No, she was exaggerating. It would probably add up to an hour. Pathetic.

It had been ten years. Ten years of awful, unfulfilling, sometimes painful, sex. The realization of how bad her sex life had been came the afternoon she returned home and thought someone was being murdered in her house.

Cries built as she'd crept up the stairs to her bedroom, carrying a cast iron bookend. It was the only weapon she could find. Having never been prone to violence, she wasn't sure what she planned to do with the heavy bookend. The capacity to bludgeon someone really wasn't in her gentle nature. But someone was definitely being attacked—or so she'd thought.

Six months later and she still couldn't get rid of the image of her husband, Kevin, drilling into Loretta like he was trying to strike oil. The disgusting sight was permanently seared into her mind's eye. In ten years, he'd never once touched her like that. Not once.

Kevin appeared in her life at the end of her senior year, right after she and her mother moved to the area. First, he'd been nothing more than her shy friend. Over time he asked her out and eventually they wound up making out in the back of her cramped Beetle convertible.

After graduation he proposed. The proposal was unexpected, but she'd said yes all the same. There was a laundry list of unsound reasons why she agreed to be his wife. All of her friends were a thousand miles away in Florida. She was lonely. She had yet to make many new friends in Pittsburgh. And, believe it or not, Kevin was nice. Now, years later and much wiser, she understood he wasn't so nice after all.

When they were kids, Kevin was still in the ugly duckling stage of life. His confidence was nil and he'd seemed surprised a girl like Becca would notice him. Not that she was anything spectacular. To her thinking, she'd always been about average.

Always the quiet type, mostly because life hadn't presented her with many exciting opportunities, Becca learned to value the small things. That made marriage very easy for Kevin—until life got complicated.

She was sick of it, sick of being the good girl, the go-to girl, the quiet, don't make any waves and take one for the team girl. That was why she'd chosen Nikki to be her wingman tonight.

The divorce papers were signed that afternoon, sealing away a decade of her life she'd never get back. Nikki was well informed about what had happened. The more Becca confessed about her marriage, the more her friend became utterly appalled. Becca now understood how truly pathetic her marriage had actually been.

As Kevin approached his thirties, he started to change. Maybe he was suffering some sort of early mid-life crisis. He'd joined a gym, bought a new car they couldn't afford, and started fussing with his hair a lot. The whole thing puzzled Becca until one day she looked at her husband and saw someone she barely recognized.

His body trimmed down and his hair magically turned a shade darker than it had naturally been. His attitude swanked of confidence he'd never displayed before. Such flagrant boasting grated on her daily. It was around that time that he'd started acting "neighborly" with Loretta.

It hurt at first. In the beginning Becca had blamed herself for his cheating, knowing she'd traded her extravagant side for jaded sensibility several years ago. But no matter how low key her life had become, nothing justified his infidelity.

Kevin was the one who needed to prove something. Not once had he come to her stating he was unsatisfied with their personal relationship.

Their lackluster marriage was an oversight, sure, but there wasn't always time to primp and prep the way a waiting mistress could—certainly not in Becca's world. But she held no pity for herself and accepted even less from others.

While some might view her life as encumbered, she was happy to carry the responsibilities piled on her.

Perhaps if her husband had lent a hand when family life turned challenging she would've been more invested in their sex life. Her lack of carnal enthusiasm was greatly *his* doing.

Nikki whacked her in the arm. "He's leaving!"

Becca glanced longingly at Mr. Beautiful. It wasn't like she was going to make the offer Nikki suggested. He was beautiful, though.

His hair was the perfect shade of blond, clipped neatly in a way that showed off the slight waves. The dark blue, tailored suit he wore matched the sharpest blue eyes she'd ever seen. No ring, but there was no way a guy that pretty was single. Either that or he was gay.

"You need to go talk to him before he gets away!"

Becca let out a disheartened breath. It was a fun fantasy, but that's all it would ever be. "No. He's not my type—" Her chair tipped and she was abruptly dumped onto her feet, luckily catching herself—none too grace-fully—on the table before she landed on her ass. "*Nikki!*"

Her friend glared at her. "Why am I here?"

"Because you're supposed to be my friend." She attempted to reseat herself only to have the seat snatched away.

Scowling, and making quite a scene, Nikki snapped, "No. I'm here to make sure you close out the last ten years of your life with a physical bang and I'm not leaving until that's been accomplished. Thoroughly. You, my friend, are banging that guy tonight."

"Will you knock it off?" Becca hissed, her face heating to an uncomfortable burn.

"Not a chance. *Look at him, Becs!* He's gorgeous. Can't you imagine your legs wrapped all around those strong shoulders and stroking against that fine, wavy blond hair? No! Of course you can't, because you've spent the last decade screwing Kevin and his pintsize penis doing a sad impression of a baby toe. Now, I refuse—*refuse*—to let you go on living, never knowing what a full body, true, scream your lungs out, orgasm feels like. And that's the guy who's gonna give it to you."

Her face had to be bright red. Her chest heaved as she caught her breath. Licking her dry lips she whispered, "Will you please stop? People are staring at us." She didn't need the whole world knowing she'd never had a real orgasm.

Nikki reached for her purse. "How much will it take?"

"What?"

"How much?" She slapped her checkbook on the table and uncapped a pen with her teeth.

"You're going to pay me to have sex with someone?"

"No, I'm going to pay you to make a proposition. One line, only a few words, to that man over there, and I'll cut you a check, whether he takes you up on it or not. Give me a number."

She wasn't doing this.

"You know what? Forget it. I know exactly what I'll do." Her hand moved quickly as she scribbled. She tore the note away and handed it to Becca. "My gift, from me to you. I'm buying you a divorce."

Becca's jaw dropped. Nikki was loaded and Becca definitely was not, but there was no way she was letting her friend reimburse her the cost of her divorce. "No, Nikki—"

"Take the check."

"No!"

"Take the check."

"No!"

"Becca, take the damn check or so help me God, I won't be your friend anymore."

"What are you, twelve?"

"Take. The. Check."

"I'm not taking the stupid check. Now tear it up or I will."

"I'll tear it up if you go proposition him." A devious smile curled the side of her unreasonable friend's mouth.

Becca's teeth clamped tight and she growled, "I hate you."

Nikki laughed. "Go on. Before he escapes. And I'll be watching, so you better offer him exactly what I said."

Becca shook her head, but grabbed her purse, hissing, "I am not saying smurf sex." Turning, she stomped over to the other end of the bar. Once she spotted the man in question her steps staggered. Turning back to Nikki, she cowered as her friend shot her a threatening glare.

Right. To the guy.

Heart fluttering in her chest like a ballistic hummingbird, her lungs drew in a long ragged breath. He was perfect. Everything about him was a masterpiece. Sluggishly, she baby stepped in his direction. Her hand casually ran over her shoulder length blonde hair and she tugged at the bottom of her shirt, trying to show the slight amount of cleavage she had to offer.

Licking her lips she jaggedly took the last step in front of his table and froze.

His head slowly turned as he sensed her presence—the moron standing across from him, gawking. Blue eyes traveled over her questioningly and she cleared her throat.

He smiled a bit nervously. "Hello."

Oh. She needed to shut her eyes for a second. That voice was so thick and smooth she nearly hummed. *Crap. Was she humming?* Her lips firmed, cutting off any accidental sounds of nervous pleasure.

Forcing her eyes to meet his gaze, she squared her shoulders. *Deep breath.* "Hello. My name's Becca. I'm here celebrating my divorce." Why did she sound like a cyborg? "I noticed you sitting here and I was wondering if you might be interested in a night of…" She could do this. "… no strings attached sex. With me. Becca. And no strings. All night. Sex. Anything you want. The smurf kind even." *Oh, my God, stop talking.* "Me. Becca."

Those blue eyes glanced suspiciously around as though he were the target of a practical joke. "Is this a joke? Where's the camera?"

"No cameras."

His teeth flashed, as the corner of his mouth hooked upward in a devilish grin. Oh, boy. He was really, really pretty. "So then *not* anything I want."

His grin was contagious, but confusion cut her smile short. "Excuse me?"

He shifted and draped his elbow over the back of a

stool. His smirk turned cocky and she shot Nikki a nervous glance. Her friend nodded rapidly and waved her on. *Dear God, she was starting to sweat.*

"So in all this no strings attached, wild, anything I want sex, no cameras are allowed? I wouldn't be able to take your picture?"

What? "Of course not! Why would you want to?"

He shrugged. "Souvenir."

"Oh." Was he serious? She couldn't tell. "Would my clothes be on?"

He chuckled quietly and she still wasn't certain if he was teasing. "If that was a condition, I suppose I could work with that."

She chewed the side of her lip. Now it seemed like the joke was definitely on her. "Okay."

His head tipped to the side. "Really?"

"Um. Yeah."

"And you said your name was Becca?"

"Yes. Becca."

He held out his hand. "Pleasure to meet you, Becca. I'm Braydon."

Braydon—such a great name—slowly reached for her wrist and lifted her limp arm, placing her palm softly against his. His fingers gave a light squeeze as he asked, "Do you live close?"

Holy Hannah, was he actually agreeing to this insanity? Did single adults really behave this way? "Uhhh…" Passing out was a definite possibility. Her belly flipped with anxious bravadoes and a touch of fear. What if he was a serial killer? What if he was the next Jeffery

Dahmer? Was she insane? She could *not* do this! Her feet shifted back a step but his fingers remained closed over hers. "Actually—"

"Because my apartment's right around the corner if you'd rather go there."

Her mouth snapped shut.

"Is that your friend over there?" he asked. "She looks like she's leaving."

Her head twisted and Nikki was indeed paying the check and grabbing her purse, a satisfied smirk on her face. She ambled over to the man's table and extended her hand. "Hi. I'm Nikki."

Braydon finally released Becca and shook Nikki's hand. "I'm Braydon."

"Nice to meet you, Braydon. I just wanted to let you know my brother's a cop and my husband's an investigator. Becca here is my best friend and I love her very much. I also collect samurai swords and know how to use them. I work in real estate, so I know lots of abandoned properties that would be great for getting rid of a body in a pinch. I think you and Becca are going to have buckets of fun tonight, but I'm gonna need your ID until she's safely returned to me."

Braydon's expression was blank. It probably matched Becca's. Nikki had the biggest heart in the world. She was a tiny thing and had no problem showing the world that little things could pack a lot of excitement. Sort of like an atomic bomb, one measly spec of nothing, cut it open and —*Boom!*—there was crap everywhere. Nikki packed a bit more punch than that.

Braydon's cobalt eyes roamed over Nikki's small frame and his mouth twitched as he chuckled. "You're serious?"

Nikki tipped her head in agreement and held out her palm. "As an enema. Hand it over, sweet cheeks, and your wish is Becca's command."

"Nikki!"

She ignored her. Leaning forward, her friend stage whispered to Braydon, "Did she mention she took years of yoga? Those legs can bend in ways you've never seen."

Braydon reached in his pocket and placed his driver's license on the table. A small squeak escaped Becca's throat as she stared in shock as Nikki pocketed his ID.

"Awesomesauce. You kids have fun now. Call me in the morning, Becs." And with that she skipped off, tapping over her pocket holding Braydon's identity.

Becca slowly pivoted and glanced at Braydon. "She was my ride."

He grinned. "I like her."

Becca laughed, sort of hollow-like. "She eats guys like you for breakfast."

He stood and slipped his arm around her waist, startling her as he drew her body close to his. "I don't scare easily." Oh, he was warm and much taller than Kevin. Pressing his mouth to her hair, he whispered, "But it's a good thing I have you to keep me safe until morning."

God, he smelled so good her body shivered. Or was that a quiver of fear? Perhaps the kind someone suffers before they enter the secret lair of a mass murderer.

"Shall we go?"

Holy crap on a stick she was really going to do this.

Blinking dumbly, a stab of something like her resurrected courage gave her a swift kick in the ass. Heck yeah, she was going to do this—after she found a pillow to scream into, of course.

Closing her eyes, she breathed and issued a fast mental pep talk. She deserved this after everything she'd been through over the years. This was her reward, her due, and her duty to women everywhere.

When she looked into his eyes again, the fanfare and trumpets playing in her head dwindled to a sound resembling a deflating balloon. How was she ever going to go through with this?

BRAYDON TURNED the key and his apartment door clicked open. Placing his hand on Becca's back, he escorted her inside. "Can I get you something to drink? Wine? Beer? Whiskey?"

She stood awkwardly, shifting as if she wasn't sure what to do—accept or bolt. Her slight fidgeting told him she was nervous enough for the both of them. It wasn't like beautiful women frequently propositioned him.

Pale blonde hair caught the light. A narrow headband held the flaxen strands away from her face. Give her a pair of patent leather Mary Janes and she'd be a grown up Alice in Wonderland. Nothing about her fit a woman familiar with propositioning strange men in a bar. Yet here she was.

"I'll just have some water if you don't mind."

Braydon went to the fridge and removed a bottle. Taking down a glass from the stainless wall rack, he tried to ease some of the awkwardness. "So…how long were you married?"

"Too long." A nervous laugh hiccupped past her lips and she blushed. "Um, a little over ten years."

Passing her the water, she tipped it back, taking steady sips until the glass was empty. "Your place is nice. Clean."

"Thanks."

The condo was nice, but not home. It wasn't what he wanted long-term. Being an architect, he hoped to one day build his own house. There was plenty of property back home in Center County to build on, but he worked out of Pittsburgh, which complicated things. Settling down was, luckily, a long way off. Still, he'd been saving for that moment since he started working.

When he was younger, he imagined himself married right out of college. He'd even found a woman he thought was the perfect girl. Only problem…she up and married his brother. That was something that left a man a bit jaded and stuck in neutral.

His attention returned to his guest. "Can I take your coat?"

Becca shifted and slowly drew her arms out of the sleeves. After folding the thin wool jacket twice, she passed it to him. Carrying the coat to the wall, he hung it next to his. Not quite sure what was going to happen here, he played it casual, but certainly hoped she'd be removing more than her coat.

"So…"

"So…" she echoed.

He sat on the couch and waved a hand for her to follow. Perching on the edge of the farthest cushion, she sat like she had a dowel up her ass. "You can relax. I'm not going to attack you."

"Oh, I know that."

"Do you?"

"Well, no, not really. But you seem polite."

Chuckling, he said, "My mum would be glad to hear that." He eased back, trying to make her a bit more comfortable. "Do you usually proposition strangers at bars?"

She snorted. "No." It was a completely unladylike sound, but he found it charming.

"Yet you propositioned me. Why?"

Drawing in a deep breath, she explained, "It's a long story. You met Nikki. She made me do it."

"Why?"

Her expression tightened as if she were hosting some sort of mental debate. "Do you ever think *this is my life* and then—*pow!*—*y*ou realize everything you based your existence on was a crappy lie?"

"Yes."

Her surprise was evident as his response caused her gaze to jerk to his. "Really?"

"Yup, but I want to hear your story first. Did your husband cheat on you?"

"You could say that. I caught him having sex with our neighbor in our bed. Apparently she wasn't the first."

Luckily, no one had ever truly cheated on him. Well, not really. "How long were you together?"

"Since high school."

That was a long time. "Have you ever been with anyone else?"

"No. It's always been him. And according to Nikki, our love life was a joke."

"Why? I mean, aside from the other women."

Her lips pursed. "If you were married—*Oh, God*—you aren't, right?"

He laughed. "No. Never been married."

"Oh, well, if you were, how often would you…you know…?"

"Fuck my wife?"

Her eyes widened.

He chuckled. "Sorry. I figured, under the circumstances, we could talk plainly. How often would my spouse and I make love?"

"On average."

He considered this for a minute. "Probably four to five times a week. If we had children I'm sure that would change slightly, but I'd at least want to…make love to her a couple times a week."

"A *week?*"

"Yeah. How often did you and your husband make love?"

Her pale cheeks turned deep pink as she looked away. "Not that often."

"A couple times a month?"

"Try a year."

His brows shot up, pulling his face tight. "Was your husband gay?"

"What? No!"

He laughed, astounded. "I'm sorry, it's just…have you seen you? You're a ten."

"A ten?"

He didn't want to come off like a creep, but the minute she'd introduced herself he'd, of course, perused her assets. Her high, full breasts looked to be a large B or small C. Her hips swelled at all the right places and her legs went on for days. Plus, she had the whole innocent Alice thing going for her. Give her an aproned dress and a sign that said "Eat Me" and he was going to Wonderland.

"Trust me, you're very attractive."

Her sensuous little mouth twitched into a nervous smile. "Thank you. You're very handsome."

Braydon grinned. "So…do you want to tell me what smurf sex is?"

"Ohmygod…" Her face fell into her palms. "I'm going to kill Nikki."

"Why?"

"Because this is all her fault. I didn't even know what smurf sex was until an hour ago."

Though he didn't know much about her, she was highly entertaining. Such capriciousness usually faded in women her age. He laughed. "I still don't know."

"It's when you…" She waved her hand in repetitious circles.

"Fuck?"

She made a sound of distaste and scrunched her nose.

"Make love?"

"Yes. Until you're blue in the face."

His head tipped back and laughter bellowed from his chest. "So you just spent the last decade having religious sex and now you're going for smurf?"

Her brow crinkled. "We didn't have religious sex."

"Sure you did. Got *nun* in the morning and *nun* at night."

Her mouth opened and she looked offended, but the truth was the truth. "Well, it wasn't always like that. In the end it turned into hallway sex."

"What's hallway sex?"

"We'd only pass each other in the hall and I'd say *screw you*." Her eyes twinkled, her disposition no longer showing offense.

Now he was really laughing. "Well, I hope you at least had good courtroom sex and screwed the shit out of him during the divorce."

Her mouth tightened in a little smirk and the slightest chirp of laughter slipped out. Her fingers covered her lips as the chirps turned to giggles and then a snort snuck out.

"You have a great laugh."

She sobered and lowered her gaze to the floor. "I shouldn't be laughing about my marriage ending."

"It's okay to laugh about it, Becca."

Her returning smile was shy at first, then beautiful, like a flower coming into bloom. "It was terrible," she softly confessed. "Sometimes I wasn't even sure if he was awake or if he'd fallen asleep on me. Do you have any idea what it's like to be almost thirty and not know what certain things feel like?"

His amusement faded. "What do you mean?"

Apparently startled by her own words, her expression paled. "Nothing. Never mind."

"No. Tell me."

Her head lowered and she flicked a speck of lint off her jeans. "It was always the same, nothing fancy, and never with the lights on."

Looking at her, seeing her delicate profile and the feminine way she held herself, it was actually quite tragic this beautiful creature had been so neglected. "Did he at least make sure you…?" He censored his language, gathering she wasn't used to crass words.

The corners of her mouth pulled tight in a sad smile, and she slowly shook her head.

Jesus. Who the hell was her husband and what was wrong with him? He considered their situation. Although *she* was the one to put the offer on the table, once he discovered how timid she was, he assumed they wouldn't go through with it. But now…

It was an absolute tragedy that this woman didn't know what good sex was. "Did you really intend to sleep with me?"

Her head snapped up and she gawked at him. Somehow, after all this, he'd managed to embarrass her. Her voice quavered. "Oh, you don't have to. I can go if—"

"I don't want you to go." Her timidity was incredibly sexy. He was honestly growing more intrigued with every word she said.

Her breasts pressed against her shirt as her breathing picked up. "R—really?"

He tipped his head. Come on. She couldn't be that naïve. She had to know she was appealing as hell. She acted like he was doing her a favor, when in reality, he couldn't think of a more attractive woman. "How would you like to do this?"

She glanced around his apartment. "Should we go to your room?"

"Depends. What are you in the mood for?"

"I beg your pardon?"

"What are you hoping to gain here, Becca? Is there something specific you always wanted to try? Maybe a fantasy you had?" Figuring this was a one-time opportunity, he went for broke.

Her little pink tongue darted out and traced over her full lower lip. "Um… I used to fantasize that Kevin—I mean—I used to think it would be fun if a guy sort of came up and was so…full of passion he'd take me like his life depended on it."

He must have done something really good to earn this sort of karma. "Do you want me to take you like my life depends on it?" He hoped she said yes, as that would be no fucking problem at all.

Her face flushed and she lifted a shoulder. "It's sort of all fake if we plan it. I don't think it would be the same."

"Why don't we kiss and see where things go?"

The narrow column of her throat moved as she swallowed. In a hushed voice, she said, "Okay."

Braydon moved to the center of the couch. The energy

of the room intensified and seemed to snap between them, turning electric and making the little hairs on his arm rise. Inflamed curiosity folded into raw desire as he breathed in her soft scent. Not wanting to startle her, he hoped she'd meet him halfway. "Come here."

Licking her lips again, she scooted close and he turned into her. Her eyes focused anywhere but on him. His fingers lifted her golden hair over her shoulder as he touched his lips to her neck, breathing in her delicate fragrance. At first, she flinched, but as his lips brushed her rapidly fluttering pulse, her posture slowly eased. "Mmm. You smell nice."

His tongue slowly flicked her ear and nibbled the tiny lobe between his lips. Sliding his fingers to her other ear, he tugged on the tiny pearl stud, massaging slowly until she shivered.

"Is this okay?"

"Oh yes." Her voice was breathless.

His palm caressed her arm, reached for her knee and gently squeezed. "Why don't you lie back and get comfortable?"

It was almost impossible to stifle his chuckle as she gingerly scooted lower on the sofa. Not much, but it was enough. Dragging his mouth over the fine contour of her jaw, he traced over the corner of her mouth. As her lips parted his lust was provoked beyond his patience. "I *really* want to kiss you, Becca."

Her chest lifted with each breath. "You do?" Long lashes hid her eyes.

His lips pressed to the crest of her cheek, dragging out

the anticipation. "Mm-hm. I want to do other stuff to you too, but right now, all I can think about is kissing you like you've probably never been kissed before."

Soft breath puffed over his mouth and he could scent the fruity traces of whatever she'd been drinking at the bar. His fingers coasted up her arm, around her neck, and through her flaxen hair. His palm cupped the back of her head as his mouth slowly slanted over hers.

A moan escaped as his tongue coaxed its way past her lips. Her mouth was soft and sweet. Kissing her slowly, he drew out her passionate side. His other hand cupped her jaw, his thumb massaging gently over the fine arch of her cheek. As her shoulders melted into the couch, she sighed, rocking his body with a responsive throb.

The first timid caress of her tongue went right to his cock. He twisted his bulk and deepened the kiss. Her lips were perfect little slices of heaven, plump and succulent. It seemed she possessed some unfamiliar quality, a perfect blend of innocent curiosity that made her angelic. Nibbling her lower lip with his teeth, he chuckled against her mouth, his thoughts slipping into whispered words. "You're an angel."

Her delicate hands hesitantly relaxed on his shoulders. Rising to his knees, he deepened the kiss, urging her lower on the sofa. Her fingers flexed into his shoulders and her breasts dragged softly against his chest.

Easing back, he glanced at her through hooded eyes. Her hair was a spiral of gilded waves fanning out beneath her, her swollen lips a shade darker from kissing. The most peculiar colored eyes gazed up at him. They were Elizabeth Taylor eyes, such a fascinating shade of blue they could be mistaken for violet.

His mouth lowered and captured her lips. Long legs shifted as he settled over her. Every kiss brought his body to life. Learning each other's touch with slow caresses, he dragged his hips seductively over hers and those violet eyes turned luminous.

Who was this woman? "You have incredible eyes."

"Thank you."

Her fingers flexed against his arms as soft keening noises traveled from her lips to his. Easing back, he slowly undid the buttons of her shirt, pausing for only a brief moment to allow any objections. Her flushed face tipped as she watched each button come undone. Spreading the shirt wide, his eyes feasted on two perfect breasts framed in soft white lace.

Trailing his fingers over the scalloped edging, she arched in response, the violet of her eyes deepening with arousal. Soft fawn colored lashes lowered as he peeled the lace cups away and lowered, catching one tiny pink nipple in his mouth.

"Oh, God," she gasped, sounding almost panicky.

Pinching the tight bud gently between his lips, he traced his tongue over the hard tip and released her. "This okay?"

"Mm-hmm." She didn't sound too sure.

"Becca, look at me." He waited until her lashes lifted. "Are you okay with this?"

She nodded tightly.

"Tell me what you want. If it's too much we'll slow down."

"I liked what you were doing."

Cupping her breast in his palm, his thumb dragged slowly over the turgid tip. Maybe she was nervous and simply not used to experiencing such things. "You have very beautiful breasts."

Her blush traveled from her cheeks, darkening her nipples a shade. "Thank you."

"Can I see the rest of you?"

She licked her lips in what he was coming to recognize as something she did whenever she debated internally. "Do you have…protection?"

He nodded slowly, his body tightening another degree at what her question implied.

"Then yes."

Easing back, his fingers went to the snap of her jeans. He dragged the zipper down slowly, her breath quickening with each whispered tick. Matching white lace panties peeked out of the V of her pants.

Sliding off the couch, he turned her so her legs were draped over the edge. Plain black pumps covered her petite feet. Removing her left shoe, he lifted her foot and placed a kiss on the delicate arch. Her toes twitched and he wondered if she was ticklish. The image of tickling laughter from her turned him on even more.

Removing the other shoe he kissed her other arch. Slowly sliding her jeans down her long legs, her posture twisted, leaving her slightly flushed and disheveled as he peeled the sleeves of her shirt from her arms.

Displayed in only a bra and panties, he took his time regarding her. She was absolutely perfect. He let out a slow breath, feeling a bit outmatched. He wanted to make it really good for her, but her beauty left him staggered.

Placing a kiss on her knee, his lips travelled leisurely up her thigh. His fingers traced the lace edging of her panties and down they came beneath a gentle tug. Brushing his knuckles over the fine patch of golden curls, he met her gaze.

Watchful eyes studied him as he slowly nudged her thighs apart. Pink, dewy folds opened and he was mesmerized. Taking his time, he kissed down the crease of her thigh, and licked over the tiny pearl nestled at the peak of her sex.

Her body jolted and he glanced up at her, but gave her no chance of escape as he pressed his tongue deep. Her mouth moved over a tangle of whispered words he couldn't make out. With soft, penetrating strokes of his tongue, he tasted her. Her head fell back and she moaned as sweet heat met his tongue.

His palms glided up her inner thighs, his thumbs parting her folds as he drove her closer to climax. Her cries increased in volume and rhythm. Sinking the first finger deep, her knees drew up and she keened. Twisting his wrist, he withdrew and entered her again. Her arms lifted, elevating her breasts as she gripped the cushion of the couch behind her wild hair.

His lips teased her clit as his fingers fed into her slit. Slicked and primed, he inserted another finger and pressed deep, brushing soft tissue hidden inside.

Her eyes flashed open. His lips held her tiny jewel tight as he watched her. Burying his fingers deep, he tickled a bit more and she shattered. Lips parted, body quivering near violently with each intense tremble, she cried out and he drank her pleasure.

Quiet, gasped breaths filled the room as he leaned back. Licking his lips, he gazed at her, lowering his weight to his heels. "I want to fuck you, angel."

Her eyes flared as his crude language penetrated. He was so damn turned on he'd forgotten she shied away from curse words. There was that little tongue again. She deliberated for only a few seconds and then whispered, "Yes."

Standing, he lifted her like a feather, her languid weight drifting easily into his arms. She modestly attempted to cover her figure, but he caught her hand and shook his head slowly. "Don't hide. You're beautiful."

Deep pink crept from her breasts to her cheekbones as her hand dropped delicately to her hip. Lowering her feet to the floor of his bedroom, he went to the dresser and removed a condom, placing it on the nightstand. Turning to face her, he slowly peeled off his shirt, and reminded himself to take it slow.

"Oh, boy..." she rasped and he almost laughed. The lights were definitely staying on.

With deliberate slowness he undid the clasp of his belt. Toeing off his shoes and socks he slid the pants to the floor.

"Ohmygod." Her mouth opened, as she seemed to take a step back, but never actually moved. That, indeed was the most flattering reaction he could ever recall earning.

Her attentive appraisal sang to him, bringing a quick rhythm to his heart and heating his blood. Those violet eyes crawled over every bit of exposed flesh like a caress.

"Tell me what you want," he whispered, voice husky under the weight of his arousal.

"I...I'm not sure." She glanced at his large bed, hesitated, and slowly took a step closer.

Her fingers stroked the duvet and she glanced over her shoulder at him. She was stunning. The long line of her back tapered to her succulent ass. Her hips flared with feminine flawlessness. Artists couldn't paint a more perfect picture.

Her body tensed when he stepped behind her, slowly dragging his fingers down her bare arm and grazing his rigid front against her delicate back. "Whatever you want, angel, it's yours. Just tell me what you like."

Slowly pivoting, she wreathed her arms around his neck and gradually leaned in to kiss him. His fingers squeezed her hips lightly, nudging her toward the bed.

"Lie back," he said, as his mouth brushed over hers.

She lowered and scooted onto the bed as he gingerly crawled over her. His cock rested at her hip as his hands learned her curves. Her body stretched and writhed beneath him as he plucked and licked at her breasts. He made quick work of removing the bra still twisted around her ribs and tossed it to the floor.

"Braydon, please..."

Reaching for the condom, he slowly slid it over his length. "May I?"

"Yes," she breathed, opening her thighs for him. His motions had turned a bit more desperate since they'd reached the bed, but he intended to give her everything she needed, his own need fueled by hers.

Lining up his cock with her sex he slowly slid in. Heat wrapped around his length like a hot glove. His spine tingled as his eyes rolled back in ecstasy.

"Oh God," she breathed.

He withdrew a few inches and slowly thrust deeper. Crying out, her fingers tightened over his back, nails pressing deliciously into his skin.

His hand coasted over her soft thighs, curling around her delicate knees as he lifted and plunged deep. His pelvis kissed hers and he held the position for a long, delicious moment. Not wanting to rush, he focused on pleasing her. As her nails scraped over his shoulders he filled her again and again. "Tell me what you want," he whispered, pressing his lips to the soft curve of her throat.

"Faster."

He increased his speed.

"Harder."

Each thrust became firmer, stabbing deep into her core, rapidly filling her with each penetrating advance. Her voice grew high in pitch as she cried out with each plunge. Her body tightened and pulsed around him as he gave her everything she begged for.

Driving deep, he rotated his hips and her composure dissolved, her body rocking with uncontainable trembles.

Her sobs filled the air, driving his control to the brink. He fought back his release, but it was impossible with her body clamping down so lusciously. His seed left him in a rush and he nearly collapsed with the force of it.

Pressing his brow into her shoulder, he breathed hard. Her arms fell to her sides as she caught her breath. After a while she sighed and said, "I've never experienced anything like that before in my entire life."

"Are you pleased?"

She laughed a bit nervously, but it was a charming sound. "Pleased isn't the right word. I'm shocked."

Pressing his smile to her neck, he chuckled. "I'll be right back. I'm going to clean up."

He withdrew and his cock twitched, already missing her heat. Her body was a sanctuary. Standing, he went to the bathroom and shut the door. Unsure how he'd tempted the gods of karma, he was certain he'd done something great.

He tossed the condom and washed up, wanting to get back to her as soon as possible. Exiting the bathroom, he asked, "Do you need any—" He frowned. "Becca?"

The door in the living room clicked. Hustling out of the bedroom, finding no evidence of her presence, he frowned.

She was gone.

DON'T STOP THERE! Download Controlled Chaos now!

9 781957 573106